A former journalist on the *Daily Mail* and *Evening Standard*, and social editor of the *Tatler* for ten years, writer and broadcaster Una-Mary Parker has crafted a dramatic, compelling and topical novel of suspense. Her previous international bestsellers, *Riches*, *Scandals*, *Temptations*, *Enticements*, *The Palace Affair*, *Forbidden Feelings*, *Only The Best*, *A Guilty Pleasure*, *False Promises*, *Taking Control* and *A Dangerous Desire*, are all available from Headline, and have been highly praised:

'A smoothly readable thriller' *Daily Telegraph*

'Romance and suspense with an unexpected twist' *Sunday Express*

'Freshness, convincing dialogue and capacity to sustain one's interest' *Sunday Telegraph*

'This novel has everything – intrigue, romance, ambition, lust . . .' *Daily Mail*

'Una-Mary's bestselling formula succeeds yet again' *Daily Telegraph*

Dark Passions

Una-Mary Parker

HEADLINE

First published in 1998
by HEADLINE BOOK PUBLISHING

First published in paperback in 1998
by HEADLINE BOOK PUBLISHING

10 9 8 7 6 5 4 3 2 1

ISBN 0 7472 5687 X

Typeset by CBS, Felixstowe, Suffolk

Printed and bound in Great Britain by
Mackays of Chatham plc, Chatham, Kent

HEADLINE BOOK PUBLISHING
A division of Hodder Headline PLC
338 Euston Road
London NW1 3BH

This is dedicated to
Clare Foss,
a marvellous editor
and a wonderful friend

One

Antonia watched as the bride and groom cut the wedding cake. The frosted sugar that covered the three tiers was as smooth as virgin snow, until the sharp blade of the knife splintered the surface of the bottom tier, cracking it like ice on a dark lake, revealing the rich fruity mixture below. Then a cheer went up and everyone raised their glasses, in the mood to laugh at the usual corny speeches and drink endless toasts.

Antonia moved closer. Susan Sinclair, who now stood before a hundred and fifty relatives and friends, transfigured for the day into a ravishing figure in a romantic bridal dress and veil, smiled with ecstatic happiness at Antonia, her friend since they'd both been twelve. Her expression seemed to say: *Isn't life marvellous?* Beside her, Andrew, her husband for the past two hours, went for the roar of instant approving laughter by beginning his speech with the words 'My wife and I . . .'

Another toast was drunk, the bride's mother wept whilst still smiling, and the pink and white marquee resounded to the cheers of those who wished the radiant couple all the happiness in the world.

By Antonia's side an elderly gentleman was looking around as if searching for someone. She'd been stuck by his side for the past fifteen minutes, trapped in a tedium of polite conversation, but now she knew exactly what he was going to say next.

'—And which one is *your* husband?'

It was a question she was often asked at parties and she was heartily sick of it.

'I'm not married,' she replied with more asperity than she'd intended.

His faded blue eyes regarded her with hurt surprise.

'What? A pretty young girl like you?'

Antonia acknowledged the compliment with a tight smile. At this precise moment she felt neither young nor pretty. Yet another of her friends had got married, while she still remained single, and how was she supposed to answer his question? Say she'd never had time because building up her own business had been all-consuming? Add she was in no hurry to settle down, and anyway, she hadn't met the right person? Or should she be honest and humiliate herself completely by admitting that no one had asked her? She didn't even have a steady boyfriend. Her last brief relationship had been four years ago and hadn't amounted to much, anyway.

Antonia forced herself to smile sweetly. 'I suppose I'll have to get around to it one day, but right now I'm happy as I am.' Who was she fooling? She looked at him and tried to gauge what he was thinking, but he too was smiling falsely and his expression had become veiled, as if he didn't want to embarrass her by making further comment. After a decent interval, he drifted off, muttering, 'I'd better go and see how the old girl's getting on,' leaving Antonia free to mingle with the other guests. This was the third wedding she'd been to in the past four months! It was almost as if an epidemic of marriage was sweeping through her friends leaving her stranded on the shelf. Only this epidemic didn't seem to be catching, she reflected dismally, as she held out her champagne glass to be refilled by a passing waiter. Of course it was ridiculous to think like that and she really had lots of time yet, but even so . . . Something uneasy niggled in the pit of her stomach and she tried to quench the tiny flicker of panic by taking a gulp of her drink. *Which one is your husband?* If only! she thought, glancing around the room at the dozens of good-looking men, made even more attractive by their smart apparel of morning coats. If only *one* of them belonged to her. He needn't be wildly handsome, in fact she had a theory that good-looking men were conceited, but it would be nice if he were taller than her, and definitely slim, but most important of all, amusing. She could forgive a man almost anything if he made her laugh. Her eyes alighted on all the couples she knew; some held hands, others trailed small children, and three of the wives were heavily and proudly pregnant. One of them, Libby Parsons, caught sight of Antonia and waddled over.

'Hello! How are you? It's ages since I've seen you,' she exclaimed. She regarded Antonia with pity. 'Are you still working terribly hard?'

'Yes, business is great,' she replied robustly. 'We've just bought a property near Marble Arch which we're going to convert into six flats. We're also about to sell a huge house in Belgrave Square, which will make a fabulous embassy

3

and which we've restored to its original Victorian glory.'

Libby's eyes gazed glassily at her and Antonia realized she wasn't listening.

'Umm. How lovely,' she said vaguely. 'Did I tell you Giles and I are buying a house in the country? Well, with a baby and everything, it will be much better. We've seen a gorgeous house near Virginia Water. It's got six acres . . . enough room for the sprog to run about,' she patted her stomach fondly, 'and Giles says he doesn't mind commuting, and it does mean we can have a couple of dogs and all that. I can hardly wait!'

'That will be lovely,' Antonia replied politely, feeling rather out of it. All her married friends were so full of their new interests these days, and so bored by what she was doing in her life, that they seemed to have little in common any more.

'Giles says he's going to buy me a car, so if he brings his up to town, I can be independent.' Libby cast her eyes up. 'Isn't life heaven?' she breathed.

'Heaven,' Antonia repeated drily.

The sight of all this togetherness depressed her so much she headed for one of the tables arranged down one side of the marquee where three young women sat on their own, exhausted by their efforts at unsuccessfully working the room in search of single, eligible young males. They were all friends of Antonia's, and although joining their coterie of despondency admitted defeat, she slumped on to one of the little gilt chairs with a sigh of relief. At least they were all bonded by spinsterhood.

'Ciggie, darling?' Denise, party girl and self-professed

'lipstick lesbian', held out her packet of Marlboro.

Antonia shook her head, helping herself instead to a tiny cucumber sandwich. 'You know I don't smoke, Denise.'

'Darling, there are lots of things you don't do,' Denise retorted slyly. 'For God's sake get a life, Tony.' She blew a perfect smoke ring and tossed back her long blonde hair. Tall, very thin and languid in a black trouser suit, she liked to be regarded as a rebel, refusing to conform, intent on shocking, but Antonia, who'd been at school with her, knew that Denise was actually deeply insecure under her bravura display of sophistication.

'Antonia's *got* a life,' interjected Barbara. 'She's cleverer than all of us put together. *Look* at the marvellous career she's carved for herself.' Barbara was a blonde, too, but very different to Denise. Willowy rather than thin, gentle and kind rather than abrasive, she'd been Antonia's best friend since they'd met at school when they'd been six. Not interested in having a career herself, she was happy to be a legal secretary with a large firm of solicitors in Gray's Inn, until she found a suitable man to marry. Antonia was amazed that Barbara hadn't already succeeded in her ambition – there was certainly never a shortage of young men drifting around – but her friend seemed unable or unwilling to commit herself to any of them, and so at thirty-three, she too was still single.

Denise snorted in a derogatory fashion. 'Oh Christ, Bar! I was joking.' She stubbed out her cigarette. 'Of course Antonia's got a life; it's just not one I envy.'

Barbara flushed, wanting to defend Antonia, but was abashed and rather scared of Denise's scathing manner.

The third member of the group, Jane, spoke for the first

time. She was dark and serene and convinced that the man of her dreams would fall into her arms one day without her having to make any effort. The others thought her optimism was awesome, but she smiled her placid smile and put her trust in horoscopes which constantly assured her that 'romance was in her birth sign next week'. Denise had once pointed out that Jane wasn't in the least choosy, so she was going to be happy with who ever came along.

'We're all longing for a knight in shining armour to come riding by,' Jane asserted now. 'There's no good pretending we aren't.'

'*You* may be,' Denise said, lighting another cigarette, 'but what's wrong with a Lady Guinevere on a white charger, turning up to take us away from this lot?' She waved her hand expansively at the very obviously heterosexual crowd. 'No risk of getting pregnant, and think of the novelty!'

Barbara turned to Antonia. 'Do you think Roland is going to get engaged to Jinny?'

Antonia looked surprised. Roland was one of her three brothers and only twenty-five. It hadn't occurred to her that either he or Leo, who was twenty-three, might get married before her.

'I don't know, Barbara,' she replied. 'I suppose it's possible.' Roland had had a succession of pretty girlfriends since he'd been sixteen, and Jinny had certainly lasted the longest so far.

'Do you approve of her?'

'Who? Jinny?' Antonia considered the question. 'I hardly know her, you know. I only go home occasionally and she and Ro are off doing something most of the time.'

'Well, she'll be a very lucky girl if they do marry,' Barbara observed. At that moment Antonia was distracted by a cluster of bridesmaids in long Kate Greenaway dresses, being chased by a little boy pretending to be Spiderman, and so she missed the wistful expression that passed over Barbara's face. But Jane noticed, and she smiled at Barbara sympathetically.

'You should have your horoscope done,' she whispered.

'Got you-u-u-u-u!' yelled the little boy, as he dodged around their table, a slice of chocolate cake in one hand, and the end of the bridesmaid's sash in the other.

'Ar-r-r-ah!' screamed the bridesmaid, feigning terror in ear-splitting tones.

'Oh God! *Children*!' said Denise in disgust. 'Who'd have them?'

The little girl's mother came hurtling through the crowds. Antonia recognized her as someone she'd been to secretarial college with, years before.

'Hello, Rosemary,' she said smiling. 'You've got your hands full, haven't you?'

'Tell me about it,' Rosemary groaned, straightening up to ease her aching back. She peered at Antonia's bare left hand.

'How I envy you still being single,' she continued with feeling. 'This lot are driving me crazy. I've been up since five-thirty this morning. I had a fight with Flora who decided she loathed her bridesmaid's dress, and George was sick in the car on the way here. We still have a seventy-mile drive to get home, and Edward will expect a three-course dinner on the table at the usual time, although I've got no help in the house, when all I'll want to do is go to bed. Alone.' She sounded bitter.

'Poor you,' Antonia murmured, but she thought the idea of cooking a cosy dinner for two, while your beautiful-looking children slept upstairs and your husband opened a bottle of wine, was something akin to paradise.

After the wedding, which was held at Susan Sinclair's parental home in Hampshire, Antonia drove back to her flat in London. Although it was a Saturday evening and most of her friends were desperate to fling themselves into the bucolic pleasures of a rustic life, spending their weekends trudging through mud, battling against winds as cold and cutting as spears and getting drenched by driving rain, all she wanted to do was get back to the solid security of the city, where the constant activity formed a stimulating backdrop to her usual weekend pursuits. It seemed to her that on Saturday, and especially Sunday, London belonged to those who lived in it and loved it; they bought their papers from the local newsagent's and walked their dogs in the park. They pottered in their gardens and polished their cars, and the hustle and bustle of the thousands of commuters who invaded the city every morning in a soulless surge, was replaced by the calm atmosphere of people with a sense of belonging.

Tonight though, as she drove along the Cromwell Road in the direction of her flat, she wasn't looking forward to the rest of the weekend with as much anticipation as usual. The wedding had unsettled her. And so had the sight of so many of her friends with their husbands and children. The most depressing part of all, though, had been seeing Denise, Jane and Barbara, sitting huddled on their own, around a table, smoking and drinking and looking quietly desperate. Am I like them? Antonia asked herself, as she parked her car just round the corner from her flat in Cadogan Square. A frustrated single woman? Longing to get married and have a family? She was a highly successful woman with her own company, Murray Properties Ltd, which she'd formed six years ago and which specialized in buying large houses which she either restored or converted into luxury flats. She herself lived in a beautiful flat in the best part of town, possessed a wardrobe full of designer clothes and could afford to take holidays anywhere in the world. *Anyone*, she told herself fiercely, would be happy to have all she'd got, but as she let herself into the Victorian building where she'd lived for the past two years, she felt a deep core of loneliness. During the twelve years she'd dedicated herself to her work, all the right sort of men seemed to have vanished from the scene, snapped up by girls who were prettier, sexier and had more time on their hands. Or maybe they'd just been lucky because they'd been in the right place at the right time, that exact moment, as precise as the moment of conception, when a male was considering settling down and was actually on the lookout for a mate.

As soon as Antonia entered her three-room apartment, which was on the first floor and overlooked the central square garden, her feelings of discontent partially vanished. She'd decorated the large airy rooms in soft shades of aquamarine, dove grey and pale sunshine yellow and she'd furnished them simply but stylishly. Vases of flowers and bowls of pot-pourri filled the air with delicate perfumes and as she turned on the lights, everything became bathed in a warm and welcoming glow.

How dare I wallow in self-pity, she chided herself, as she went straight to her bedroom to change into more comfortable clothes. *Some people work hard all their lives and never attain all I've got.*

At that moment the silence was broken by a loud clattering coming from the direction of the kitchen. Antonia went back into the hall and saw that the kitchen door, at the far end of a corridor, was ajar. Coming from within was a soft thumping noise followed by the sound of something else being smashed.

Charging down the passage, she pushed the door wide open and switched on the light. A broken cup and saucer lay on the floor, its fragments scattered wide.

'Crash! I wish to goodness you'd be more careful,' she scolded loudly.

A Persian cat of incredible beauty, with large golden eyes, gazed up at her unapologetically, and rubbed himself against her legs.

'You're so clumsy. That's the third thing you've smashed this week.' Although she spoke crossly, she nevertheless scooped the cat up in her arms, where he proceeded to push his ice-cold nose against her cheek, while purring like a motor mower.

'Oh, Crash. Why can't you look where you're going?' she crooned, rocking him lovingly now. 'The trouble is, you've got no coordination.'

Crash purred louder than ever.

'Come on then. Let's watch some television,' she said, switching off the kitchen lights. 'And if you knock anything else over,' she added with mock sternness, 'you're going straight back to the kitchen.'

Antonia looked at her reflection in the bathroom mirror as she got ready for work on Monday morning, as if to seek reassurance about her appearance. Her make-up was immaculate and subtle and her long brown hair with its blonde highlights hung smoothly to her shoulders. She wasn't beautiful, she decided, but there was a vitality about her face which was attractive; her mouth was full and humorous, and her skin had a healthy glow. She also quite liked her eyes, which were a warm brown and almond-shaped, like her mother's. And she was slender with long slim legs, which suited the sharp suits and high heels she always wore to the office. Crash hovered in the bathroom doorway, watching her, anxious to be given his breakfast before she departed.

'I haven't forgotten,' she told him, bending down to stroke his beautifully soft coat, 'and I've cleaned out your tray, so you're a lucky cat, aren't you?'

He jumped up on to the bathroom stool with a little chirrup of pleasure and promptly sent her make-up bag flying. Then he peered down at it in great surprise, as if it had nothing to do with him at all.

'Now look what you've done!' she exclaimed, planting a kiss on the top of his head. 'I really wish you'd look where you're going.'

It took her only five minutes to walk from Cadogan Square to her office, which was situated on the ground floor of a new building at the bottom of Sloane Street. It was a prime site, a modern edifice of smoked glass and steel and the rent was enormous, but it gave Murray Properties Ltd the necessary *gravitas* when raising financial backing for a project.

Twelve years before, Antonia had started out as a secretary at Hutton, Datchet & Compton, estate agents with branches throughout the south of England, dealing in middle-of-the-road residential property. She'd watched and learned every aspect of the business during the six years she worked for them, and had become their chief negotiator. When advising someone on selling their house, she'd make sure they put into practice all the tricks of the trade to tempt potential buyers: the rooms were to be tidied and cleared of all clutter and if necessary redecorated, lights should be turned on, window boxes and garden should be blooming, there were to be flowers and plants in every room, and the delicate fragrance of coffee and freshly baked bread should permeate the house just as clients were due to arrive.

When Antonia decided to start out on her own as a property dealer, everyone told her she was crazy. She lost count of the negative objections to her plans, which ranged from there being too much competition in that field, the economy not being right for her ambitious schemes – and what made her think she'd succeed when others were going bankrupt at an alarming rate? – And how was she going to finance office premises, staff salaries and running costs, not to mention the capital required if she was intent on buying large properties and then spending hundreds of thousands of pounds renovating them? Think of the interests rates! people warned, and what happens if you can't sell the property?

And think how long it might be before you got a return on your investment.

Within two years she'd proved the sceptics wrong. Thanks initially to a bank manager who had faith in her, and some contacts in the business world who were ready to back her, she was able to finance first one deal and then another. Now, working in conjunction with architects, builders and decorators, designers and antique dealers, she was able to restore a property and then put it on the market ready to move straight into, right down to bars of Chanel soap in the bathrooms. Once, a Belgian millionaire contacted Antonia on 10 December, saying he was coming to London and wanted a fully furnished house, ready to move into for Christmas, for him and his wife and three small children. She not only, by sheer luck, had a newly decorated and furnished house ready to put on the market, but by 21 December, when the family arrived, she'd installed an eight-foot, decorated Christmas tree in the spacious hall, food and drink in the fridge and freezer, chocolates and the latest magazines and books in the drawing room, toys and a rocking horse for the children in the playroom, and a beautifully gift-wrapped present for each of them under the tree, which, as she told her father, was the least she could do having sold them the house for six point four million pounds.

The irony of the situation was not lost on her, though. While she created homes of exquisite taste and style, it was always for other people with families, and not for herself. The warm and functional kitchens were not for her to cook in. The nurseries, with their hand-painted furniture and dado of Beatrix Potter characters, were not for her babies to sleep in. And the beautiful master bedrooms, with marble bathrooms en suite, were not for her and an adoring husband, but for another couple, people she didn't even know. At times the thought was so depressing she found herself quite jealous of her clients, because most of them were living the life she'd begun to long for.

Now though, as she swung through the double glass doors into her open-plan office, she felt a frisson of excitement. A new week had begun and there were properties to view, clients to see, designs to select, colour schemes to choose and advertising layouts to approve. Whatever happened, she loved her work and she planned never to retire.

'Good morning,' she said, going to her desk, beside which stood an easel with an architect's drawing for the conversion of three houses into de luxe apartments.

There was a chorus of greeting from the three women and two men who worked for her. They were all in their early thirties, all hungry for success, but they worked as a good team under Antonia's direction. She inspired, cajoled, encouraged and when necessary told them where they were going wrong. Not afraid to criticize, her criticism was nevertheless constructive.

'Any messages, Linda?' she asked her secretary, opening her mail and glancing at a surveyor's report on a house she was interested in purchasing.

'Your three o'clock meeting with the solicitor about the Wilton Place property has been postponed until four o'clock, and Jane English says the curtains for eighteen, Eaton Place are going to go over budget, and she needs to know whether you want her to go ahead or not.'

'Thanks.' Antonia reached for the phone. 'I could die for a cup of coffee, Linda, and then I want to go through the ads for July with you.'

For the next four hours she worked steadily without a break, asking for more coffee from time to time, but then getting so absorbed in discussions with the others that she forgot to drink it and it grew cold. They all had so much on hand at the moment, in various stages of development, that she felt like a juggler, trying to keep all the balls in the air. When she realized it was nearly one o'clock, she gave an exclamation of dismay.

'Oh, God! My *mother*! I'll be late if I don't hurry,' she said, grabbing her handbag. 'Linda, you did book a table at Daphne's, didn't you?'

Linda, small, dark, neat and unruffled, looked up from her computer keyboard and grinned. 'Yes. Table for two. One o'clock.'

'You're a star!' The glass doors into the street flashed open and shut and Antonia was gone.

'Ma! I hope you haven't been waiting long?' Antonia kissed her mother and noted with satisfaction that they'd been given a good table. The restaurant was already packed with fashion-conscious women and rich-looking men from both sides of the Atlantic and the atmosphere was heady with celebrities.

'Darling, don't worry,' Hilary Murray replied calmly. 'I ordered myself a glass of champagne and I'm fine.'

Antonia smiled at her mother with a pride that was almost maternal. In the past few years there'd been a definite shift in their relationship, as Antonia became protective and indulgent towards Mrs Murray, while herself becoming the strong one. Not that there was anything frail about Hilary Murray. At almost sixty, she was as active as she'd ever been, running the family home in the country, which she jokingly said their three sons used like a hotel at weekends, bringing their girlfriends and their washing with them, and working in her beloved garden for several hours each day. Married to Quentin Murray for nearly forty years, she'd retained a warm and radiant charm that attracted people towards her, and that emanated from her own contentment with life.

'How's everything going, darling?' she asked after they'd given their order.

'Fine, Ma. We've got a lot on but things are going very well.'

'Have you been going out much?'

Antonia knew exactly what her mother was getting at, but chose to sidestep the underlying issue.

'I went to Susan and Andrew's wedding on Saturday and saw masses of people. It was a gorgeous wedding and Susan looked really lovely. Yesterday I had a blissfully quiet day, recharging my batteries.'

Hilary Murray smiled and sipped her champagne.

'Otherwise I've been very busy,' Antonia added unnecessarily.

'Are you coming down this weekend?'

'I don't think I can, Ma. I've got to work on Saturday and on Sunday I'm having lunch with some clients; they're German and rather important and I don't think I can get out of it. I've sold a couple of flats through them.'

'You work too hard, darling. I hope you're going to take a break this summer. You really should arrange a good holiday.'

Antonia smiled, at a loss as to how to reply. For the first time in their lives a barrier had sprung up between them because they were both aware of her single status, but neither could bring themselves to talk about it; Antonia because she was proud and felt her mother saw it as some kind of failure, and Hilary Murray because her policy, once her children had grown up, was never to interfere in their lives. So now they moved around each other, engaged in a verbal pavane, anxious not to tread on each other's toes, their movements sometimes stilted for fear of causing hurt.

'I might be able to manage the following weekend,' Antonia remarked, seeing the fleeting look of hope that crossed her mother's face. 'Once Eaton Place is finished, things won't be so hectic.' But of course she knew they would be, because she seemed to fill every waking moment of her life with work.

'Well, it would be lovely to see you whenever you can manage it,' Hilary Murray replied warmly. Then she looked around the restaurant, and at the tall, handsome waiters who dashed to and fro with trays laden with platters of exotic food. 'Are they always as busy as this?'

Antonia nodded, grateful to her mother for changing the subject. 'This is the "in" place,' she said laughingly. 'I think we booked this table two weeks ago.'

'My God!' Mrs Murray looked stunned. 'How different things are in London, aren't they? I don't think I could bear to live up here again. Give me my peaceful garden any day.

Daddy was only saying the other day . . .'

Antonia nodded, smiling automatically as her mother continued to talk, but her thoughts were far away. She was remembering Barbara and Jane and Denise, with her nervous chain-smoking, sitting around the table at the wedding and it suddenly struck her that they'd never find anyone with their negative attitude. Failure breeds failure, she reflected, just as success breeds success. It was no good just *sitting*, hoping for a miracle to happen, you had to *make* it happen. Just as she'd made Murray Properties Ltd happen, so she was going to have to make finding someone to love happen.

The idea took hold as she sat there, oblivious to the chattering and clattering around her. With a businesslike attitude, she would set about finding someone.

'. . . So we're thinking of getting a part-time gardener to do the heavy stuff,' Hilary Murray concluded.

Antonia blinked, trying to drag her mind back to the present and concentrate on what her mother had been saying, remembering how Libby had switched off when she'd been talking to her at the wedding; now she'd become just as bad. Was life divided up into such closed sections that people were only interested in hearing about things they could relate to themselves?

'That's a good idea, Ma,' she agreed, feeling guilty. She saw so little of her mother these days, the least she could do was pay attention to what she was saying when they did meet.

'I'll really try and come down in a couple of weeks,' she promised.

Hilary's face lit up. 'That would be lovely, darling. You

need to relax a bit. You work far too hard.'

Antonia's three brothers, Tristram, Roland and Leo managed to go home almost every weekend, safe in the knowledge that Quentin and Hilary would be there, ready to administer sympathetic council, hot meals and long rambling walks with the dogs, plus a welcome for whatever females they might have in tow at that precise moment. In the summer they lazed on the lawn with glasses of Pimm's, and in the winter they clustered around great log fires, roasting chestnuts and drinking mulled wine. The Murray sons basked in the security provided by Hilary and Quentin, charming their way through life and making little effort to justify their existence, except for being delightful company. Only Antonia, the workaholic in the family, preferred to keep busy, helping her mother in the garden, suggesting games of tennis, dinner parties which she offered to cook, and getting up a petition to persuade the local council to allow gypsies to camp on a stretch of wasteland on the outskirts of the village. In truth, she liked the buzz of city life better, finding the very beauty and stillness of the countryside melancholic. To please her parents, though, she stayed at Clifton Hall on average one weekend in four, arriving in time for lunch on Saturday, and leaving Sunday afternoon— 'Because I can't leave Crash on his own for too long,' she always said. Much as she loved time at home with her family, the feverish activity of urban life beckoned and she couldn't wait to get back to the comforting knowledge that she was surrounded by a mass of other people, even if she stayed in her flat all weekend and didn't actually see anyone. On a high from the driving energy of city life, stimulated by the charged atmosphere, she felt she could conquer the world when she was in London. Murray Properties Ltd would never have been born if she'd stayed at home, because life there was too easy and the atmosphere too leisurely to encourage ambition.

For the next few days after lunch with her mother, Antonia continued to worry about her future. Suddenly, gaps were appearing in her life which Murray Properties wasn't filling. At moments, she even had to stifle pangs of fear that she might never find the right person with whom to share her life. Was it Susan Sinclair's wedding that had brought on this anxiety about still being single? Or Barbara's question that Roland might be getting engaged to Jinny? She knew she must do something to improve her social life, so that she could meet more people, but what? Then one morning she felt a resurgence of alarm when she saw yet another old school friend's engagement announced in *The Times*.

'It'll happen to us, too,' said Jane confidently, when Antonia mentioned the news. They belonged to a gym club in Chelsea, which they and several of their friends had joined the previous summer. They mostly met on Sunday mornings, which was a very popular time, though not, unfortunately, for young men.

'Nothing just happens,' Antonia retorted, putting on her dark blue leotard. 'My business didn't just happen. I worked like a dog for six years, eighteen hours a day, to get up to speed. My flat didn't just happen. It took me years to afford it, six months to find it and another six months to decorate it.'

Jane studied herself sideways in the changing-room mirror

because that way she looked slimmer. 'But falling in love is different. You *can't* force it to happen, like looking for a flat. Do you think my thighs are getting too muscular?' she added in a worried voice.

Barbara joined them, hair fetchingly pinned up on top, her slender body in its pale pink leotard drawing irritated looks from some of the other women. 'Your thighs are fine, Jane,' she assured her, sweet and supportive as ever.

'Are you sure . . . ?' Jane turned the other way, flexing her knee. 'I don't want to get chunky legs.'

'You won't,' Barbara and Antonia chorused in unison.

Loud music could be heard along the corridor.

'Come on, the class is starting,' Antonia told them.

When they entered the large studio the room was already full. This was the most popular aerobics class of the week, and heavily subscribed to by women who ranged in age from seventeen to seventy and in size from ten to eighteen. Antonia, Barbara and Jane managed to squeeze along the back row. Denise was already there, ensconced in the front row, in a dazzling blue leotard, white leg warmers and blue and white trainers. She was flirting outrageously with a muscular girl called Pam, who was the chief aerobics instructor, and when she saw then she waved gaily.

'Are we all ready, then?' Pam boomed, flexing her biceps. 'We'll start with the warm-up routine. You all know it, so let's go! go! go!' With the flip of a switch she turned on the loud, pounding music, and the room began to vibrate as the decibel level reached the point where Antonia's eardrums began to ache.

'One, two, three, *four*!' yelled Pam, as she stamped her

way through the set steps, and forty-three bodies of varying ability tried to follow her, goggle-eyed and soon breathless.

'Jesus,' Jane puffed, in a loud aside. Her face had turned scarlet and sweat was trickling down her throat.

'The woman's a power freak on a trip,' Antonia agreed.

The music continued to blast out of the speakers, as Pam relentlessly exhorted them to 'Stretch, one, two, three, *four*,' and '*lift*, one, two, three, four.'

Behind her, the floor-to-ceiling mirrors reflected them all in their various stages of collapse; there were some seriously unfit newcomers, and Antonia wondered what the procedure was if someone had a heart attack. Her own reflection, in a blue leotard and thick tights, showed that her thighs were definitely too flabby. Something had to be done about that, she thought in alarm. It's all that sitting at a desk that's the problem. Redoubling her efforts, she swung her arms and stamped her feet . . . whoever said this was a low-impact form of exercise? Cellulite or no cellulite, Antonia began to wonder what on earth she was doing in this place. It was eleven-thirty on a Sunday morning, and when she'd been a girl she'd have been in church at this time, singing hymns and saying her prayers. And what was she doing now? Worrying about the state of her thighs instead of the state of her soul! If someone was going to love her, surely the state of her spiritual being was more important than her outer bulges? Out of the corner of her eye she saw that Jane had now turned pale and was gasping like a fish out of water. Barbara, she noticed, looked as if she was enjoying herself.

'Let's get out of here,' Antonia shouted above the din.

The relief that swept over Jane's face was comical. 'Oh,

yes,' she wheezed, 'before I need an ambulance.'

They stumbled from the studio, trying to ignore the disapproving glare of Pam, while Denise, they noticed, was now pretending she didn't know them.

'What a nightmare,' Jane said, when she was in a fit enough state to say anything. They'd had a shower, and changed back into jeans and T-shirts.

Antonia nodded. 'That's the first and last time I'll do *that* class. The woman's a sadist. Let's go back to my place. I could do with a strong Bloody Mary, couldn't you?'

'Bliss.' Jane sounded dreamy.

Antonia's car was parked outside the club. On the way home, she stopped to buy the Sunday papers.

'I think we deserve a lazy afternoon after all that.'

'But we'll undo all the good that class just did us.'

'Good?' Antonia asked incredulously. 'What good? I'm not sure I'll ever be the same again. I joined the gym partly to improve my figure, but also in the hope of meeting some nice chap; I didn't go to kill myself.'

'Then why not do some evening classes? They might be less strenuous.'

Antonia sighed. 'Jane, I'm thirty-two. I look upon evening classes as being for old ladies who want to learn basket-weaving, or teenagers who can't afford to go to art school. I really don't think I qualify. In four months' time I'll be thirty-three.' She found it an appalling and rather scary thought. In silence they returned to her flat, made a large jug of Bloody Mary liberally laced with freshly ground black pepper and Worcester sauce, and then settled themselves in the drawing room.

'This is more like it,' Antonia observed, curling up on the sofa, with Crash snuggled against her knees.

'I must spend more weekends in London,' Jane agreed. 'It beats trekking around the countryside every time.'

But Antonia's gloom soon returned. It seemed that every newspaper and magazine she picked up echoed her consternation at being unattached.

'Listen to this, Jane,' she said, and read aloud. 'Statistics show that a woman's chance of finding a husband drops dramatically after thirty-five, and practically vanishes off the graph after forty. As to pregnancy, a woman over thirty is regarded as "old" and requiring special antenatal care. Isn't that an appalling thought?'

Jane regarded her with calm blue eyes. 'But what can you do about it? My favourite clairvoyant says there is someone out there for everyone; by the law of averages, we're bound to meet Mr Right sooner or later.'

'I don't know about you, but I'd rather he arrived before I get my Zimmer frame.' Crash chirruped as if in agreement, and moved himself into a more comfortable position.

'Friends keep giving dinner parties and inviting me to meet their single friends,' Jane said hopefully.

'*Tell* me about it,' Antonia intoned. 'I've had more blind dates than Cilla Black's had hot dinners! It's a recipe for disaster. The trouble is, one's expectations are unrealistically high.'

'What else can we do?'

'I'm working on it,' Antonia replied firmly.

A few nights later, Antonia remembered their conversation

as she climbed into her car, which she'd parked up the street from Kay and Melvyn Buxton's dinky little house in Campden Hill. They'd been married for eighteen months and were expecting their first baby in two months' time. Meanwhile, Kay was determined to cram in twelve months' entertaining in the next eight weeks, because she knew she'd never have time once the baby arrived. Tonight had been the night when she wanted to 'do a favour for her dear old friend Antonia Murray'.

What a ghastly evening! Antonia thought, as she turned the car into Sheffield Terrace, easing her way past rows of parked cars. Street lamps were reflected in the wet road and the rain on the windscreen blurred her vision. Switching on the wipers, she swore that never again would she let herself be persuaded to 'meet a charming man', and for once she was thankful to be going back to an empty flat and an even emptier bed.

What was Kay thinking about, inviting that fat toad to meet me? she sighed inwardly. I'm not *that* desperate! What was the dreadful man's name? Todd something? Yes, that was it. Todd Mackenzie. She sighed gustily and, revving the engine, shot along Kensington Road towards Knightsbridge, thankful that she'd driven to the dinner party. There'd been a nasty moment when Todd had suggested they 'go on somewhere for a drink and I'll drop you home afterwards'. Then, to make matters worse, Kay had started making encouraging noises.

'Oh, I'm sure Antonia would love to, wouldn't you, Antonia?' in a nudge-nudge, wink-wink way.

At that moment, Antonia realized there were too many

Todd Mackenzies in this world and too few really attractive hunks, and the fact that Todd was obviously an old friend of Kay's was unnerving in itself. Had pregnancy so altered her friend that she'd lost all sense of judgement? Most alarming of all was Kay's presumption that she'd find Todd attractive.

'He's awfully eligible, you know,' Kay whispered, when Antonia went to get her coat. 'He's a successful barrister and he's got a lovely little flat near Regent's Park.'

'How nice for him,' Antonia replied sweetly, thinking of her own beautiful and roomy flat in Knightsbridge.

'He's a *very* nice person. You didn't give him a chance,' Kay replied firmly, as they came back down the stairs from her bedroom, which Antonia knew was shorthand for: *At thirty-two you can't afford to be choosy.*

Stung by the truth of this, Antonia ignored the remark because she didn't want to be rude. The fact that Kay had changed since the claims of matrimony and maternity had turned her into an airhead probably wasn't her fault. She'd secured her man and she wanted all her girlfriends to be as happy as she was. Which, Antonia said to herself, was patronizing in the extreme, even if well meant.

There was no doubt about it: these 'dates', fixed up in an unsubtle way by married friends, were an embarrassing disaster.

By the time she'd parked her car, let herself into her flat and endured Crash flinging himself off the kitchen table in welcome, breaking a butter dish in the process, she'd made up her mind. It was time to take her future seriously in hand. One thing was certain. She already had the cat. What she didn't want was to end up a lonely old maid as well.

* * *

'Call for you, Antonia,' Linda announced the next morning. Antonia, absorbed in writing the blurb for a whole full-page advertisement for a house she was putting on the market, in *Harpers & Queen* magazine, looked up from her desk, which was cluttered with photographs of the property.

'Can you take it?'

'It's Roland.'

'OK.' She grabbed the phone. 'Hi, Ro! How are you?' If Leo, the baby of the family, was her kid brother, and Tristram, at thirty-four, her protective mentor, Roland was her soulmate. When he and Leo had been babies she'd hung around the nursery, begging to be allowed to bathe them and feed them and play with them, and even now, she still felt faintly maternal towards them.

'I was wondering if you were going home this weekend?'

She paused. 'I think I'm going to be too busy.'

Roland seemed slightly evasive. 'We haven't seen you for ages. You always seem to stay in London at the weekends,' he added, slightly accusingly.

'Well . . .' She felt guilty because it was true. 'OK. I'll come down, but I can't make it until lunchtime on Saturday.'

'Great.' He sounded really pleased and she felt touched.

'Is everything all right, Ro?'

'Couldn't be better. How's it with you? Busy as ever, I suppose?'

'Frantic.'

'See you Saturday, then.'

'Yes. Tell Mummy I'll be down, will you?'

'Sure.'

'Thanks. See you then. Bye, Ro. Lots of love.'

The Murray family had lived at Clifton Hall, on the borders of Hertfordshire and Buckinghamshire, for nearly a hundred years, but inheritance tax on the death of Antonia's grandfather had left the family impoverished by their standards. Where once there had been six full-time gardeners to tend the twenty-acre grounds, there was now just Hilary Murray and a part-time lad from the village. Indoors, three village women came in every day to cook and clean, whereas originally there had been ten servants, whose living quarters were above the stables.

The years of financial decline had been gradual at first, after Quentin Murray had inherited the place from his father in 1964, but then had escalated into a haemorrhage as repairs to the old house became vital; it needed rewiring, a new roof was required, a boiler had to be replaced and finally the building needed underpinning. By the time it was all paid for, Hilary and Quentin were having to make sacrifices if they were going to keep the property in the family. There was never any question of selling Clifton Hall, though. They all loved it too much for that, and it had been in the family for so long they felt it was an important part of their heritage. One day it would belong to Tristram, the eldest of their four offspring, and to avoid further inheritance tax when Quentin died, the house had already been put in Tristram's name. Meanwhile, they enjoyed the privilege of having such a beautiful home to return to, whenever they could.

It was noon by the time Antonia drove up the wide tree-lined drive to Clifton Hall. There were already five cars parked on the forecourt, and she recognized three of them as belonging to her brothers.

'Hiya!' Roland was standing in the open doorway of the porch, arms folded across his chest as he watched Antonia climb out of her car, looking trim and vibrant in designer jeans and a navy-blue blazer over a white T-shirt. A moment later he was joined by Leo with the family's three brown and white spaniels.

'Hi!' she called back. Roland was the image of their father, Quentin; tall, thin, dark-haired and hollow-cheeked, resembling more a poet than an accountant, while Leo still had the soft blushing skin of an adolescent, and the brown eyes and light brown curly hair of their mother.

Leo helped her take her case out of the boot of her car, while Amber, Jacko and Rags sniffed her ankles suspiciously, wondering why she smelled of cats, and Roland gave her a hug.

'How are you, Ro?'

'Never been better,' he replied, grinning broadly.

Antonia looked at him curiously. 'What's up?' she asked, instinctively knowing he was up to something.

His grin broadened, so that it seemed to split his face in two, and his eyes glittered with merriment.

'Nothing's up.' He tried to sound nonchalant.

'Why should anything be up?' Leo asked, also hugging her.

'*Something* must be up! That's the first time you've ever offered to carry my case,' she joked. She looked from one to the other, but they continued to smile blandly.

'Anyway, how's it all going in the great metropolis?' Leo

asked. 'How many millions are you worth now?'

Antonia laughed. 'Where's Mum?'

'Where do you suppose? In the garden or the greenhouse, of course. Is she ever anywhere else? Dad's in the study though.'

'Is Tristram around?' Tristram, the serious one, and probably the brainiest of the family, was a lecturer at the London School of Economics.

'I'm not sure where Tris is.' Hands deep in the pockets of his jeans, Roland sauntered off in the direction of the kitchen. 'Lunch won't be for ages and I'm starving. Want anything?'

'No thanks. I'm going to see Dad.'

Antonia found Quentin sitting at his desk, writing letters.

'My darling girl!' he greeted her warmly. Rising, he put his arms around her and held her close for a moment. 'It's so good to see you. Are you well? Come and sit down and tell me all your news.' He looked taller and thinner than ever, his angular frame gaunt under his baggy trousers and open-necked shirt.

Antonia, his only daughter, was his favourite child although he wouldn't admit it. From the moment she'd been born he'd loved her fighting spirit, so strong and bright, so clear-thinking and hard-working, so full of joy and a love of life. And as the years had passed – God! is she really thirty-two? he asked himself – she'd grown stronger and brighter with a smile to gladden his heart each time he saw her; his only regret was that she hadn't yet found someone to share her life, and he simply couldn't understand why. What was wrong with the young men of today? Why hadn't Antonia been snapped up years ago? It was a mystery to him. She'd make such a marvellous wife and mother. Quentin's only remaining ambition now was to live long enough to see her settled and to know her children.

As he sat down opposite her and took in her glowing face and sparkling eyes, he longed to hear what she'd been doing.

'Business is good, Dad,' she assured him. 'The Belgrave Square property is now under way.'

'That's the big job, isn't it?'

She nodded enthusiastically. 'It will make a fantastic ambassadorial residence, or a small embassy. I've already had enquiries from the governments of Oman and Austria. It's going to be restored to a very high standard, and I've got some brilliant builders on the site because not only do we have to do up the place to perfection, but we have to install a state-of-the-art security system as well, especially if I'm going to sell to a foreign state.'

Quentin nodded. 'I can see that. It's a lot of work, isn't it?'

'Yes, and a very expensive exercise, too, but I should make a packet and that will make the bank manager happy.'

At that moment the study door burst open and Hilary Murray came hurrying into the room, a large plastic apron over her tweed skirt, her grey hair wind-blown.

'Darling! How lovely to see you,' she exclaimed, as she removed her gardening gloves and kissed Antonia warmly on both cheeks. 'Have you heard the exciting news?'

Antonia turned to look at her father questioningly. He smiled and nodded in the direction of his wife.

'It's supposed to be a surprise, Hilary.'

Mrs Murray hesitated, suddenly unsure. 'Haven't you seen Roland?' she asked Antonia instead.

'Yes. He was outside in the drive when I arrived. Why? What's Roland got to do with . . . Oh!' Enlightenment dawned and her eyes widened. 'Why didn't he tell me?'

Her mother laughed conspiratorially. 'That's why I'm so thrilled you're here. Granny will be arriving any time now.'

'Granny?' Antonia was stunned. The Honourable Mrs Henry Cope, autocratic and snobbish mother of Hilary Murray, practically never came to stay. She lived in a rather imposing flat in one of the crescents in Bath, now that she was a widow and no longer occupied the nearby Ripple Manor, a fact she was anxious to impress on meeting people for the first time for fear they wouldn't realize just how grand her life had been.

'Why's Granny coming to stay?' Antonia asked in dismay. That meant changing for dinner and not being able to lounge around in jeans and bare feet. In fact it meant being on one's best behaviour all the time, as if one was spending the weekend with someone else's family.

'Granny's here! The car's coming up the drive,' they suddenly heard Roland shout from the hall.

Mrs Murray hurriedly removed her apron and shoved it and her gardening gloves behind the sofa. Quentin Murray rose to his feet and placed his arm around Antonia's shoulders.

'Roland wants to surprise you,' he murmured softly, giving her a reassuring smile. 'Don't let on that Mummy's let the cat out of the bag.'

Antonia nodded, as a lump formed in her throat. This

was something she'd been dreading for a long time, knowing it was inevitable and that when it happened she must play the part of the overjoyed sister. But it meant the first of the birds was flying the nest, and things would never be quite the same again. She glanced at her mother as she hurried into the hall, trying to gauge her feelings but as usual Hilary Murray was smiling, her features arranged with such mastery that none would guess that her warm smile of delight often covered deeper feelings.

Antonia and Quentin Murray followed her. Lavinia Cope, in an old-fashioned mink coat and dark red felt hat, was stepping out of the car she'd hired to bring her to Clifton Hall, and as she looked at them all they could sense a discontented querulousness in her demeanour. Roland, ever the diplomatic one, reached her first.

'Granny darling! You look marvellous. Thank you for coming.' He kissed her rouged cheeks carefully, and taking her by the elbow, guided her towards the others, as if she were special, as if she belonged only to him.

Slightly mollified, Lavinia Cope allowed herself to be greeted by her daughter, and then Antonia, before regarding Quentin with cold eyes, button-bright and sharp.

'Are you well, Quentin?' she asked, but without interest.

'All the better for seeing you, my dear Lavinia,' he replied, smoothly. Many years ago they'd formed a truce of mutual dislike, which they cloaked with formality and perfect manners.

Antonia gave her father a fleeting wink behind her grandmother's back, as they trooped into the hall and then Hilary hurried ahead, to lead the way into the drawing room, where they would have drinks before lunch.

'Of course, I can guess why I'm here,' Lavinia Cope remarked, as Roland took her heavy coat and Quentin came forward with a tray set with a decanter of sherry and glasses. 'Where is the girl?'

A frown flickered across Roland's handsome face. 'Jinny will be down in a minute.' He caught Antonia's eye and grinned. 'It's not much of a secret I suppose, but I thought it would be fun to make a formal announcement.'

She smiled back, pleased for him, happy for his sake, but wishing with all her heart that Jinny was someone she really adored.

It was now nearly one o'clock, and as if attached to some homing device, Tristram sauntered into the house from his walk, just in time for drinks. Leo was with him.

'Sherry?' Tristram said, after he'd greeted his grandmother and Antonia. 'Ugh! I think I'll have a whisky if you don't mind.' He strolled over to the drinks cabinet at one end of the drawing room.

As Hilary sipped her Dry Fly, vaguely wondering why she'd accepted a glass because she really didn't care for sherry either, she looked around, relishing this moment of having the whole family around her. But where was Jinny? Shouldn't she be down by now? She seemed to spend an inordinate amount of time doing her face and hair and so she supposed she was still stuck upstairs in front of a mirror. Then Hilary's eyes alighted on Antonia and she felt a deep pang of pain that they weren't going to be announcing any exciting news about *her* future. It was so easy for the boys. They would always find as many girls as they wanted to bring them happiness, but Antonia . . . Hilary stifled a sigh and wished she could wave a magic wand and make everything perfect for her adored daughter.

'Am I not to be shown to my room before lunch?' Lavinia Cope was asking in a loud voice.

Hilary got to her feet. 'Of course, Mother. I'll take you up right away.'

They climbed the stairs to the first floor, side by side, and yet the gulf between them was like a deep abyss. There were moments, like now, when Hilary felt her mother was a stranger; remote, cool and uncaring. As always, though, she tried to reach out and be the sort of daughter any parent would be proud to have.

'Your usual room is all ready for you, Mother,' she said ingratiatingly.

Lavinia Cope ignored the remark. 'One of your women will do my unpacking, won't they? Simpson packed for me, of course. She really knows how to do it properly.' Mrs Simpson, who had originally been a parlourmaid at Ripple Hall now worked for Mrs Cope as a general dogsbody, and Hilary felt sorry for her because she had no family and nowhere else to go.

'I'll unpack for you, Mother, after lunch.'

Lavinia stopped at the top of the stairs and stared at her daughter. 'Why can't one of your women do it? What do you pay them for? I never believe in paying the dog and barking yourself.'

'Mother, they're basically cleaning women from the village. One of them happens to be an excellent cook. They're not ladies' maids.'

Mrs Cope appeared not to hear because she paused and pointed to a closed door halfway down the landing.

'Who's in that room?'

'No one. That's the other spare room, Mother. You're the only guest this weekend apart from all the children.' Hilary was just thinking how absurd it was to refer to Tristram, Antonia, Roland and Leo as 'children', when Lavinia Cope laid a hand on her arm, pulling her back.

'You're surely not letting them sleep together *under your roof*!' She looked shocked and scandalized. Standing rock-still she glared at Hilary as if she expected her to face damnation.

For a second Hilary looked bemused, before realizing what her mother was referring to: Roland and his girlfriend Jinny. They'd been living together for the past two years and neither she nor Quentin had any objection to them sharing Roland's old room when they came for weekends. In fact, Hilary thought, to have done otherwise would have been hypocritical.

'Mother, things are different these days. Why put them in different rooms? What would be the point?'

The Honourable Mrs Henry Cope moved on towards her own room with frigid dignity as if she couldn't bear the proximity of her own daughter.

'They should respect the fact that this is your house, and you should not be seen to condone immorality. There are such things as standards.'

'Hi, Antonia!' Jinny swept into the drawing room as if she owned the place. Small, dynamic and with a strong, square jaw and determined blue eyes she radiated self-confidence although she was, as Antonia reminded herself, only twenty-two. Her hair, drawn back into a ponytail, was streaky blonde, and her only make-up was a touch of frosted pale pink lipstick. Exuding energy in tight white jeans and a navy-blue shirt, she strode about in search of a gin and tonic as if she were prospecting for gold.

Roland quickly came to her rescue with a brimming cut-crystal tumbler, topped by a slice of lemon trapped in a miniature ice floe. 'Here you are, darling.'

'Thanks.' Jinny took it from Roland without looking at him. She turned back to Antonia. 'Has old Daggers turned up yet?' Ever since she'd first met Lavinia Cope she'd referred to her as Daggers, 'because of the way she looks at you', she'd explained.

Antonia's smile was polite. 'Yes.' She glanced at her watch. She could tell it was going to be a very long weekend.

An hour later, as they all sat having lunch in the Jacobean-style dining room, Roland gently tapped his spoon against his glass to call for silence.

'I expect you can guess why I wanted you all here, today.' There was a ripple of amused assent and he looked bashful. Quentin and Hilary, seated at either end of the long refectory table, smiled at him encouragingly while Tristram and Leo hurriedly refilled their wine glasses. Lavinia Cope looked, as always, as if she had a bad smell under her nose but was too polite to mention it, but it was Antonia who braced herself, knowing that whichever way she looked at it, this was going to be an emotional moment for them all, made worse by the knowledge that Jinny would not have been their first choice of a wife for Roland. It felt as if he were leaving them all behind. Never again would he come home for weekends and at Christmas by himself. Never again would he belong just to them; there would always be someone else, from now on, who came first in his life.

This was the beginning of the family breaking up, and suddenly Antonia felt her eyes sting with unshed tears. She avoided looking at her mother, because she knew they shared the same feelings.

'I'd like you all to know . . . that Jinny and I . . . have . . . that is, we're engaged. We hope to marry in the autumn.' The words came out in a rush, tumbling over each other, leaving Roland scarlet in the cheeks and sweating. He held Jinny's hand tightly.

She's as cool as a cucumber, Antonia thought, glancing at her future sister-in-law, who looked composed and even a little triumphant. Then the awful thought crossed her mind that perhaps Jinny wasn't truly in love with Roland. Maybe she was just marrying him because she wanted a husband, like . . . Jane and Barbara and even Denise, though she'd hotly deny it. And like me, too, Antonia reflected.

'Congratulations!' everyone was saying, 'Here's to your future happiness . . .' Glasses were raised, Hilary reached over and kissed her son gently on the cheek before kissing Jinny, and Quentin left his seat to embrace them both. Amid loud chatter, everyone was soon kissing everyone, and Tristram and Leo were thumping Roland on the back and talking cheerily about 'making the most of his last few months of freedom', which Jinny didn't think was funny.

'Show them your ring, darling,' Roland told her. There was excitement in his voice, reminding Antonia of when he'd been a little boy, telling them about the shelter he'd built in the woods, before dragging them all off to see it.

Jinny delved down her front and withdrew a fine gold chain on which hung a ring.

'Let's put it on now,' Roland urged her eagerly. He slid a gold ring with a cluster of tiny diamonds on to her third finger. Antonia watched, filled with a protective tenderness.

'Oh, it's beautiful,' Hilary exclaimed warmly. 'Did you choose it together?'

'No, I got it as a surprise for Jinny.' Again the pride in his voice.

'It's sweet,' Lavinia Cope observed, glancing down at the large diamonds in her own rings. 'Sweet.'

Absurdly, Antonia wanted to weep for that little boy of long ago because his joy, now, at getting engaged to Jinny, was so touching. If Jinny didn't make him happy . . .! Antonia clenched her jaw, determined not to cry.

Lavinia Cope, feeling left out because she wasn't the centre of attention, something she couldn't bear, suddenly spoke.

'And when on earth are *you* going to get married, Antonia?' she asked accusingly. 'You'd better hurry up, you know, or you'll be left on the shelf. You're already over thirty, aren't you?'

Hilary glared at her mother in horrified silence, but Quentin spoke calmly and serenely.

'Antonia will marry when she feels like it, and *if* she feels like it. It is no longer an essential move for a woman these days and if she wants to be a career girl, that's all right with me.' Then he smiled fondly at his daughter, feeling the depth of her anguish because they'd always been close, determined she would not be humiliated by her bitch of a grandmother. He'd never liked Lavinia, who'd told him often over the years that Hilary had made the worst mistake of her life by marrying him, but he did his duty as a son-in-law and host when she came to stay. He could not, however, allow her to get away with talking so woundingly to Antonia.

There was an awkward silence.

Tristram, sensitive to the situation, suggested they have coffee in the drawing room. 'I'll bring yours up to your room. I'm sure you will want to have a rest, Gran,' he added affably, winking at Antonia.

Lavinia looked at him stonily. 'Why should I want to rest? I want to watch racing on the television.'

'At least it will keep her quiet,' Leo whispered to Antonia, as they left the dining room. She shot him a grateful look.

'I think I'll take the dogs for a walk,' she murmured.

'I'll come with you,' said Leo.

'So will I,' Tristram announced stoutly. He looked at Amber, Jacko and Rags. 'Walkies? Come on, then.'

Roland rushed up and caught Antonia's hand as she headed for the front door.

'Are you all right?' he whispered. 'Don't pay any attention to Granny, you know how she goes on.'

Jinny, beside him, looked at Antonia with patronizing sympathy. 'So unnecessary of her to talk to you like that, though,' she added with a smug little smile.

Antonia raised her chin. 'Let's not make a drama out of

it,' she said lightly. But nevertheless she was deeply hurt by her grandmother's spitefulness. Her words had hit their mark, making Antonia wonder if other people regarded her as 'left on the shelf'. And why did it seem that, quite suddenly, everyone had marriage on their minds in one way or another? Including herself? The pressure was definitely on to get married and start a family before it was too late. Get your skates on it, the pundits warned, or you'll miss that fictional boat which seemed to spend its time leaving people stranded on the quayside.

Crash was so pleased to see her when she arrived back at her flat on Sunday afternoon, that he came running down the corridor, miaowing loudly and dribbling all over her new suede boots.

'How's my sweetheart?' she murmured, picking him up and holding him in her arms. His whiskers tickled her cheek as he rubbed his head against hers, purring all the while with ferocious passion. 'Has Mrs Miller given you your lunch?'

Antonia's neighbour, an elderly widow who lived in the flat above and who adored cats, always came in to feed Crash when she was away.

His feeding bowl contained the last few shreds of a chicken breast which he sniffed but disdained to finish.

'Chicken! So who's a spoiled boy?' She had a suspicion Mrs Miller sometimes gave the cat her own lunch. There was also cream in his drinking bowl. 'I'm surprised you don't leave home and move in with *her*,' she remarked, rinsing the bowls and giving him fresh water which the vet had told her was much better for cats. Crash regarded her action with silent disapproval and then suddenly remembered he'd been grooming himself when she'd interrupted him. Turning his back on her, he stuck one of his hind legs in the air, and resumed his toilette.

Flinging her weekend bag on to her bed to be unpacked later, she took the Sunday papers into her living room, and with a sigh of relief, curled up on the sofa. Oh! the utter bliss of being back in her own flat. She stretched luxuriously, stuffed a cushion under her head and started to read the *Sunday Express*, in the knowledge that she wouldn't be disturbed for the rest of the evening. It wasn't that she didn't care for her family; she did, very much, and she knew they cared deeply for her, but this weekend had been particularly stressful.

At half past six, the phone rang. Dislodging Crash from her lap, she got up to answer it.

'Antonia? Oh, thank God you're in.' It was her friend, Emma Hall, whom she'd met when they both worked for Kensington estate agents Hutton, Datchet and Compton.

'Hello, Emma! How are you?'

'Terrible.' Emma's voice broke and Antonia could tell something was very wrong.

'What's happened?'

'Tom's left me.'

'*What?* Oh God, I'm so sorry.'

Emma was sobbing so hard she could hardly speak.

'Can I come round . . . to see you? I don't think I can bear . . . bear being alone.'

'Of course. Come over right away.' Antonia felt shocked.

42

Tom was one of the nicest men she'd ever met; fun and with a great sense of humour, good-looking and kind. It had been taken for granted, in their circle of friends, that he and Emma would get married one of these days.

Antonia got out the gin, and some ice and lemon. From experience she knew this was going to be an evening of indulgence. Five of her friends had been dumped by their respective boyfriends over the years, and she was an expert at bringing out all the words of wisdom such as: You're better off without him. I never liked him in the first place. You never know, he may come back. He'll live to regret this.

It had all been said before, and no doubt it would all be said again.

Twenty minutes later Emma came stumbling into her flat, bent over like an old woman and her face ravaged with crying.

'I wish I were dead,' she wailed dramatically, sinking on to the sofa. Her short dark hair, usually sleekly brushed, was sticking up in tufts. She gazed at Antonia, eyes blurred with despair. 'What am I going to do?'

Antonia put her arm around Emma's shoulders. 'Poor lamb. What happened?'

'He asked me out to dinner, said he had something to tell me. I was . . . so excited,' she sobbed.

'And . . .?'

'I thought he was going to ask me to marry him. We have been going out for three years . . . and I thought . . . at *last*!' She reached in her pocket for a sodden wodge of tissue. 'I was *so happy*.'

Antonia could guess what was coming.

'But instead,' Emma sobbed, 'he said he just didn't fancy

me any more and he told me right at the start of dinner. Can you imagine? I had to sit there, weighing my way through *Escalope de veau*, while I was choking with misery. I could have killed him for telling me in a public place.'

'Oh, Em, I'm so sorry. What a swine.'

'I think he's met someone else.'

'I don't suppose he has,' Antonia said comfortingly.

'Then why? *Why*?' Renewed sobs overcame Emma again. 'I feel such a failure. What can I do to get him back?'

Antonia spoke carefully. 'Have you thought that you might be better off without him . . .? in the long run?'

Emma shook her head miserably. 'I'll never find anyone like Tom again. I love him and I know he loves me. I *know* it. Someone must have poisoned him against me; some bitch who wants to get her claws into him.'

As Antonia had anticipated, it was a long evening and there seemed to be nothing she could do or say to comfort her friend. All Emma wanted to do was talk, so Antonia let her hash over the past twenty-four hours again and again, relive the dreadful moment when Tom had told her it was all over, and speculate about the future.

'How am I ever going to find anyone like Tom?' she kept saying. 'I don't think I've got the energy to do it all over again, either. You know, meeting someone, then getting to know them, then deciding when to go to bed with them. Then all those *years* of trying to be the perfect partner. Always striving to look one's best. Always being nice to his mother. God, the time and effort I've *wasted* on Tom, and it's all been for nothing.'

Eventually Emma realized it was after midnight.

'You can stay here if you like,' Antonia suggested. 'This sofa turns into a bed and it's quite comfortable.'

Emma gave a deep sigh. 'Thanks, but I think I'd better be getting back. I'll call the office tomorrow and say I'm ill.'

'Are you sure you'll be OK?'

'As OK as I'll ever be.'

Antonia called her a taxi and made her promise to keep in touch. 'I don't want you to be on your own, Em, if it all gets too much.'

'Thanks. Don't tell Jane and Barbara, will you?'

Antonia looked puzzled. They'd all been friends for a long time, and usually told each other everything.

'. . . Or Denise,' Emma added with feeling. 'She'll say "I told you so", and try to enlist me in her lesbian movement.'

Antonia laughed. 'Denise doesn't have much use for men, does she?'

'That's only because she can't get one,' Emma replied crisply.

Antonia lay awake for a long time after Emma had left, saddened by the news of Tom's departure. That was one relationship she'd been sure was going to work. Maybe falling in love was not the right way to go about finding a life partner? Maybe it should be approached in a more matter-of-fact way, as they did in some other countries, where marriages were not left to chance, but arranged with care. Was it such a frightful idea? As the hours passed, and she was still wide awake, a plan was forming in her mind. She personally didn't know anyone who'd done it, but it might just work, and what had she to lose, providing she kept it a secret? But wasn't it risky? And where should she start? Still in a state of indecision she finally fell into a troubled sleep and dreamed that her grandmother had already booked Westminster Abbey for her wedding.

Two

Antonia spent a long time wording her advertisement, which she did, for the sake of privacy, when she got back to her flat the following evening. But even on her own, curled up on the sofa with her supper on a tray, she felt curiously embarrassed and self-conscious about the whole thing. It seemed such a calculating way of trying to find a life partner. Somehow it also felt shameful. No one must ever know, she thought, as she read dozens of advertisements in what was now referred to as the *Kindred Spirits* column in the upmarket newspapers, in order to get some inspiration.

'Attractive redhead, 5ft 4, desires tall dark handsome man with GSOH . . .' What was that? 'Intelligent cultured lady, 63 . . .' *Sixty-three!* . . . 'I have everything but you . . .!' 'Looking for Prince Charming, frogs need not apply . . .' And to have to resort to the Personal column, in the first place, indicated total failure. Pretty young women never had to take an ad to find a man. Pretty young women had men falling over their own feet in their eagerness. Pretty young women could pick and choose. Then she was struck by another thought. Supposing even this method of finding someone didn't work? Supposing dozens of men replied, but after the first meeting, never wanted to see her again? Going, in turn, hot and cold, she tapped away at her laptop. After all, as she reminded herself, what had she to lose? It took her two hours to get it right.

> *Tall, slim, town-dwelling career girl, 32, with own company, seeks man of similar age with sense of humour, for serious relationship. Likes children & animals, theatre, music, good food. Photograph please.*

Antonia read it several times, trying to see it from a man's point of view. It was honest, she reflected, and showed that she was a working woman who was not likely to abandon her career in exchange for an apron and a washing-up bowl, yet she did eventually want children. It also showed that she wasn't just out for an adventure.

Tomorrow she would arrange to put it in the *Sunday Telegraph*, with a PO box number, and then wait and see what happened. What would it be like, meeting a total stranger with a view to a relationship? And how on earth should she handle that first meeting?

On the following Sunday her advertisement appeared, surrounded by rather more, she thought, tantalizingly worded pleas for partnership. She'd got up early, leaving Crash glaring at her accusingly because she hadn't yet given him his breakfast, and rushed round to the local newsagent's. The newspapers were stacked in a row and as she went to pay for them, she felt sure everyone in the shop knew all about her advert and knew that that was why she was buying that particular paper.

Once back home, she scanned the column. God! There were so many ads! 'Home alone last Christmas . . .' 'Attractive shapely blonde, 27 . . .' 'Creative black female . . .' Row after row of little ads, making her realize there were a lot of lonely people out there.

Then her heart gave a great nervous leap as she recognized her own wording. It was the same sort of frisson she'd experienced when her first advertisement for Murray Properties Ltd had appeared. Only this time it wasn't a house or a flat she was offering.

She'd taken the plunge and now would have to wait and see what happened, she reflected. And how soon could she expect a response? Quelling a burning desire to confess what she'd done, and share her feelings, part excitement, part fear, with someone else, she fed Crash and decided to spring-clean her flat. 'Nesting', her mother would have called it, and perhaps, Antonia thought, ironically, that was exactly what she was doing.

Within a week Antonia received thirty-seven letters of response. Some had typed envelopes, others were addressed to her in a range of handwriting, some of it quite feminine, and a variety of inks, from black and blue through to red, green and purple to one scrawled in gold.

Spreading them all on the floor one evening, with the photographs that had been enclosed placed on top of each letter, she surveyed them with fascination, hardly knowing where to start. There were older, balding men in their fifties and adolescent-looking boys who had hardly begun to shave. Then there were academic-looking men with glasses, and arty types with beards, making her wonder if she should have specified the sort of man she was attracted to. None of these fitted the bill and that was for sure, she thought with disappointment. One of the photographs showed a gross-looking man with a neck like a bull; he must have weighed twenty stone. In stark contrast, a skeletal face leered at her from the four-by-six print; he was the one who'd written in gold ballpoint.

At that moment Crash padded softly into the room, and surveyed this new strange carpet-covering with curiosity. After sniffing one of the photographs he started to walk across them in a deliberate fashion.

'Off!' Antonia scolded. 'Get off there, Crash!'

He ignored her until he came to the picture of the twenty-stone man. Then he sat neatly on the face and started washing his nether regions.

'Crash!' Antonia dissolved into giggles. 'So that's what you think of him, is it?'

The main front doorbell rang at that moment. Alarmed at being caught with her secret spread out before her, she gathered up the pictures and letters into a heap, mixing them all up, but what did it matter? There wasn't one she even wanted to *meet*. Stuffing the pile into the hall cupboard, she answered the intercom.

'Hello? Who is it?' she said in a fluster.

'Hi! It's me.'

'Roland! What a surprise! Come up.' She pressed the

switch and heard the street door buzzing. A minute later Roland came bounding up the stairs, taking them two at a time.

She greeted him with a hug. 'What are you doing up in London?' The firm of accountants he worked for was in St Albans and he hardly ever came to town.

Roland grimaced. 'Jinny's uncle has invited us to dinner at Claridge's. She's awfully anxious to go because he's rich, and as both her parents are dead she thinks he's going to leave her everything.'

Antonia led the way into the drawing room. 'Can I get you a drink?'

'Yes, please. I've come to ask you a favour, actually.' He hovered over her as she got out a bottle of gin and some tonic water from the drinks cupboard, in the bottom half of one of the bookcases she'd had built on either side of the fireplace.

'Where's Jinny?'

'She's meeting me there. She had things to do in town today; getting her hair done, and buying some clothes.'

Antonia handed him a drink. 'So what can I do for you, Ro?'

He sat in one of her large comfortable armchairs and looked slightly sheepish. 'The thing is, sis, we're planning to get married in October.'

'I know.' The weekend of his engagement, there'd been a lot of discussion about when and where the marriage should take place. As Jinny had no proper home, and no family to speak of, it was finally settled that it should be held at Clifton Hall, with a marquee in the garden and a local firm to do the catering.

'Mum wants to make all the arrangements,' Roland continued.

'So what's the problem? It seems perfect to me. Where else would you hold the reception?'

Frowning, he took a quick gulp of his drink. It was obvious he was embarrassed by what he was going to say, but at the same time, felt compelled to get it off his chest.

'The thing is . . . Jinny's not terribly happy about things.'

'What exactly is she not happy about?' Antonia spoke carefully.

He gave slight shrug. 'Oh, you know what it's like. She doesn't want the whole thing taken out of her hands. After all,' he continued loyally, 'it is *her* wedding, and she really wants to have a greater say in how it's arranged.'

'Who's paying for it all?'

Roland looked stunned. 'Does that matter? Jinny hasn't got any money. When her father died he only left a few thousand pounds and a cottage that wasn't worth anything. She's had to work, you know, jolly hard, to keep herself afloat.'

Don't we all? Antonia thought. Aloud, she said with equal loyalty: 'Mum's a brilliant hostess. Any arrangements she makes will be wonderful. And a wedding is a fairly straightforward occasion. I don't know what Jinny's worrying about.'

Roland flushed at the implied criticism in the tone of Antonia's voice. 'Jinny says she won't feel it's *her* wedding if someone else makes all the decisions,' he rejoined anxiously.

'But I'm sure Mum will consult her, Ro. Why doesn't

Jinny go through all the plans with Mum the next time you go home?'

'She doesn't want to do that.'

'Why not?' Antonia was genuinely amazed. None of this boded well for the future, either. If their parents were going to be kind enough to arrange *and* pay for the wedding, surely Jinny should be grateful?

'One only gets married once,' Roland protested. 'At least, that's the big idea. Jinny wants it to be *her* day and special. If her mother was alive, it would be different, but she isn't even particularly close to Mum.'

Antonia only resisted asking whose fault that was by biting her bottom lip and counting to ten. What was Jinny's problem? She and Roland had only just got engaged, her parents had bent over backwards to make her welcome in the family and had promised them both a beautiful wedding, and already she was complaining.

'Can you have a word with Mum,' Roland said persistently. 'Explain, you know, how Jinny feels. I'm sure every bride feels the same.'

'As far as I know, Mum is probably expecting Jinny to help plan it all,' Antonia argued. 'Why doesn't she have a word with Mum herself? Get it sorted?'

'I told you, she doesn't want to do that.'

'So what does she want to do?'

Roland looked embarrassed. 'She'd like to do it all herself. Choose the colour scheme for the marquee and the flowers . . . and decide on the menu and have a disco dance in the evening, after the reception . . . you know the sort of thing. You go to hundreds of weddings. She wants it to be different.'

'I'm sure,' Antonia said quietly. And Jinny obviously wants to make a big splash, she reflected silently. Aloud she said, 'Ro, I don't want to be drawn into this; you and Jinny must talk to Mum yourselves. What are you scared of, anyway? Mum's not a control freak. I expect she thought it would be a relief to Jinny to have all the arrangements taken care of.'

'Humph.' Roland didn't looked reassured. Then he looked at his wristwatch. 'Christ! I've got to go or I'll be late.' Jumping to his feet he gazed out of the window. 'Oh, shit! It's raining cats and dogs.'

Antonia followed his glance. The rain was falling like silver stair-rods through the still evening air.

'Can I borrow a brolly?' he asked. 'I promise not to lose it; otherwise I'll be soaked to the skin before I reach the end of the street in this downpour.'

'Yes, of course you can.' Antonia turned to leave the room, but Roland sprinted ahead into the hall, and then opened the cupboard where he knew she kept raincoats and umbrellas.

'What the . . .?' An avalanche of photographs of men and letters cascaded to his feet. Roland looked at Antonia with a shocked expression. 'What on earth are these?'

Scarlet-faced, Antonia couldn't think of any excuse that he'd believe. Even as a child she'd been a hopeless liar. Roland knew her too well, too. She'd never get away with some fabrication.

'Yes, well . . .' she began lamely.

He grabbed her wrist and his eyes were stricken. 'Oh, love, it's not as bad as that, is it?'

His sympathy made her want to cry. 'Please, Ro, please don't tell anyone. I haven't answered any of them. I probably won't either . . . just forget the whole thing. It was only done for a lark, anyway.'

Roland was skimming one of the letters. 'Christ! How pathetic.' He picked up another from the heap by his feet. 'I bet they're all losers. Men don't have to apply to lonely hearts ads unless there's something wrong with them.'

'That doesn't mean there has to be something wrong with me.' For some reason she felt deeply ashamed, as if her brother had caught her out doing something dishonest.

He immediately put his arms around her and hugged her close. '*Of course* there's nothing wrong with you, love. The trouble is there's a shortage of good men around. That's why there are so many girls in the same boat as you. But this is not the way to find a husband. Burn all these letters and pictures, Antonia. Forget the whole thing.'

A tear trickled down her cheek. 'But I do so want to get married and have children . . .' Her voice trailed off brokenly.

'You will. I promise you will.'

'But when? I'm working so hard, I don't even get to meet the right sort of man. Do you know it's about two years since I was even asked out on a date? So many of my friends are married now, and having babies, and the worst part of it all is that I feel so isolated when I'm with them. We don't seem to have anything in common any more.'

'It'll be all right, love. Don't worry. Someone fantastic will come along one day.' Roland glanced at his wristwatch again. 'I've got to fly or I'll be late. Now promise me you'll bin this lot.'

Antonia nodded. None of them appealed to her in any case.

'You won't say anything, will you? Mum and Dad would die if they knew. And I don't want you to tell Jinny.'

'OK. No problem.' He'd grabbed her big black umbrella and was hurrying to the front door.

'You promise, Ro?'

His kiss on the cheek was perfunctory. 'Promise. See you soon, and if you can have a word with Mum about the wedding . . .'

'You and Jinny must talk to Mum yourselves. She'll understand, Ro, but don't hurt her feelings. It's very kind of her to go to all the trouble of arranging your wedding in the first place.'

'I know. Now I really must go. Bye. And don't forget to bin all that rubbish.' He was running down the stairs as he spoke, shouting back over his shoulder.

After she'd heard the main street door bang shut, she bent down to pick up the scattered photographs and letters. What she'd said had been true; there wasn't one she liked the look of. So that, she thought, is the end of that.

To Antonia's surprise, she got a second batch of letters two days later, forwarded to her from her PO box number. She knew she was running late to get to the office, but she couldn't resist ripping them open to have a quick look. The first one showed yet again a middle-aged balding man with weary eyes and a disappointed mouth. The second looked like a grim schoolmaster with a beady expression. The third was bearded, no doubt to hide his mean mouth, and the fourth looked so lecherous that she guessed there was only one thing he was interested in, and it wasn't love and companionship. With a sinking heart she discarded them, without even bothering to read the accompanying letters. Maybe Roland was right; perhaps only hopeless losers replied to requests in the lonely hearts column.

When she opened the fifth envelope she gave the enclosed photograph a cursory glance, expecting it to be another man who would be a complete turn-off. But then she looked again, studying the face that smiled back at her with mounting interest. Dark humorous eyes and a generous mouth was what attracted her initially. That, and a regular bone structure, and the easy, unaffected way he was looking into the camera. His hair looked thick and dark and was well cut, and his open-necked shirt added to the casual air of someone who is comfortable in their own skin. Quickly she read his letter, handwritten in black ink on plain white paper. His name was Colin Holbrook, he was thirty-five, and English by birth. He'd been working in Canada for the past eleven years and had only recently been transferred to Britain to take up a post with a firm of stockbrokers in the City. He went on to say that his family came from Yorkshire, but as both his parents were dead, and he was an only child, he found himself living alone in a rented flat, without the time or the opportunity to make friends. He, too, apparently, liked children and animals, was an avid reader and music lover and had reached the stage in life when he longed to settle down and have a family. He ended by saying he'd very much like to meet her and hoped she'd phone him at home, any evening after seven-thirty. His address, she noted, was in Islington.

Antonia looked at his photograph again, suddenly feeling rather breathless. Everything about him was right. His face, his age and his business background. He looked as if he could be fun to be with, and his interests sounded akin to hers.

Most important, she thought, which set him apart from all the others, was that he had a real reason for wanting to meet someone. Anyone who had been away from the country for eleven years and had no family was naturally going to be out of touch. And love London though she did, she was also aware that if you didn't know many people, it was one of the loneliest cities in the world.

She didn't bother to look at the rest. Already late for work, she propped up the photograph of Colin Holbrook against a lamp on a side table, and decided she'd phone him during the evening.

Crash, watching with interest, rose from his position in front of the fireplace, and seemed to be gauging the height of the table.

'Don't even *think* about it!' Antonia warned. 'If the picture isn't valuable, the lamp is.'

He chirruped in answer and then casually sashayed his way out of the room, as if he'd never had an interest in the photograph in the first place.

There was a stack of messages on her desk when she arrived at work, and Linda seemed to be cheerfully coping with three incoming phone calls at the same time. Mark Gillingham and Guy Ramsay were both out of the office, showing clients, respectively, the Wilton Place property, which was in the final stages of being decorated and furnished, and a flat in Chelsea which Antonia had recently converted. Sally Adamson, the senior negotiator, apart from Antonia, was discussing a property with their most valued German client, whose Berlin company wanted to purchase an apartment. Carina Knight, sitting at the desk nearest Antonia, was in charge of building; she was giving the foreman detailed instructions about fittings for the Belgrave Square mansion, which was nearing completion and scheduled to go on the market in three months' time.

Throughout the day, which never seemed to come to an end, Antonia kept thinking about Colin Holbrook, and in her mind's eye seeing his face in the photograph. From the moment she'd set eyes on it that morning she'd felt drawn to him. He was just her type, good-looking without being too handsome, with nice dark hair and intelligent eyes. Good-humoured too, yet with enough command about him to be taken seriously.

As soon as she got back to her flat she picked up the photograph again and studied it for a while. It was a heart-stopping thought to realize that she could be looking at the man with whom she might spend the rest of her life. It was time to phone him. How would he sound? Would his voice be as nice as his face? Little shivers of excitement made her heart race and the promise to her brother was forgotten. Not that she didn't understand Roland's reservations. This was a step in the dark. For all she knew a psychopath might have answered her advertisement. Or someone who thought 'career girl' meant rich. Or a criminal recently released from prison who needed a roof over his head.

On the other hand, she reasoned, Colin Holbrook was different. His description of himself and what he'd done was both plausible and likely.

Antonia glanced at her wristwatch. It was fifteen minutes to eight. Taking a deep breath, she seated herself on the living room sofa and picked up the phone. As a precaution, she dialled 141 before punching his number, thus ensuring he wouldn't be able to trace her call.

'Can I speak to Colin Holbrook, please?' Antonia tried to keep her voice steady, casual even, while her heart thumped and she felt as if she'd forgotten how to breathe.

'This is Colin Holbrook speaking.' The voice was warm in timbre and educated.

'Oh, hello. This is the box number you wrote to . . .' and then she had a moment of panic as it suddenly struck her that he might have replied to several box numbers and how would he know which one she was?

'. . . I'm the one that said I was a slim, town-dwelling career girl . . .' she said hurriedly.

'. . . Looking for someone with a sense of humour?' he broke in and there was laughter in his voice.

'Yes. And I'm only interested in having a serious relationship . . .'

'That's right. And you like children and animals.'

Unexpectedly Antonia found herself blushing hotly at the mention of children. It sounded so incredibly intimate coming from someone she'd never even met. Someone who might become her lover and the father of her children.

Then she heard him chuckle. 'Don't worry. Yours was

the only one I replied to. The only one that struck a chord. Can we meet, d'you think?'

'Yes. Yes, of course.'

'How about a drink after work? Is tomorrow evening any good? Where do you live?'

Antonia felt he was taking the initiative away from her, and that was not what she had intended. Neither did she want, at this stage, for him to know where she lived or worked.

'I live in town,' she replied non-committally. 'I suggest we meet somewhere central; how about the bar of the Chelsea Hotel? In Sloane Street?' She knew it well, as it was five minutes' walk from her office and she often met clients in its pleasant but impersonal ambience. There was also the added advantage of the bar being an open space on the first floor by the staircase, so if the meeting was a disaster it would be easy to make a graceful exit.

'Fine,' Colin was saying. 'I'll be coming from the City so I won't be able to make it until seven. Will that be OK?'

'Yes. That would be perfect.'

'Seven o'clock it is, and can I take you out to dinner afterwards?'

This is going too fast, she thought. It's as if he's already made up his mind . . .

'Let's see how it goes,' she said firmly.

'OK.' He didn't sound at all put out. 'There's just one thing . . .'

'What's that?'

'How will I recognize you? You've got my picture so you'll know me, but I don't even know whether you're blonde

61

or brunette!' He laughed in such a relaxed and easy fashion that Antonia wished she had as much composure. As it was, her hands were shaking and her stomach was tied in a tight knot. She could hardly believe she was *doing* this . . . and then she thought, *what shall I wear?*

'I'll be wearing a cream suit,' she replied with outward calm, 'and I'm sort of brownish-blonde.'

'. . . and tall and slim; I remember you put that.'

'Yes.'

'Then I'll very much look forward to seeing you tomorrow evening. By the way, what's your name?'

Now she felt vulnerable and exposed. Once she told him her name he'd be able to trace her . . . and if she didn't like him when they met, but he became more persistent . . .

'Susan.' It wasn't a lie. She'd been christened Antonia Susan.

'Susan . . .?'

'Just Susan.'

He chuckled. 'OK. Then you have the advantage over me. I'll greatly look forward to seeing you tomorrow evening and, well, we can take it from there.'

'Exactly. I'll see you then.'

When they'd said goodbye Antonia sat still for several minutes, staring at the photograph of Colin Holbrook. His face held her spellbound. It seemed so incredibly unrealistic that one could change the whole course of one's life – who one lived with, where one lived and everything one did – by putting a small advertisement in a newspaper. Was this what fate was all about? Life's lucky dip? Had she been destined to meet Colin in any case? Would she have met him at a dinner party if she hadn't used a lonely hearts column? Or bumped into him in the checkout queue at a supermarket? Might he have been a friend of Roland or Tristram or Leo?

Had this meeting which was to take place in the bar of a swish hotel the next evening been predestined all along? It rather seemed to her that it might be so, because now that she'd spoken to Colin and heard his voice, she felt convinced that this meeting between them had been meant to happen. Perhaps, for the past few years, it had been ordained that she should remain on her own, awaiting the ultimate agency that finally predetermines the course of events. But surely it couldn't be as easy as all that? And as effortless? When she considered how long it had taken her and how hard she'd worked to get her business off the ground, it seemed ridiculous that one advertisement, which had taken a few hours to compose, could bring her everything she wanted.

Of course it was Jane, she reflected, who in her laid-back way had always said that there was someone for everyone, and that sooner or later that person would come along. Perhaps she was right?

When the mobile phone rang, Antonia jumped. If it was Roland he'd know something was up by her voice, and this was something she definitely wanted to keep to herself. Apart from her promise to Roland, she wanted to make sure she wasn't making a complete fool of herself over Colin Holbrook. He might turn out to be a real *nerd*! Snatching up the phone she pulled out the aerial and switched on.

'Who is that?' she asked carefully.

'Hi! This is Jane.'

'*Jane?* I don't believe it . . .!'

'What's the matter?'

'I was thinking about you this very minute,' Antonia exclaimed, stunned.

'Were you?' Jane sounded gratified. 'Why?'

'Er . . .' She realized she couldn't tell Jane what she'd been thinking about without giving her activities away. 'I was thinking . . . I must give a dinner party soon. And you must come.'

'That sounds fun, but I thought you hated giving dinner parties. You always say there aren't enough interesting single men and you don't want to end up with nothing but lovey-dovey newly married couples.'

'That's right. I don't.'

'Then why are you bothering?'

If there was one thing about Jane that annoyed Antonia it was that she always took everything absolutely literally and with total seriousness. She was the sort of person who would spend ten minutes splitting a restaurant bill when they went Dutch, even down to details like who'd ordered a second glass of wine or a pudding, instead of just halving the amount.

'Maybe I won't,' Antonia replied.

'Then why were you thinking of it in the first place?'

Oh *God*! Antonia groaned inwardly. 'Perhaps I'll make it a drinks party instead,' she said feebly.

'That's a good idea. When will you give it?'

'God knows. Listen, how are things with you?'

'That's why I'm ringing.' Jane sounded mysterious. 'I've met someone.'

'You have? That's great, Jane. What's he like? Where

did you meet?' Antonia felt genuinely glad for her. It also reinforced her belief that Jane *had* been right; there was someone for everyone.

'It's too embarrassing . . . you'll never believe this . . . I mean, it's like that film, you know, when the—'

'Jane, where did you meet him?'

Jane spoke so low Antonia could barely make out what she was saying. 'My washing machine broke down, so I went to the local launderette . . .' Then her voice faded away altogether.

'. . . You met him in the launderette?' Antonia shrieked in delight. 'But that's terrific. Tell me all about him! What's he like?' She was bursting with curiosity. Was it possible, she secretly conjectured, that in a few weeks' time she could introduce Colin to Jane? And Jane could introduce . . .?

'What's his name?' she interjected.

Jane seemed to spend some time clearing her throat before she muttered something unintelligible.

'Sorry. I didn't catch that,' said Antonia.

'I said his name is Percy.' Jane sounded uncharacteristically defiant. 'Percy Beresford. He's thirty-eight and he's a tax inspector.'

'Sounds great.' Antonia winced inwardly. Tax inspectors, as far as she was concerned, should be eliminated from the face of the earth. Never mind: Jane was obviously happy. 'Where does he live?'

'In St John's Wood.'

The kiss of death, Antonia reflected, remembering the dreary house an ancient aunt of hers had lived in, in Acacia Road.

'But his mother left him a large house with a garden,' Jane continued. 'It's very nice, with some lovely big rooms.'

'So . . . you can just imagine yourself ensconced, can you? Living in a ten-bedroom house with—'

'Oh, it only has five bedrooms,' Jane cut in earnestly, 'but it does have two bathrooms and space for a third.'

Antonia was beginning to get the distinct feeling that Jane was actually looking for a des res rather than a husband.

'How lovely,' she remarked sweetly. 'And no doubt there is a nursery, too?'

Unabashed, Jane laughed. 'A *huge* nursery,' she admitted ingenuously. 'I can't wait for you to meet Percy. He's so *nice*, and *kind*.'

'I am glad for you,' Antonia said with sincerity. 'You deserve someone nice.'

'I wondered if you'd like to come to drinks tomorrow night? It's not a party, but I've invited a few old friends; Kay and Melvyn Buxton, Barbara, Emma, Denise . . .'

All the old gang, Antonia reflected, Barbara and Emma were certainly going to feel left out if Jane got married before them, even if Percy was a tax inspector.

'I don't think I can make it,' she replied, feigning regret. 'I'm already doing something.'

'You and your work! What are you doing? Meeting clients?'

'That sort of thing.'

'Why don't you get someone else in your office to meet them? Surely you can get out of it?'

'I'm afraid this time I can't. They're . . . um . . . Japanese, and they're looking for a house in central London,' she explained, horrified at herself for being able to lie to an old friend with such glibness.

'Oh, *dear*!' Jane sounded disappointed. 'I did so want you to meet Percy, so you could tell me what you think of him.'

'I'd really love to meet him, Jane, but it shouldn't matter what anyone else thinks.'

'Oh, but I think it does. I don't know how good my judgement is and I'm so desperate for it to work. We're so right for each other, and he's the man I've been waiting for all this time.'

'Then you've nothing to worry about, have you?'

'No . . .' Jane hesitated. 'But I would still like one of my friends to confirm that he's right for me.'

'If he's right for you, you'll know it. You won't need anyone to tell you,' said Antonia, quoting from one of the endless articles she'd read in women's magazines about finding a mate. Fleetingly she let herself dwell for a moment on her meeting with Colin Holbrook the following evening; would she know if he was right for her?

'I'll tell you what I'll do, Jane. If my meeting doesn't last long,' *because Colin is not what I'd hoped for*, she secretly thought, 'I'll come along later.'

'Oh, will you?' Jane sounded pathetically grateful.

'Yes, but I'm not promising. You know what these clients are like.' *Supposing I really like Colin and he asks me out to dinner . . .*

'I do understand, Antonia. I know how important it is to you, but it would be lovely if you could join us, as soon as you're through.'

'I'll do what I can,' Antonia promised, and that much was true, she reflected. If Jane were to know her real reason for refusing the invitation, she'd be even more understanding. But that was something Antonia was going to keep to herself. For ever. No matter what happened.

Antonia dressed with care the next morning, putting on the cream suit as she'd said, and choosing a becoming pair of gold earrings. With the suit she teamed pale tights and cream shoes, and then she tucked her make-up into her briefcase so she could freshen up before she left the office to meet Colin.

It was hard to concentrate on work. Through the large windows of Murray Properties Ltd, she found herself gazing vacantly at the constant flow of traffic passing up and down Sloane Street, and at the shoppers, mostly well-dressed ladies, laden with Peter Jones and General Trading Company carriers bags, and the beatific smiles of women who know they have run up large amounts on their husbands' credit cards.

'. . . And the builders want to know whether to go ahead or not.'

Antonia suddenly realized Linda had been talking to her, but she'd been so immersed in her own thoughts she hadn't heard a word.

'I'm sorry, Linda. What was that?'

Linda grinned and started again. 'The builders who are working on the Belgrave Square property have found a problem with condensation in one of the bathrooms and they want to know whether to go ahead and insulate the walls, before it's decorated, or not?'

'Which bathroom is it? There are five in the house,'

Antonia replied, pulling herself together with an effort.

Linda consulted her notepad. 'The one on the third floor at the back.'

Antonia nodded knowingly. 'The problem with that one is that it has three outside walls, so the moment you put on any heating, when it's cold outside, the walls start to stream. Get a quote from them, will you, Linda? Don't let them go ahead without a written sanction from us. I know what these builders are like. Just because I'm a woman they think they can blind me with science. Look out the surveyor's report, too. I think he warned us about this problem when we originally bought the property.'

Forcing herself to concentrate, although Colin Holbrook's face in the photograph kept filling her mind, she worked steadily all day, having takeaway sushi from Prêt à Manger for lunch with a bottle of mineral water. Shortly after six, the others started to clear their desks and collect their things. Sally was going to the theatre with her boyfriend, and Carina was off to a party, while Mark was taking his girlfriend out to dinner and Guy was rushing back to his wife who was pregnant and not feeling well. Linda was usually the last to leave. Her husband, Robin, was a banker and also worked late most evenings, and so she was happy to stay until all the loose ends had been tied up.

Antonia sometimes wondered if Linda didn't stay on to keep her company, knowing she had no one to rush home to. Except for Crash.

Tonight, though, Linda seemed anxious to be off. She was gathering up her things and kept looking at her watch, and her expression was slightly anxious.

'Is it all right . . .?' she began.

'Of course it is,' Antonia assured her warmly. 'I've got to meet someone at seven o'clock so I'm leaving in a few minutes anyway.'

'Are you sure?'

'Absolutely. You get off. I'll lock up. It's no problem.'

Linda looked relieved. 'Thanks so much.'

'Are you and Robin doing anything special tonight?'

'No. Not really. I just have to get a lot done,' Linda replied vaguely. Her hands shook as she took her car keys out of her handbag.

'Is everything OK, Linda?' Antonia suddenly asked intuitively. She could sense something was wrong. In all the years Linda had worked for her, she'd been the most placid one in the office; always cheerful in a matter-of-fact way, always calm and unfazed by anything. Tonight, though, she seemed edgy, almost nervous about something.

'I'm fine,' Linda replied briskly, eyes averted. 'I'll see you tomorrow. Have a good meeting.' Without looking back, she swung through the glass doors and was gone.

Antonia sat for several minutes, puzzling over Linda's unusual behaviour. Perhaps she'd been too absorbed in her own thoughts about meeting Colin Holbrook to have noticed something was wrong? Perhaps Linda was having problems with Robin? Or maybe – horror of horrors – she'd been offered a better job. Antonia felt a dart of alarm at the thought of losing her righthand person. She depended on Linda so much, perhaps too much, and she knew it would be hard to replace her if she left. Making a mental note to have a quiet word with her in the morning to find out what was going on,

Antonia hurried to the cloakroom to redo her make-up. It was now twenty minutes to seven. With hands that shook every bit as much as Linda's, she noticed with something akin to amusement, she washed her face and applied fresh foundation and blusher and a coral-coloured lipstick. Then she brushed her shoulder-length hair until the blonde highlights gleamed under the cloakroom spotlights, and regarded her reflection critically. There was no doubt about it. She looked good. The cream suit gave her skin a pearly glow and flattered her figure.

It was five minutes to seven. Turning off the lights, she threw the alarm switch and locked the heavy glass doors behind her. If she hurried she could be at the hotel in three or four minutes. She decided to take the short walk at a steady pace. Better to make an elegant late entrance than be on time and breathless.

The brightly lit windows of the shops in Sloane Street displayed their luxurious wares with tempting panache, but this evening Antonia's thoughts were on other things. With barely a glance at the designer clothes and shoes and jewellery that would have normally caused her to pause and look, she walked briskly towards the Chelsea Hotel, and as she informed herself dramatically, her future.

Once inside the glittering marble lobby, she turned to her left and slowly climbed the open-style staircase to the first floor, to a gallery with a mirrored bar and a selection of small tables and comfortable armchairs. She paused to glance around, her heart hammering uncomfortably, hoping to see the now familiar face of Colin Holbrook. She'd been waiting for this moment for twenty-four hours now, and her expectations grew higher by the moment. The place was full of couples, except for a group of four businessmen who were engaged in serious talk, and two women who, judging by the packages at their feet, had obviously dropped in for a restorative cocktail after a hard day's serious shopping.

Then she saw a man sitting up at the bar. His hair was dark, and although he had his back to her, she felt a frisson of excitement, certain that this was Colin Holbrook. He was sipping what looked like a whisky and soda and as she started walking towards him, on legs that felt as heavy as if she were treading waist-deep in treacle, she heard the clatter of high heels on marble as a small woman with a mass of red hair propelled herself past Antonia in the direction of the man, exclaiming loudly: 'Piers! I'm so sorry darling! The wretched traffic . . .'

The man swung round on the stool to greet the woman and Antonia realized it wasn't Colin Holbrook at all, but a much older man with a swarthy complexion.

Antonia dropped swiftly into a chair, blushing at the realization that she'd been about to go up to the wrong man.

'Can I get you anything, madam?'

A tall, good-looking waiter in black trousers and a white jacket hovered in front of her, with a silver tray on which stood bowls of olives and nuts. These he placed with reverent care on the table.

'I'd like a gin and tonic, please.'

'With ice and lemon, madam?'

'Yes, please.'

He withdrew on silent feet and a moment later she heard

the refreshing clink of ice on glass coming from the bar.

The momentary respite gave her the opportunity to look around. Soft music was being played on a nearby black grand piano, giving the bar area a romantic atmosphere with its pyramids of scented flowers and flickering candles. From where she sat she also had an uninhibited view of the open-plan staircase so she could look down and see people from the moment they entered the lobby below. She glanced nervously at her wristwatch. The tiny hands pointed to ten minutes past seven. He was late.

Jane carefully poured the golden sherry into an engraved Victorian glass and handed it to Barbara, who'd been the first to arrive.

'Is that all right?' she enquired, her brow puckered. 'Do you really like sherry?'

Barbara nodded cheerfully. 'You bet!'

Jane hovered by the side table on which she'd placed bottles of red and white wine, and spirits for those who wanted them.

'What does Percy drink?'

Jane smiled fondly. 'Mostly white wine, though he's fairly abstemious, actually. He should be here in a minute. I'm longing for you to meet him.'

Barbara perched on one of the arms of the sofa and sipped her drink. 'You don't think he'll be . . . well . . . scared off by meeting all your friends like this?'

Jane looked abashed. 'Oh, I don't think so. I mean, I've got all sorts of people coming this evening; it's not like he's being inspected for suitability, or anything.'

'I thought that's what *was* happening.'

'*He* doesn't know that, though,' she replied, shocked. 'I just want him to realize I've got lots of nice friends that I'd like him to get to know. All my horoscopes say this is a good week for socializing. Did I tell you he's a Virgo? That's a wonderful sign for me. Our charts are most compatible. I'm sorry that Antonia can't come because she's always good at parties.'

'What's she doing?'

'What does Antonia *ever* do? Work, work, work. She doesn't give herself a chance. Apparently she's meeting some Japanese clients and she'll join us if she can but I bet she won't.' For once Jane sounded disgruntled. 'She'll *really* find herself on the shelf if she doesn't give more time to her social life. I suppose you saw the announcement of Roland's engagement?'

Barbara looked crushed for a moment, then she made an obvious effort at pulling herself together. 'Yes,' she replied in a small voice.

Jane looked at her curiously. 'You didn't fancy him, did you?'

'I thought he was awfully nice,' she replied lamely. 'Younger than me, of course. By several years.'

'Did you ever go out with him?'

'Not on his own. We sometimes went for walks when I was staying with Antonia in the country. I don't think he really noticed me.'

'I expect he saw you only as Antonia's school friend,' Jane pointed out, trying to be consoling.

Barbara shrugged. 'I expect you're right. I've had a thing

about him for years. I remember going to the party the Murrays gave for his twenty-first . . .' Her voice drifted off, on the verge of tears. 'He was the best-looking young man I've ever met. And awfully sweet, too.'

'Does Antonia know you were in love with him?'

'God, no! She must never know, either. I suppose I'll be invited to the wedding but I think I'll arrange to be away on holiday. Go to Spain or something. I know I couldn't bear to sit and watch him getting married to someone else.'

'Oh dear!' Jane looked distressed and was just about to say something when she was interrupted by the ringing of the front doorbell.

'Oh! That will be Percy,' she exclaimed, hands fluttering with excitement.

Instead it was Kay and Melvyn Buxton, robustly full of themselves and bursting with the news that the scan had shown that their baby, due in four weeks, was a boy.

'Isn't it lucky I chose eggshell blue for the paintwork in the nursery?' Kay squealed. 'I just had a *feeling*, but now we don't know what to call him because Melvyn's very stuck on the name Wanda.'

'*Wanda*?' Jane and Barbara exclaimed in horrified unison.

'I think it's sweet,' Melvyn protested, not at all put out. 'But of course it won't do for a boy.'

'Maybe the next one will be a girl,' Kay said consolingly.

Melvyn's sandy eyelashes blinked rapidly. 'Hang on, darling. Let's get over the arrival of the first one before we start talking about the next. I think Kieran is a nice name for a boy.'

Kay giggled complacently. 'It sounds like a footballer.'

More guests were arriving, and she was dying to regale them with her exciting news.

Within twenty minutes Jane's small living room seemed full. Emma arrived, and a moment later Susan and Andrew, just back from a holiday in Greece, swept in looking deeply tanned and glowing with happiness.

'You've *got* to get married!' Susan gushed to anyone who would listen. 'It's utter, utter bliss.'

'Chance would be a fine thing,' Emma muttered bitterly.

Denise, arriving at that moment with an exotic-looking Japanese girl in tow, overheard the remark and looked smug.

'What for?' she purred. 'Only a woman knows what another woman wants, so why get married?'

'What on earth's happened to Percy?' Jane kept muttering nervously, her head cocked to one side as she listened for the bell. 'I told him to come early.'

More people arrived, mostly women with the eager air of someone on the prowl for a mate, but there weren't enough men to make the numbers even, and of those that were there most were married, two seemed to be totally asexual, which Denise observed could only happen in England and was a product of the public-school system, and three were rampantly gay, standing in a corner talking to each other and shrieking with laughter at their in-jokes.

When Percy finally arrived, fifty minutes after the party had started, he was steered by Jane to the centre of the room where she proceeded to introduce him to everybody as if they were commoners and he was visiting royalty.

'. . . and this is Barbara Ramsay . . .'

Barbara looked up into the pale, tired face of a man in his

late thirties, with sticking-out teeth, thick glasses and soft wisps of hair sprouting from his balding head.

'. . . This is Percy Beresford,' Jane said proudly.

Barbara smiled at him politely and remembered how Jane had always said there was someone for everyone in this world . . . but what sort of someone? Faced with the prospect of spending the rest of her life with someone like Percy, or remaining on her own, Barbara had no problem in deciding which she'd prefer.

It was seven-thirty, and there was still no sign of Colin Holbrook. Tense, and aching with disappointed anxiety, Antonia ordered another drink and finished off the bowl of olives. So what if the waiter did think she was a lonely alcoholic? The bar was crowded now, and she felt embarrassed by the curious stares she was getting, aware she'd commandeered two chairs and a table, while there were people standing around with nowhere to sit.

I'll give him until seven-forty-five, she thought. Perhaps he's got caught in traffic. Maybe he's been delayed at the office. Or been taken ill. She knew she was fooling herself, but pride forbade her, even in her innermost thoughts, to face the fact that he might have chickened out, met someone else in the past twenty-four hours, or gone off the whole idea.

The waiter brought her drink and she asked for her bill. If Colin Holbrook did turn up she didn't want him to know she'd been drinking steadily while she'd been waiting for him.

The buzz of voices was drowning out the tinkly piano as

she strained to listen to the music, and she couldn't remember when she'd felt so isolated and awkward in her whole life. Accustomed to being in control of most situations, whether in business or socially, she now felt adrift and unsure of herself. She also felt vulnerable and exposed, sitting here, by herself, in this crowded bar. She got the feeling everyone thought she was a hooker waiting to be picked up.

When the waiter returned with her drink and the bill, she put her American Express card on his tray and told him she was in a hurry. Colin Holbrook obviously wasn't going to turn up now and she felt like getting the hell out of this place and sneaking back to the safety of her flat. Her self-confidence was at rock-bottom. If she couldn't secure a relationship through a newspaper column there wasn't much hope for her, she reflected despairingly, as she gulped down her gin and tonic and gathered up her things. Then, with her head held high and pretending to look as if she'd never intended to meet anyone in the first place, she walked nonchalantly out of the bar and down the stairs. She could still get to Jane's party if she hurried but somehow she couldn't face it now. Disappointment dampened her spirit and she suddenly felt very tired.

He was six foot four, thin, slightly stooped, and although in his mid-fifties, he looked older. The sallow skin of his face hung from his cheekbones in drooping lines of disappointment and his bottom lip jutted loosely. Small grey eyes glinted watchfully through brass-framed glasses. Sparse grey hair grew round the back and sides of his bald head, and was exactly the same shade of grey as his single-breasted suit which looked limp and slightly creased.

Keeping his distance, and with his hand in his trouser pocket to suggest he was taking a casual stroll, he never took his eyes off Antonia, pretending to look in a shop window when she did; quickened his pace when she hurried on, lagged behind when she dawdled.

He'd been watching her for some time in the bar, sizing her up, realizing she was exactly right. Now all he had to do was find out where she lived. As she turned right down Pont Street he hovered on the corner, wondering which way she'd go. When she crossed over to the south side, heading in the direction of Cadogan Square, he followed at a discreet distance. Halfway along he saw her climb the white marble front steps of one of the red-brick Victorian houses which, he was pretty certain, had been converted into flats. He paused, pretending to look for something in his wallet until she was safely inside, then he walked across to the other side of the square, so that he could observe the building through the foliage of the trees and shrubbery in the central garden. Most of the windows were veiled with fine net curtains, but on the first floor, the two french windows which led on to a balcony had no such device. He could see clearly into an elegant interior and a moment later, there was Antonia herself, holding a cat in her arms as she sauntered slowly across the room.

Then he watched as she opened her french windows and stepped out to inspect her tubs of flowers. That done, she paused to glance down into the square, but there was no one about as far as she was concerned, except for an old lady walking her Pekinese. A moment later she turned and went back indoors.

Three

'Damn you, Colin Holbrook!' Antonia threw the photograph on to the floor and scooped Crash up into her arms. For a few minutes she paced up and down her living room, appalled at her own disappointment. She'd been so sure . . . Well, that's the end of that, she decided determinedly. Nobody, not anybody *ever*, had stood her up, in the entire course of her life. This was a first. And one she definitely didn't like. Plonking Crash into one of her cushioned armchairs, she went to the kitchen, and, filling her galvanized watering can from the tap over the sink, decided that tending the plants on her balcony would be therapeutic. She only had a few tubs, containing impatiens, geraniums, petunias and nicotiana, and a couple of formal bay trees, but she found it very relaxing to potter about, dead-heading and watering and smelling the tobacco plants as their perfume pervaded the evening air.

Tonight, though, her vexation was too acute to be soothed by mere horticulture, and having given the containers a perfunctory sprinkling of water, she wandered disconsolately back to the kitchen. Another lonely evening lay ahead, and an even lonelier night. Her anger gradually gave way to sadness as she made herself an omelette which she then proceeded to share with Crash. Her longing for someone and the emotional emptiness of her life was proving too heavy a price for her to have paid for the success of her business. She'd given her all to Murray Properties, and now she had this ghastly nagging feeling that perhaps it had not been worth it. No! She would *not* be negative, she chided herself. She'd made a lot of money, owned her flat and furnished it with fine antiques, bought some lovely clothes and a few pieces of discreet-looking jewellery, had a new car and could holiday where she chose . . . but it wasn't enough. As she sat there with Crash on her lap, licking the remains of egg on her plate, it dawned on her that not all the material comforts in the world would compensate for the lack of someone to love. Suddenly her eyes brimmed as she thought of the husband she might never have; the children who would never be hers; the grandchildren she could never spoil. A deep sense of grief and loss swept over her at that moment. *She was going to die without ever knowing what it was all like*. Her eyes fell on to the photograph of Colin Holbrook, still lying on the floor, one corner bent back now from the roughness of her treatment.

Slowly, she picked it up and looked into the face again. Oh, God, he was so attractive. She liked the dark eyes which held that hint of humour and the generous smiling mouth. She liked the curve of his high cheekbones and the cleft in his chin. She liked the ruggedness of his demeanour, and yet there was something sophisticated about him, too.

For a moment she felt tempted to phone him and demand to know why he hadn't turned up. It was rude, apart from anything else. Then she realized that of course he had no way of contacting her if something had gone wrong because she hadn't given him her number; but he could still have phoned the head barman at the hotel and asked him to give a message to 'Susan', who was 'a tall, slim lady with brown-blonde hair wearing a cream suit'.

Then, her anger unabated, she decided it would be better to write him a short, curt note, saying she was very disappointed that he should have behaved with such lack of courtesy, and no matter what excuse he might come up with she did not, in the circumstances, wish to have any further contact with him. She figured that would show him what she thought of him. Teach him a lesson, so that if he embarked on further dates with unknown women he wouldn't insult them, too, by not turning up.

Antonia opened up her laptop computer, indignation giving her a burst of energy. She had to do *something*, and this seemed as good a way as any to exorcise her frustration. She slid a sheet of plain white A4 paper into the printer and set to work, inspired as if she were wording the description of an important property for an advertisement. The words flowed as she tapped away. At that moment Crash, who'd been sitting beside her, giving a delicate pedicure to his hind paws with his sharp little teeth, decided he was bored. Regardless of what she was doing, he walked straight in front of her, and the next moment, there on the screen was . . . sdxc t67, kmnj p0oi][;-ppppppppppppppppppp.

'Crash! What are you doing?' she yelled, pushing him away. 'Why can't you look where you're going?'

Crash stalked away, tail in the air, head held high, every line of his body registering pique. Languidly, as if he didn't care what she thought of him, he attended to the toilette of his front paw, his pink tongue making soft rasping noises on his fur.

'Oh, Crash!' Relenting, because she could never resist him when he looked so sweet, she leaned forward and, gathering him up in her arms, buried her face in his warm back. 'I love you, Crash, although you're so clumsy,' she murmured. She looked back at the screen. 'And you're absolutely right. This letter is a load of pompous crap. Colin Holbrook owes me nothing.' She pressed the delete key, wiping the screen blank. 'Let's forget all about him, shall we?'

Crash, forgetting his huffiness, pushed his cold nose into her cheek, purred gently, and then dribbled with ecstasy.

'And whoever I eventually marry, that is, if I do, is going to have to love you as much as I do,' she added firmly.

In the shadows of a chestnut tree, the balding grey-haired man, still in his grey suit but this time covered by a grey raincoat, stood with the stillness of a sentry, watching the windows of Antonia's flat. It was seven o'clock the next morning, and a pearly-pink dawn had awakened the birds in the gardens of Cadogan Square, who were giving vent to their joy at being alive by singing with piercing persistence. The milk float had already been and gone; so had the boy on a bicycle who delivered newspapers. At this hour the square was deserted and the houses still, their curtains drawn and their front doors locked.

The man never moved, and his grey eyes remained fixed on their target. He was prepared to wait for as long as it took.

* * *

Antonia awoke feeling more cheerful than she'd expected. She'd slept surprisingly well and as she stood in the invigoratingly hot shower, with the scent of gardenia soap permeating the steamy air, she made a mental list of what she had to do today. She wanted to see how the flat conversion at Marble Arch was getting on; there was the Belgrave Square house to inspect to check on the builders' progress; and if she had a moment she wanted to take a look at a derelict property on the Embankment, not far from Chelsea Harbour. It had previously been a warehouse, but with the right architect she could just visualize it being made into three or four studio apartments, each with a magnificent view of the Thames. At moments like this, when the adrenalin rushed and her head buzzed with exciting, creative ideas, she knew the past eight years of hard graft had been worth it. Nobody could have everything. She determined to enjoy all she'd got. After all, she told herself, being miserable wasn't going to help.

When she arrived, walking the short distance to her office at a brisk pace in spite of her high heels, Linda greeted her with the news that her brother Roland had phoned only a moment before, having missed her at her flat, and would she ring him back; that the soft furnishings at the Wilton Place house were ready to be installed, providing the painters had finished; and that there was already someone interested in buying one of the three flats in the Eaton Place conversion.

'Great,' Antonia enthused, seating herself at her desk. Everything seemed to be going well, and she'd ring Roland in a minute, but meanwhile she looked closely at Linda. She still looked edgy and there were dark smudges under her eyes.

'Can we have a moment's talk?' Antonia suggested in a low voice, so the others wouldn't hear.

Linda looked at her cagily. 'All right.' Her tone was reluctant. She seated herself on the opposite side of the desk, facing Antonia.

'I was just wondering . . . . is anything wrong?' Antonia asked.

Linda raised her eyebrows, her ruddy complexion turning to an even deeper red.

'No. Why should there be?'

'It's because you seem . . . well, unhappy, actually,' Antonia said with sympathetic honesty. 'I first noticed it last night. Have you some problem? Is there anything I can do, perhaps?'

Linda gave the ghost of a smile, as she sat twisting the gold rings on her fingers.

'I'm fine,' she said shortly.

'Robin's all right, is he?'

'Of course.'

'You are still quite happy working here?' she persisted.

The eyebrows shot up even higher. 'I *love* working here, Antonia. There's nothing wrong, I assure you.' Linda gave a forced laugh. It sounded more like a bark. She rose to go back to her own desk. 'All I need,' she continued jokily, 'is a few early nights! I have been rather burning the candles at both ends. You know how it is.'

Antonia said nothing. According to Linda last night, she'd been going home 'to get a lot done'. That sounded more like attending to household chores than painting the town red. There was nothing more she could do, however. If Linda didn't want to confide in her she couldn't force her. She only hoped it wasn't something really serious.

Roland was at his desk when she got through to his office.

'Hiya Antonia! How are things?'

'Everything's fine. Business is good,' she replied, glad for a moment that she didn't have to lie to him about having met an applicant to her lonely hearts appeal. 'How are things with you and Jinny?'

'That's what I was ringing about. It's this wedding. Jinny really doesn't want Mum making all the arrangements. We're going down next weekend to talk the whole thing through and I wondered if you'd come down, too.'

'Ro, I really don't want to get involved, you know,' Antonia replied. 'This is between you both and Mum.'

'But you're so good with Mum. You'll be clever enough to come up with a compromise, which will keep everyone happy.'

'But it's none of my business – can't you see that, Ro? If Jinny isn't happy with the plans it's up to her to say so.'

'She can be tactless, though, Antonia. I don't want her to hurt Mum's feelings. Suggestions coming from you would go down much better. Come on, be a sport. Come down on Saturday, you can always leave early on Sunday if you must.'

Antonia sighed. Damn Jinny and her awkwardness.

'If I *do* come down for the weekend, Ro,' she said after a pause, 'it will be to protect Mum from being hurt. You know what my feelings are on the subject. If she's being kind enough to give you this wedding and reception you should both say thank you very much, and be grateful.'

'I know, I know,' Roland wailed in contrition. 'I feel bad about it too, but what else can I *do*?'

'I could tell you but I won't,' his sister informed him good-humouredly. 'OK. I'll phone Mum and Daddy later on today to say I'll be coming down on Saturday, but mind, I'm not going to be taking Jinny's side against Mum's.'

'No. I promise I understand. Thanks a lot, sweetheart. You're a pal.'

'I'll see you then, Ro.' Antonia grinned at Linda when she hung up. 'Brothers!' she exclaimed. 'And worse . . . future sisters-in-law! What am I letting myself in for?'

Linda, who looked composed again and whose colour had returned to normal, laughed. 'I suppose you'll be the essence of diplomacy.'

At that moment the glass doors to the street swung open and everyone in the office fell into serious, businesslike mode at the arrival of a client.

'Can I help you?' Sally asked, looking helpful.

The middle-aged man was grey and balding, with sharp grey eyes and brass-framed glasses. His grey raincoat was belted. His gaze flickered around the office, taking in Carina, Mark, Linda, hovering for a second longer on Antonia, moving on to Guy, and then coming back to rest on Sally.

'I'm looking for a suitable house to buy, in this area preferably,' he said. The mouth with the loose, jutting-out bottom lip gave a wintry smile.

Sally, blonde and perky and particularly good with male clients, invited him to take a seat at her desk.

'If you'd like to tell me exactly what you have in mind,

I'm sure we can help,' she said, pulling a large pad of plain paper towards her. 'We have several properties, although I must point out that we're not estate agents as such.'

'That's all right. My wife and I have just sold our house in Essex, because she wants to live in London, and we want a house, rather than a flat, somewhere in the centre of town.'

Antonia, going through her mail, eavesdropped with interest, wondering how much this man was prepared to pay. He certainly didn't look wealthy; his black shoes were cheap-looking and his raincoat old and worn.

'May I take your particulars?' Sally asked. 'Then we can send you the details of anything suitable we may have.' She picked up her pen. 'What is your name, sir?'

'Preedy. Alec Preedy.' His voice was low and nasal, with a tinny inflection.

'And your address, Mr Preedy?'

He seemed to pause for the fraction of a second before saying, 'Grosvenor House Hotel, in Park Lane. My wife and I are staying there until we find a suitable house.'

Sally didn't flicker, but Antonia's head jerked up in surprise as she looked at his back view more closely, reminding herself that there were some rich people who were extraordinarily eccentric, and even went about in rags while sitting on small fortunes.

'Couldn't you give me any details now?' Mr Preedy asked. He was sounding less agreeable now. 'Something I could look at, even if it's not ready for habitation?'

'I'll see what we've got, Mr Preedy.' Sally stabbed at the keys of her computer and shot Antonia a secret questioning look. In reply Antonia gave a little nod, signifying that Sally could show him the details of any property she liked. Mr Preedy caught the subtle exchange, and spun round to look penetratingly at Antonia. Her expression was bland as she smiled at him politely. He stared back at her, his sallow face almost glittering with a sickly sweat, like someone with a high temperature.

'There are a couple of houses you could see right away, Mr Preedy,' Sally said brightly, summoning a printout from the computer. 'They're almost near completion.'

'Good.'

Sally looked across at Mark. 'Can you show Mr Preedy Wilton Place and Victoria Road, Mark?'

Mark Gillingham nodded in agreement but Mr Preedy looked furious.

'Why can't *you* show them to me?' he demanded of Sally.

Sally didn't want to go into the explanation of Antonia's policy that no unaccompanied female should show a male client around a property.

'Mark Gillingham is our chief residential negotiator,' she lied smoothly. 'He knows more about the houses than anyone else.' She turned to Mark. 'Your car's just around the corner, isn't it? Could you take Mr Preedy now?'

'I'd be delighted,' Mark replied, sounding as if it were a great honour. He rose, car keys clinking in his hand.

Mr Preedy rose also, his lower lip jutting out more than ever. He glanced at Antonia once more and their eyes locked, then he turned abruptly, and followed Mark into the street.

Work was the best antidote for depression, Antonia reflected, as she moved steadily through the day. She'd attended to all the most pressing jobs that had to be done, and now, by mid-afternoon, as she bit hungrily into a smoked-salmon and cream-cheese bagel, she decided to postpone her inspection of the Marble Arch and Belgrave Square properties, and take a look at how the house in Wilton Place was getting on. The decorators should be finished in another three days. Providing they'd done the work properly, the curtains and carpets could be installed at the beginning of next week. But first she had to phone her parents, to tell them she'd be down for the weekend.

Quentin Murray answered. 'My darling girl! How splendid to hear from you,' he greeted her warmly. 'How's everything going?'

'Fine, Daddy. Are all of you OK?'

'We're all very well. When are we going to see you again?'

'This coming weekend, if that's all right.'

'It's more than all right, sweetheart. Any chance of you coming on Friday evening?'

Antonia hesitated, reluctant to leave London a moment before she needed, but she knew her parents would like to see more of her and she felt a pang of guilt at going home so rarely.

'If I can arrange for Mrs Miller to come in and feed Crash, then I could come down on Friday.'

'Fantastic, my darling. Oh, your mother will be thrilled. With any luck we'll be by ourselves. Roland and Jinny are coming down early on Saturday, and Tristram's going to Hereford. I'm not sure what Leo's up to, but I don't think he'll be here until Saturday, either.'

'That'll be great, Daddy, I'll bring some dressed crab with

me, shall I? I know it's your favourite.'

'Dressed or naked, sweetheart. I love crab any which way! Put it in a bikini, for all I care.'

They both laughed, comfortably and entirely at ease with each other.

'That's settled then, Daddy. I'll see you and Mummy at about seven-thirty. Will that be all right?' As she spoke she scribbled a shopping list in her diary for Friday morning which, apart from the crab, included champagne, a whole ripe Stilton, some smoked salmon, which they could have on brown bread and butter with their drinks before Sunday lunch, a yard of Bendick's chocolates and some out-of-season strawberries.

If there was one pleasure, she thought, about earning a lot of money it was being able to afford to give her family and friends the special things they liked most.

Having said goodbye to her father, she cleared her desk because she hated to leave it in a mess, and checked with everyone else in the office to make sure they were up to speed before she left.

'How did you get on with Mr Preedy?' she asked Mark when she got to him.

Mark's expression was both surprised and impressed. 'He's a genuine buyer, all right, though you wouldn't think it to look at him, would you? He was telling me all about the house he's sold in Essex. A lot of land went with it and he got a very good price for it.'

'So he's definitely interested in one of our properties, is he?'

Mark nodded. 'He liked the house in Wilton Place and I

showed him the outside of Belgrave Square but we didn't go in, because it's obviously far too big for him and his wife. What actually interested him most, although he wanted to look at some houses, was the flats conversion near Marble Arch. He's going to phone, later in the week, and arrange for us to show it to his wife as well.'

'Great,' Antonia said approvingly. 'You never can tell, can you? I thought he looked like a real loser. Keep in close touch with him, Mark, in your usual charming way, and butter up his wife when you meet her.'

'Will do,' he replied, grinning. 'I'll make sure he spends the proceeds from his house with us.'

'I'm off to Wilton Place myself, actually, and I might pop along to Chelsea Embankment afterwards to look over that warehouse.' As she spoke she buttoned up the jacket of her grey suit and knotted a pale green scarf at the neck.

'I'll call in on the mobile later on,' she added, picking up her briefcase and making sure she had all the keys she needed.

'See you in the morning, then,' Linda remarked, looking more cheerful than she'd done earlier that day.

As soon as Antonia arrived at the elegant house in Wilton Place she realized the painters had gone for the day. It was later than she'd thought, but it didn't matter. What she wanted to see was how the rooms looked now they'd been decorated in the pale shades of oyster, pearl, sepia and cinnamon that she'd chosen. As she stood on the front doorstep, unlocking the front door, she suddenly had the unpleasant feeling that she was being watched. She looked across the road to the Berkeley Hotel, where the doorman was ushering people into and out of taxis. No one was even looking in her direction.

Still with a feeling of unease, she glanced in the direction of St Paul's Church, which was adjacent to the hotel, but the heavily shadowed and gloomy forecourt was deserted. Frowning, because she could have sworn her movements were being observed, she let herself into the house. Why would anyone be watching the comings and goings of an empty house, she wondered? Unless to steal the builders' tools, or perhaps some of the fittings?

A moment later, as she switched on the lights, she forgot her suspicions. The rooms looked magnificent, a real triumph of architecture and interior design. As she ran up and down the stairs of the house, she could see that what she'd set out to do had worked. There were four floors, and the five bedrooms and reception rooms were small, but she'd managed to create an effect of space and light, and even formal grandeur on a small scale. The white marble fireplaces she'd had installed fitted perfectly. The cornices were spectacular, picked out in dazzling white and mushroom. And the oak banisters, restored and polished, gleamed like the genuine antiques they were. No wonder Mark had said Mr Preedy liked the house! If she were to get married and have a family it was exactly the sort of town house she'd choose for herself.

Antonia took a deep breath of satisfaction as she looked around one more time. She was going to have no problems in finding a buyer, whether Mr Preedy wanted it or not.

There was a package waiting for Antonia when she got home from work a couple of days later. A swift glance showed her it had been forwarded from the PO box number she'd used for her advertisement. Thanking Mrs Miller for taking it in for her, she ripped open the brown wrapping paper, wondering why an applicant should have sent her something large enough to have constituted a parcel; was it an album of photographs? or a couple of videos? Intrigued, she found a box of handmade chocolates, and tucked under it a letter.

> *Dear Susan,*
>
> *I don't know how to begin to apologize for not turning up to meet you on Tuesday evening. My boss suddenly called an urgent meeting which I couldn't get out of, and which went on until nearly eight o'clock. Can you believe my bad luck? I had no idea how to get hold of you. I even phoned the bar of the Chelsea Hotel to try and get them to give a message to someone of your description but you must have already left, because when I arrived at eight-thirty, you'd gone! Entirely my fault, I'm afraid, and you can imagine my deep disappointment, and worse . . . The realization of what you must think of me. I enclose, as a small token of my deepest apology, some chocolates which I hope you will accept. I do hope we can still meet and that you will get in touch with me again. I would really like to meet you so much.*
>
> *Best wishes,*
> *Colin Holbrook*

Antonia read the letter several times, with a growing sense of delight. So he hadn't stood her up, after all? And she could understand and empathize with his predicament. So often in the past, just as she'd been leaving for a private meeting with a friend, something urgent had come up and she'd regretfully had to cancel. But at least she'd always had a contact number for a phone, a car mobile or a fax. Colin had had nothing. He'd done his best by ringing the hotel but had obviously missed her.

Antonia sat in thoughtful silence for a while, although her mind was made up. She'd phone Colin in a few minutes but first she must look at her diary to see when she was free. This week was hopeless. Tomorrow night she'd promised to have supper with Jane, and having missed her drinks party she couldn't very well cancel, and the next night she was going home for the weekend. She flicked over the pages of her Filofax. Monday was a reception given by the Knightsbridge Association, Tuesday was a charity auction she'd promised to attend, having taken advertising space in their gala brochure and Wednesday . . . 'Oh, hell!' she muttered in annoyance; on Wednesday she was taking four of her Japanese clients to dinner at The Collection. That meant she wouldn't be able to meet Colin Holbrook for over a week, she realized with dismay. She was going to have to make it clear to him that she wasn't playing hard to get, and stress that all these business engagements were the very reason she'd had to advertise for someone in the first place.

Pouring a glass of wine to give herself confidence, she took a deep breath and dialled 141 followed by his number. Until she met him she knew it was only sensible to protect herself. After several rings he answered.

'Hello, this is . . . Susan speaking,' Antonia said, remembering to use her second name.

'Oh, Susan!' Colin spoke her name in tones of relief.

'Thank God you've phoned. I was so afraid I'd never hear from you again, and I wouldn't have blamed you either. Am I forgiven? I can't tell you how sorry I am—'

'It's all right, Colin,' Antonia cut in. 'I do understand . . .'

'. . . You do? Oh, thank heavens . . .'

'It's happened to me, too, but I've been lucky enough to be able to get hold of the person.'

'Susan, I was frantic! I can't tell you how I felt when I finally got to the hotel and I realized you'd gone. I thought perhaps you'd changed your mind, or met somebody else. Oh, I don't know! I felt as if my one opportunity of finding happiness had gone.'

'Not quite,' she laughed teasingly.

'Then we can arrange another meeting?' he asked eagerly.

'I don't see why not,' she replied, trying to sound calm, though secretly she felt thrilled. Colin sounded even nicer than on the last occasion she'd spoken to him, and she loved the richness of his voice. It was very sexy.

'The thing is,' she continued, looking at her Filofax again, 'I'm chock-a-block with boring engagements until next Thursday; that's my first free evening.'

He sounded disappointed. 'Really? We can't even meet for a quick drink before then?'

'Not a hope,' she replied, although she knew a quick rendezvous would have been possible, but it was not what she wanted. You couldn't really tell anything about a person in a few minutes, and from his obvious desire to meet her she felt she'd got nothing to lose by holding out until the middle of next week.

Colin interrupted her thoughts. 'Could we meet for lunch

instead of in the evening? Would that be easier for you?'

'No, I'm afraid I rarely stop for lunch. Why don't we make it next Thursday? I've got to look at a property in Green Street, just off Park Lane . . . so why don't we meet at Grosvenor House? In the bar? Shall we say seven-thirty this time, in case you're kept late at work again?'

'If my boss keeps me late again I'll shoot him,' Colin joked. 'I promise I'll be there. I really am longing to meet you, Susan.'

'I'm looking forward to meeting you too.'

When they'd said goodbye, Antonia hung up feeling happier than she'd felt for a long time. She had yet to meet Colin, but judging by his photograph and the way he spoke, she felt almost in love with him already. His voice was so warm, and yet there was a boyish charm about it. He'd been genuinely upset at messing up their last date, and although it hadn't been his fault, she liked his attitude. If he were *half* as nice as she thought him to be, she'd seriously consider getting to know him better with a view to . . . The wording of her advertisement came back to her. *For serious relationship.* Could this be it?

Crash jumped up on to her knee, laddering her tights with his sharp little claws.

'Crash,' she wailed angrily. 'Look what you've done! They were new this morning!' He chirruped conversationally as if it had nothing to do with him, before curling up on her lap. 'But,' she continued, stroking his velvety head, 'you write better letters than I do. Thank God we didn't send that angry missive off to Colin, or I'd certainly never have heard from him again.'

* * *

'I'm driving up to Hertfordshire this afternoon,' Antonia informed Linda on Friday morning, 'and I want to clear my desk before I go.'

'Right.' Linda nodded in understanding. She still looked stressed and tired, and Antonia was glad the weekend lay ahead. With any luck, Linda might be back to her usual energetic and cheerful self by Monday. If she wasn't, she thought worriedly, something must definitely be wrong.

'On the way, I want to stop and see how the Marble Arch conversion is getting on.'

'Right,' said Linda again.

'And I'll probably call you from the car with notes, which we can attend to on Monday morning.'

'Right.'

'Linda, are you OK?' Antonia asked after a pause, during which she'd seen Linda staring into space, glassy-eyed.

Linda started, and then blushed guiltily. 'Yes. Yes, I'm fine.'

'I don't think you are,' Antonia said softly, so Sally and Mark, whose desks were nearest, couldn't hear. She leaned forward on her elbows, looking anxiously into Linda's face.

'I've never seen you like this. Has something happened? Do you feel ill? You haven't been yourself for a couple of weeks, Linda. Something must be wrong.'

Linda turned her head sharply away. When she looked back her face was contorted as if she were in pain, and her eyes were brimming with tears.

'*Linda* . . .!' Antonia whispered, appalled. She gathered up her handbag. 'Let's go and have a coffee at the General

Trading Company. We can't talk here.'

As they left the office, she remarked casually to the others that she needed Linda's help over the furnishing of the Belgrave Square house.

'We won't be long,' she added lightly. Gripping Linda's arm as they crossed Sloane Street to the other side, she guided her up the steps of the General Trading Company and through to their garden at the back, where tea and coffees and snacks were served all day. They found a table for two in a secluded corner and gave their order.

'Now, tell me what's wrong,' Antonia said.

The tears that had been held back now flowed down Linda's cheeks, and she wiped them away ineffectually with the back of her hand.

'I've made such a mess of everything,' she said brokenly. 'I've really screwed up.'

Antonia looked at her sympathetically. 'How?' It was so unlike Linda to screw anything up. She'd always been the epitome of efficiency, accuracy and professionalism.

'Robin's found out I've been having an affair.'

Antonia stared at her as if she couldn't believe her ears. If Linda had said she was flying to America to join NASA because she wanted to be an astronaut, she couldn't have been more stunned.

'I see,' she managed to say. 'So what's going to happen?'

Linda was weeping bitterly now. 'I've been such a fool. Robin says he's going to divorce me.'

'And does that mean you're going to marry the . . . er . . . man you're having an affair with?'

'I c-can't!'

Antonia fished in her handbag for a tissue and handed it to Linda. 'Why not?' she asked gently. 'You obviously must love him, to have had an affair with him?'

'Oh, I do. I'm crazy about him.' Linda blew her nose.

'Then why . . .?'

'He told me last week that he can't leave his family. He and his wife have got five children. I realize now he was probably just u-using m-me. I've l-lost everything,' she sobbed.

Appalled, Antonia gazed at Linda in sorrow. To see the normally cool and collected woman she'd known for six years disintegrating into someone who had lost control of her emotions, her self-respect and her life was the saddest thing, and she felt helpless in the face of such heart-wrenching despair.

'Maybe Robin will get over . . . I mean, he's bound to have been shocked, and you know what the male ego is like and all that, but I'm sure when the dust settles he'll realize your marriage is more important than his hurt feelings . . .' Antonia knew she was gabbling in her effort to sound positive but she didn't know what else to do.

Linda wiped her eyes with the sodden tissue. 'He's already kicked me out of the house and I know he won't have me back. He's always been a very unforgiving man.'

'Then where are you staying?'

'With my mother.'

Antonia's concern increased. 'But she lives out at Redhill, doesn't she?'

'Yes. I've been commuting to work for the past week.'

'Oh, Linda! Look, why don't you get off home now, and

spend the weekend resting. You can't go on like this or you'll have a breakdown.'

'But there's so much work on. I can't just abandon everything,' Linda protested.

Antonia laid her hand on Linda's arm. 'You can and you will,' she said firmly but gently. 'And next week why don't you stay in the Wilton Place house? We can arrange to have a bed delivered and at least it will be a roof over your head for the time being and save you having to commute. The electricity's laid on, and the bathrooms and kitchen are in working order and it will be quite good to have you there, because you'll be in a position to spot any flaws in the renovations we've carried out.'

Linda looked at her with red-rimmed eyes. 'That's terribly kind of you. It would be a relief to be in town, and to get away from my mother's prying interference. She simply can't understand how I could have let this happen. She always liked Robin.'

Privately, Antonia couldn't quite see how Linda had let this happen either. Robin was a kind, easygoing man, warm and affectionate, happy for Linda to work, and undemanding as far as she could see. They'd been married for six years and there were no children; Antonia had never liked to ask whether they hadn't wanted any or if there was a problem. But certainly Linda had seemed contented with her comfortable life, and that made this revelation all the more shocking.

'These things happen, I suppose,' Antonia said lamely.

Linda nodded. 'I didn't plan to fall in love with Angus. It just happened. The moment I saw him I was bewitched. It sounds so clichéd, doesn't it? To him I was a bit on the side and I don't think he ever intended to leave his wife, and to me it was like meeting the other half of myself; the love of my life . . . Oh, Christ,' she started to weep again, 'what a nightmare it all is.'

'Why don't you call it a day here,' Antonia suggested. 'I'll tell them at the office that you weren't feeling well, and you've gone home. Then you can collect your things from your mother's house and move into Wilton Place. I think I've even . . .' she fished in her handbag. 'Yes! Talk about luck! I thought I might have the keys to the house and here they are. I was there the other evening, having a look around, and it really is super.' She handed Linda two keys on a brass ring with a tag that merely said W. P.

'I wish I didn't have to go away for the weekend,' Antonia continued regretfully, 'but it's family business and I can't get out of it.'

'Oh, you've been so kind already. Please don't worry about me. I'll soon sort myself out,' said Linda, in an attempt at appearing brave. 'I'm going to have to rent a small place to live, and I suppose . . .' she shrugged, on the brink of tears again, 'and wait for Robin to divorce me.'

'It may not come to that.' Antonia tried to sound reassuring. 'I'm sure Robin's not going to throw away six years of marriage because of one mistake on your part.'

For a moment there was a flicker of the old humour in Linda's eyes.

'Some mistake!' she said drily.

'Yeah. Well. You never did do things by halves.' Antonia grinned at her sympathetically. Linda was well known in the office for being an all-or-nothing person, tackling whatever she had to do with force and verve.

At two o'clock Antonia left the office, having explained that Linda had gone home because she was ill. There were murmurs of sympathetic concern from Sally, Mark, Carina and Guy, but no one seemed to guess at the truth. Good old Linda. There was never much wrong with her. She must have caught a touch of flu.

Getting into her car, which she'd managed to park nearby, she set off for Marble Arch, glad for once to be getting out of town. She'd already stowed her suitcase in the boot that morning, and as it was a beautiful, warm day, she wound down the windows, letting the breeze waft through the car, ruffling her hair. Driving through Hyde Park, which looked lusciously green, she arrived at the house, a few hundred yards from Marble Arch, which was in the middle of being converted into six flats. As she drew up outside, a taxi screeched to a halt behind her, almost running into her back bumper.

Antonia jumped out, fright making her angry. 'What the hell do you think you're doing?' she demanded.

'It ain't my fault, missus!' the driver shouted, sticking his head out of the cab window. 'This bleeder I got 'ere yells "stop", sudden like, right in my ear and . . .! Oi . . .! *Oi!*' He spun round in his seat to look over his shoulder, just in time to see his passenger slip out of the offside back door, and hurry away in the direction they'd just come.

'Did you see that?' he yelled in fury.

Antonia could see the back view of an elderly man walking

briskly away. A moment later he'd disappeared among the crowds.

'What's going on?'

The cab driver was incensed. 'The bleeder never gave me no fare! 'Oo does 'e think 'e is?' He glared at Antonia as if it were all her fault. 'Rotten bugger. I'm goin' after 'im to see if I can't catch 'im up.' With that, he swung the taxi round with a squeal of rubber and shot off back towards Marble Arch.

Shrugging, Antonia entered the property where the builders were not so much hard at work, as sitting on the stairs having one of their tea breaks. They looked startled to see her.

'Are you OK, miss?' the foreman asked immediately, as he rose to his feet. 'We heard something going on outside in the street, but I didn't know it was you.'

'I'm fine, though for a moment I didn't think the back of my car was going to survive.'

'What happened, miss? You should have called us.'

'I don't *know* what it was all about. Anyway, the passenger made off without paying, but I can't think why the driver was so angry with me. It wasn't my fault.'

'But *you're* OK, miss?' the foreman insisted. Murray Properties Ltd were valued customers, and Antonia Murray kept them employed all year round on her various projects.

She smiled, knowing what was behind his concern, but nevertheless touched by his solicitude. 'Yes. Absolutely. Now, can I have a look at how everything's going? I want to get out of London before the Friday evening exodus starts and the traffic jams become impossible.'

'Right, miss.'

For the next hour they toured the building from its sixth-floor attics, to the damp-riddled basement, which would eventually become a 'garden-level London pied-à-terre of great charm'.

'It's coming on very well,' Antonia commented, after they'd discussed some of the finer points. 'Are you going to be able to keep to the original completion dates?'

'With any luck, yes, miss. Providing we're not let down by delays in the delivery of any of the fittings.'

She nodded in understanding. They'd all had bad experiences with taps that turned up but baths and basins that didn't; glass that had been delivered, but not the window frames; and when it came to things like tiles, slates, boilers and radiators, the rest of the house could be finished before they arrived. Once there'd been an occasion when the carpets were ready to be laid in a house in Kensington before the floorboards had even been delivered.

With a final wave of her hand, Antonia said goodbye and then she was on her way at last, heading up the Edgware Road to join the A5. At this rate she'd be home by six o'clock.

'I'm not quite sure what Jinny's problem is,' Quentin said, as he and Antonia sat having a drink on the terrace, while Hilary had a bath before dinner. The sun hadn't yet set, and it was a still, balmy evening, with the long shadows of the trees casting dark bands across the lawn.

As she sipped a glass of chilled white wine, Antonia had lightly touched on the subject of the forthcoming wedding but before she'd had time to say anything more, Quentin had remarked that nothing Hilary suggested in the way of arrangements seemed to meet with Jinny's approval.

'Your mother's rather hurt, actually,' he continued. 'She's aware that Jinny hasn't got a mother, and therefore she thought it would be rather nice to give her a really lovely day. All she's had, though, is rather unkind remarks about not wanting a formal, old-fashioned sort of "do".'

'I didn't know Jinny had actually said anything,' Antonia said in concern. This was the very situation she'd hoped to head off.

'Let's say it's been more insinuation than outright rudeness on her part,' Quentin admitted. 'But she has made her feelings clear in a roundabout way.'

'I think that's so ungrateful,' Antonia exclaimed indignantly. 'Roland told me there was a problem, but I'd hoped that a compromise could be reached; you know, arrangements that made both Mummy and Jinny happy.'

Quentin sighed. 'I'm afraid I don't think that's going to be possible. In fact, I don't think Jinny wants Hilary involved at all, except for paying for everything.'

'Oh, dear.' Antonia gazed at the wooded horizon beyond their garden, stretching away in the evening light.

Quentin glanced at her profile. 'What's that for, darling?'

'I do hope Roland's not making a mistake.'

Her father sat in silence for a moment. 'There's nothing we can do about it if he is,' he said at last.

Antonia turned to him, alarm showing in her eyes. 'You think he's making a mistake, too, do you?'

'Jinny would not be my choice of wife, but then it's not me who's marrying her. She may be perfect for Ro. Let's hope they'll be terrifically happy. I know one thing, though; I'll be damned glad when this wedding's over.'

'Have the invitations gone out yet?'

'That's another thing. Jinny hates the traditional design of a wedding invitation. She wants some sort of jazzy card with something like: "Roland and Jinny invite you to their nuptials and a disco bash afterwards".' Quentin took a quick swig of his wine. 'Can you imagine anything more ghastly?'

Antonia grinned ruefully. 'It's so awful it's almost funny,' she said.

'In that case I think your mother's about to suffer from a huge sense-of-humour failure,' he remarked drily.

'Poor Mummy. She works so hard to make sure everyone's happy.'

'Well, at least you're here for the weekend, darling, and that's lovely. We don't see nearly enough of you. Now let me top up your drink.' He reached over and refilled her glass. 'How is everything going?'

Antonia had a sudden urge to tell him about Colin Holbrook and how she was longing for their meeting, but then she decided it would be madness. They were not a family who went in for secrets; everyone knew exactly what everyone else was doing, and it wouldn't be fair to ask her father to keep something from the rest of them. Especially something that would initially horrify him. Maybe she'd never be able to tell any of them how she'd met Colin, and that gave her a strange, lonely feeling. As if she was ashamed of what she'd done. As if it was a sign of her own failure to secure a husband in the way all her friends had done. In the way Jinny was about to. Did Jinny, she wondered, realize how lucky she'd been?

When Hilary joined them on the terrace a few minutes later, wearing a silk kaftan in soft shades of burnt umber and jade green which she'd bought on a holiday in South Africa, they were discussing the progress of the mansion in Belgrave Square.

Sinking into one of the cushioned wicker garden chairs, Hilary gave a sigh of contentment. 'Bliss,' she said, smiling at them. 'That hot bath has really helped my back.'

'You do too much gardening, Mum,' Antonia pointed out, while Quentin poured his wife a glass of wine.

'I know,' she agreed, 'but at this time of year there's such a lot to do, and I do enjoy it so. You know I'm never happier than when I'm up to my elbows in earth.' She patted her daughter's hand. 'Tell me all your news, sweetheart. As we're on our own this evening we can really catch up on everything.'

When they'd finished their drinks, they had dinner at one end of the long refectory table in the richly panelled dining room that smelled of roses and wax polish and scented candles. Even though they were on their own, Hilary liked standards to be observed, and being a very romantic woman she'd placed the bowl of pink roses on the table, chosen the dinner service with the pink and gold rim and the wine glasses for their cranberry hue, so that everything harmonized and the atmosphere was seductively warm and snug. Antonia looked around appreciatively. Ever since she could remember, her mother had paid attention to the smallest detail in the running of her house. There were always lovely arrangements of flowers and leaves in each room; Chinese bowls of pot-pourri filled the air with fragrance, and in the winter the aroma of apple wood burning in the open grates, pervaded the house.

'It's so nice to be home,' Antonia said impulsively.

They both smiled. 'I can't tell you how lovely it is to have you here,' Hilary said. 'You know that Ro and Jinny are coming down tomorrow?'

Antonia nodded. She and Quentin exchanged looks. Hilary, noticing, spoke again.

'You've told Antonia we have a slight conflict of, shall we say, style?'

'Yes,' Quentin replied.

'I think you should offer Jinny an ultimatum,' Antonia said firmly. 'You either do it the conventional way and pay for it all, and I'm sure that's what Ro wants, or she does her own thing and she pays.'

Hilary looked troubled. 'But she's penniless, darling. I don't think she could afford a drinks party for ten people.'

'All the more reason for her to cooperate with you. Has Ro even been asked what he'd like?' Quentin asked. 'I can't see him relishing the idea of a "disco bash", can you?'

Hilary put down her knife and fork, and, placing her elbows on the table, clasped her hands, roughened by years of gardening, together, as she leaned towards them.

'We do have to remember it's their wedding, though,' she said in conciliatory tones. 'If Jinny really wants everything to be different from the usual traditional style, then maybe I shouldn't insist on organizing it at all. Perhaps I should give her a budget to work within and let her get on with it.'

'But it's also your *son* who's getting married. As *his*

mother, if not hers, shouldn't you have a say? It's your house that's going to be used for the reception,' Antonia declared, angrily. 'If she doesn't like it she can lump it, as far as I'm concerned,' she added.

Hilary shrugged and suddenly she looked very tired and quite old. In the candlelight, there were dark smudges under her eyes.

'There's no point in our going on about it now,' she said wearily. 'Let's have a discussion when they arrive tomorrow. We've got to make decisions, though, if they still want to get married in October. That's only . . .' she counted on her fingers, 'only three months away.'

'Well, I can promise you one thing,' Antonia told her sturdily. 'When I get married, I hope you'll be kind enough to arrange every single detail for me, because nobody could do it better.'

Hilary looked startled, and turned to gaze at her daughter, wide-eyed with curiosity. 'Darling, are you trying to tell us something?'

Turning scarlet, Antonia gave a forced laugh. 'Of *course* not!' she exclaimed, wishing she hadn't made the remark. She'd meant it as a joke, a way of cheering her mother up, but because she'd been thinking of Colin Holbrook when she'd said it, she felt hot with embarrassment. 'I'm just hoping that *one* day I might get hitched. When I meet the right person, that is. Not that I've met anyone yet.' The more she tried to explain away her remark, the deeper she seemed to be digging herself in.

Quentin, sensing her discomfort, came to her rescue as he always did. 'When the time comes I've no doubt you and your mother will agree on everything,' he said smoothly. 'Meanwhile we've got to decide how best to deal with *this* wedding.'

'So when are they arriving?'

'In time for lunch, Ro said,' he replied.

'We'll start with those beautiful crabs you brought down,' Hilary observed. 'And the champagne. Really, you spoil us, darling.'

'That's what it's all about, though, isn't it? I honestly get more fun from buying bits and pieces for you both, than spending money on myself,' Antonia asserted with genuine feeling. It was true. She sometimes felt quite guilty when she'd bought an expensive suit to wear to the office or an objet d'art for her flat. Something, she supposed, to do with the puritanical outlook of the vast majority of British people. Her grandmother, and her mother too, had been brought up to regard extravagance as rather a sin; and if not sinful, then vulgar.

That night, in the room she'd occupied since she'd been born, with its deep, mullioned windows overlooking the terrace, and oak-beamed ceiling, Antonia dreamed it was her wedding day and she was putting on a glorious dress made of white chiffon. Her mother was helping her fix the flowers in her hair when the door opened and Colin Holbrook came into the room. 'I just want to see what you look like,' he said. 'Go away!' Antonia replied. 'It's unlucky to see me before the wedding.' Then her mother had looked at her and said: 'Don't *you* want to know what your future husband looks like?'

* * *

It was with a sense of excitement that Antonia awoke the next morning. The dream had been so vivid it was almost as if it had happened, and in this very room too. She'd been standing over there, in front of the dressing table in this beautiful white dress . . . and her mother, wearing blue, had been beside her when the door had opened . . . She glanced over at her bedroom door now, almost as if she expected Colin Holbrook to walk into the room. She could see his face in her mind now, and in her dream he'd been smiling broadly, as if he were glad to see her.

She sat up slowly, shaking her head in order to bring herself back to reality. Had the dream been a good omen? or a case of wishful thinking? The conversation last night had been all about weddings, so she supposed it had got mixed up in her mind with thoughts of Colin Holbrook. Nevertheless, the sense of the dream was so strong she couldn't help feeling a thrill of anticipation, coupled with nervousness, that in five days' time she'd actually be meeting him. Sliding out of bed, too restless to go back to sleep, she pulled on her jeans and a sweater and hurried down to the kitchen where the dogs slept in their baskets near the Aga. Startled to be disturbed from their slumbers so early, they quickly roused themselves, and there was much tail-wagging and grinning.

'Come on then,' she said, putting on her green wellington boots which were kept with a collection of Barbours and waxed stockman's coats in the lobby by the back door. Amber, Jacko and Rags flung themselves into the garden as she unlocked the door, and tore around for a few minutes with the sheer joy of being let out.

Antonia's favourite walk was through the wooded part of their land, and she set off at a brisk pace, taking deep breaths of the cool, clear morning air. While her mother tended the garden, Quentin supervised the care of the fifty acres of forest in which grew oak and beech and birch, lime, horse chestnut and pine. Over the years he'd planted holly, rhododendron and camellias to create shape and interest, and in a secluded dell hundreds of azaleas formed an explosion of rich colour when they flowered. Led by the dogs, Antonia followed the wide grassy paths that cut a swathe through the tall avenue of trees, which, as she got deeper into the wood, became a network of springy woodchip tracks, through glades which in the spring were awash with bluebells while thick clusters of snowdrops frosted the grass with their pure whiteness.

Although she'd always preferred town life, because it was so much more stimulating and challenging than the countryside and gave her such a buzz, this morning Antonia felt a strange tender stirring, somewhere just below her heart. It was as if she were suddenly seeing everything through an enriched perspective. Were the leaves a brighter green today, as the morning sun shone down from a rich blue sky? Was the grass more lush? The stillness at the centre of the forest more profound? And the song of the thrush more piercingly ecstatic?

She strode on, enveloped in a strange feeling of well-being, while Amber, Jacko and Rags ran about pursuing their own interesting trails, delighted at having been taken for this early-morning walk.

When she got back to Clifton Hall, she was assailed by the aroma of fried bacon drifting from the kitchen, where

Mrs Evans, Mrs Dixon and Mrs Porter, from the village, were already at work. Mrs Evans, who did all the cooking, was busy at the stove, while Mrs Dixon laid the table in the dining room and Mrs Porter, armed with the vacuum cleaner, had made a start on the downstairs rooms. A moment later Hilary and Quentin appeared.

'You're up early, darling,' Hilary observed, giving Antonia a hug.

'It's such a wonderful day I couldn't stay in bed.'

'What a treat for the dogs,' Quentin remarked, stroking Amber's ears, as she sat gazing up at him in adoration. 'Don't you wish you had a dog, Antonia?'

She raised her eyebrows. 'Crash would never forgive me,' she laughed. 'As it is, he'll sniff me with great suspicion from top to toe when I get back. He strongly disapproves of dogs.'

At noon, Roland and Jinny arrived, and as it was another gloriously warm day, they all sat on the terrace before lunch, while Quentin opened the champagne Antonia had brought with her. Jinny appeared sullen and watchful, hardly entering into the conversation, but Roland was in ebullient form and obviously relieved to see Antonia.

Drawing her to one side, he linked her arm and walked her down the stone path that lay between fragrant borders of lavender.

'Thank God you're here,' he murmured in a low voice so the others couldn't hear. 'We've got to get these wedding arrangements sorted out once and for all. You will help, won't you?'

'Help *who*, Ro?'

'Well . . . you know, make suggestions and all that sort of thing. Jinny really isn't happy with what Mum's planning.'

'Why don't we wait until we hear what Jinny has to say and then take it from there? As I said to you the other day, this is Mummy and Daddy's house and they're going to be paying for everything, and you can rely on them to arrange everything with great taste and style, so maybe there won't be too much conflict,' she replied evenly.

Roland made a little grimace. 'I know they're not going to do it the way she wants.'

'And what do *you* want, Ro?'

'Whatever makes Jinny happy. It is her day, after all.'

'Forgive my saying so,' she said carefully, 'but I'd have thought it was your day, too.'

He shrugged. 'This sort of thing means more to a girl than it does to a man. I'm counting on you, Antonia. You've got a way with Mum. She'll listen to you.'

Antonia paused and turned to look at him. 'I'm not going to say anything I don't mean,' she replied. 'I'd really rather keep out of the whole discussion. After all, it's got nothing to do with me. It's not as if it's my wedding.'

He looked at her sharply. 'You've not done anything more about all those ghastly men who replied to your lonely hearts ad, have you?'

'Of course not,' she lied.

'You must never do anything so silly again,' he continued, as they slowly retraced their steps back to the terrace. 'It's so dangerous.'

There's nothing dangerous-looking about Colin, she thought.

'God only knows what these fellows that reply are like.'

Colin sounded like he was a good, straightforward chap.

'One wonders where the hell they come from, in the first place. And why on earth do they need to find someone through a newspaper column?' His tone was dismissively derisive.

Because if you've been abroad for years, you might have difficulty in meeting someone.

'I hope you threw out all those replies, Antonia.'

'What?' She started, brought out of her reverie by his insistent voice. 'Oh, yes. Of course I did. Now stop talking about it or the others will hear.'

'Yeah. Right. Jolly nice of you to bring down champagne. It certainly beats the hell out of sherry!'

They rejoined the others and to Antonia's relief the conversation stayed on generalities until Mrs Evans banged the gong in the hall to announce lunch was ready.

It wasn't until lunch was over that the topic of the wedding came up again.

'Shall we go through all the details, Jinny?' Hilary asked, smilingly. 'Time's getting on, and we should be sending those invitations out.' She led the way to Quentin's book-lined study where family conferences always took place.

'If you want,' Jinny replied ungraciously. Roland put his arm round her shoulders in a reassuring gesture, and Quentin and Antonia followed, glancing at each other apprehensively.

Seating herself on the leather sofa which stood in the bay window, Hilary opened a folder on the cover of which she'd written in large letters: *Jinny and Roland's Wedding*.

'Right then,' she began, adopting a businesslike manner. 'Saint Mary's is booked for Saturday the eleventh of October at half past two, and the Reverend Philip Atwell is expecting you to call him so you can arrange to see him about the service and the hymns and psalms you'd like.' There was a stony silence, and so she continued. 'The marquee has been hired, but you need to choose whether you'd like blue-and-white or yellow-and-white-striped lining.'

Jinny spoke for the first time. 'I want black, with a black ceiling studded with those tiny lights like they have in nightclubs; you know, it looks like thousands of stars in a night sky. And a dance floor, of course.'

Hilary's face remained impassive. 'You don't think it'll be a bit dark, darling?'

'Surely the caterers can provide lots of candles, black ones?' Jinny retorted.

'Well, we can come back to the colour scheme in a moment,' Hilary said smoothly. 'Meanwhile, we've still got to decide on the food, and I suggest lots of beautiful canapés, and a three-tiered wedding cake . . .'

'I don't want any of that white icing, you know. I want something original. I'd like a pyramid of leaves made of chocolate, tipped with scarlet, and perhaps touches of gold. It doesn't matter what's in the middle; sponge would do, but I'd like the cake to give the effect of a bonfire. The wedding is in the autumn, isn't it, so it's quite appropriate.' Jinny looked defiantly at her future mother-in-law. 'In any case, I'm not wearing all that conventional white stuff. I want a dress of gold lace over flame-red silk, and I want to wear gold leaves and red berries in my hair, and carry a spray of autumn berries.'

Roland looked at Jinny, entranced. 'You're so *creative*,

my darling,' he enthused. Then he turned to his mother. 'Isn't she marvellous, Mum? I think she ought to be a stage designer.'

Hilary looked at him and her expression was sadly sympathetic. 'I think she probably should,' she said calmly. She closed her file. 'I think I'm rather out of my league, here, Roland. I'm obviously being very old-fashioned because I see country weddings in very different terms. Why don't we work out a budget, and then Jinny can organize it just the way she wants and I'll leave the two of you to get on with it?'

For a moment Roland looked stricken: the little boy whose mother has pushed him from the nest, Antonia thought, watching the dynamics between mother, son, and fiancée. Jinny's expression was triumphant.

'We must agree to differ,' Hilary continued, without a trace of animosity. She was smiling warmly at Jinny as if she admired her artistic talents. 'The only thing I think we should seriously review is the guest list.'

Quentin spoke for the first time. His voice was dangerously controlled but his eyes smouldered. 'I think we should review the *whole* thing,' he said flatly. 'This is *our* home, and half the guests will be *our* friends and relatives. If you want a disco party why don't you hire a club where they already cater for that type of thing? Why don't you have it in St Albans, where you both work and live, instead of here? Why don't you have a register office wedding in the late afternoon, where it won't matter if you choose to wear fancy dress, and then invite all your friends to bop the night away, afterwards? And that being the case, because we are an old-fashioned, out-of-date conventional couple, why don't you leave us out of it completely?' His hands were shaking with rage as he looked at them all from behind his desk, and Antonia had never seen him so angry.

'Dad . . .!' Roland looked at him, appalled.

Hilary's eyes brimmed with tears. 'Quentin, there's no need to—'

'I think there's every need! If we're kind enough to finance this wedding, and you're prepared to work yourself to death organizing it, I think there should be *some* common ground on which we can agree how it should be done. Marriage is a holy estate which should be taken seriously, not an excuse for a tawdry shindig!'

Jinny looked not in the least abashed. 'It is *our* wedding and I think we should do it the way we want.'

'Exactly. So get on with it, but don't expect us to help,' he retorted, rising and leaving the room.

'Oh, dear.' Hilary dabbed at her eyes with a small white handkerchief. 'I didn't want this to happen. I'd no idea your father would get so angry.'

Roland put his hand on his mother's arm, his expression wretched. 'Mum, I'm sorry. We didn't mean to upset you.' He turned to Jinny. 'Did we?'

'I don't know what all the fuss is about,' she said sullenly. 'What difference does it make?'

Antonia, who had been listening intently, spoke.

'May I make a suggestion that would perhaps make everyone happy?' she asked.

Hilary looked at her hopefully through tear-blurred eyes.

'Go on,' Roland urged.

'Mum, how many relatives and friends of yours and Daddy's do you really need to ask?'

'About forty, fifty, maybe.'

'Then why don't you give a little champagne reception after the service at St Mary's, in the drawing room, here? You can fit in that number without a marquee. Make it a glamorous drinks party. Then Ro and Jinny can do the traditional 'going-away' bit, and have their *own* party at a club in St Albans, that night? In that way, everyone gets what they want.'

Roland's face lit up. 'You're brilliant!' he exclaimed. 'Why didn't we think of that? And, Mum,' he continued contritely, 'if you're kind enough to entertain fifty people here after the church, Jinny and I will pay for the disco party at night. That's only fair.'

Jinny turned sharply to stare at him with astonishment, and Hilary started weeping again.

'Oh, darling Ro, you needn't do that . . .'

'Of course we will,' he said firmly. 'Is that all settled, then? Shall I go and find Dad and tell him we've sorted out everything?'

Hilary nodded, unable to speak, and Antonia flashed her brother a look of approval. He charged out of the room leaving the three women alone.

'I don't know how he thinks we're going to pay for the party,' Jinny grumbled.

'I'm sure he'll find a way,' Antonia replied sweetly. 'It's a sign he's growing up at last.'

Four

Antonia arrived at the office early on Monday morning, emotionally drained by her weekend at home. Linda was already at her desk, going through the mail and looking more composed.

'How's everything?' Antonia asked immediately, as none of the others had arrived yet.

'I've moved into Wilton Place, and it's wonderful,' Linda replied. 'I can't tell you how grateful I am, Antonia. It's giving me the breathing space I so badly need, and this week I'm going to start looking for a place I can rent.'

'You certainly look more rested,' Antonia replied approvingly. 'If you're not doing anything tonight, why don't you come with me to the Knightsbridge Association's reception and then join me for supper at my flat? It'll only be Crash and me, but we can watch a video or something. Probably better than staying in an empty house on your own.'

'Thanks, I'd like that. I don't mind being alone, actually. That house has a really good atmosphere. You've done a brilliant job.'

'Let's hope we can sell it soon. That middle-aged man . . .

what's his name? . . . Mr Preedy. Have we heard if he wants it?'

'Not so far. Mark also showed him the house in Victoria Road but I think he thought that one was too big.'

'I'd have thought a flat would have suited them better. They're obviously not that young and with all those stairs . . .' Antonia said thoughtfully. 'Tell Mark to try and interest him in one of our conversions.'

A moment later Linda gasped. 'Oh, my God! How awful!'

'What is it?'

Linda had picked up the *Daily Mail* and was reading the story on the front page. 'That's the *third*,' she exclaimed.

'What are you talking about?'

'There have been three murders in central London,' she explained, looking perturbed, 'and they think they've been committed by a serial killer. The victims have all been women, in their mid-thirties, all with high-profile careers. The body of the third one was discovered on Saturday evening, and she'd been strangled like the others.'

Antonia, who was reading a letter, was only half-listening. 'How awful,' she said automatically.

Linda read on, aloud. "'*The body of the first victim, thirty-four-year-old Pauline Ashford, was found in a deserted car park near High Holborn four weeks ago, near where she worked as an account manager at Stroud Investments. The second, Valerie Martin, the thirty-three-year-old managing director of Wagner's chain of hotels, was found ten days ago. She'd also been strangled and her body had been dumped in a builders' skip near Shaftesbury Avenue. The body of the third victim, Roxana Birch, who was thirty-*

one, and who had recently been appointed Overseas
Manager of Jupiter Pharmaceuticals, was also found to
have been strangled and her body was discovered in the
basement area of the Pimlico house where she lived." It
says here that the murderer seems to have a grudge against
successful businesswomen. Isn't that terrible?'

'The world seems to be full of psychos these days,' Antonia
remarked. 'Listen, Linda, I've had a quote for the carpets for
Belgrave Square. It's going to cost thousands, but it's the
best one I've had so far. Will you write and confirm that they
can go ahead?' She handed the quote to Linda, who discarded
the newspaper with its lurid headline. The day's work had
begun.

After lunch, which today had consisted of chilled potato and
leek soup and a banana, Antonia walked the short distance
to Eaton Place, anxious to look over the property now the
conversion into three grand apartments had been completed.
The builders and decorators had gone, clearing away all their
paraphernalia. Tomorrow the carpets would be laid and the
curtains hung in each apartment and then the furniture would
be delivered, before she added those special touches that
had made Murray Properties Ltd such a success over the
years. Letting herself into the main hallway, where she
planned to put a console table with a large mirror above, she
opened the inner door that led to the ground floor and
basement flat first, pleased that it was no longer dark and
poky. Enlarged windows overlooking the patio at the back
and the demolition of two interior walls had opened it up
quite remarkably, and now it seemed light and airy and would

be put on the market not as a basement flat, but as a 'garden-level apartment', thus increasing the asking price by twenty thousand pounds. The first- and second-floor apartment was the best, of course, with a large front room leading on to a balcony, and an equally large master bedroom on the floor above. The bathroom was a luxurious mix of onyx and gilt; not her personal style but she knew the commercial value of over-the-top vulgarity with certain overseas clients. Finally the two top floors combined made a light and airy apartment with a stunning Mary Poppins view of the chimney pots and church spires of London, and although the bedroom ceilings were slanted she'd chosen wallpapers that enhanced and made a feature of the shape of the rooms. With any luck, she'd be able to put the whole property on to the market within a couple of weeks. Having walked up the stairs, she decided to try out the new lift she'd had installed, which brought her down to the main hall again. Lined with dark cigar-coloured suede, it glided downwards and the gates, she observed, opened equally smoothly.

Just as she was about to let herself out of the building, she realized she'd left her file concerning the property on a window sill in the basement, when she'd needed both hands to try out the wooden shutters.

'Damn,' she swore in annoyance, letting herself in to that apartment again. She'd just reached the room which led out on to the patio when she heard footsteps crossing the bare floorboards of the room above. The heavy ponderous steps stopped, and then started again as if someone was looking for something.

Antonia froze. Who could have got into the house? And

why? There was nothing to steal. The builders had dropped off the keys at the office late on Friday evening, and they'd had the only set. The set she had in her hand right now. Over her head the heavy footsteps paused again, seemed to shuffle for a moment, and then she could hear the person leave the apartment and climb the stairs to the flat above.

Antonia dashed up the stairs, back to the main hall. She must phone the police, but first she had to get out of the building. Slamming the door of the apartment behind her, she ran across the hall to the main street door not daring to look up the stairs. Just as she was about to open the door the piercing *drring*! of the bell echoed with startling clarity throughout the empty house. Startled, she flung the door wide, and found herself face to face with Bert, the foreman of the building company. He was an old friend – they'd worked together on dozens of properties over the years, and she nearly fell into his arms with relief.

'Oh, Bert! Am I glad to see you,' she gasped.

He looked at her white face with concern. 'What's up, miss? I was just passing this way and I saw through the window there was someone in the house, so I thought I'd better just check that it was OK.'

'There's an intruder. I went down to the basement and I heard footsteps in the room above.'

Bert was a short, rotund man with thinning hair, and round blue eyes set in a round, rosy face.

'What . . . in the lounge?' He cocked his thumb, indicating the large ground-floor room. 'Is he still there?' he asked urgently, bracing his shoulders as if for a fight.

Antonia shook her head, while reaching for her mobile

phone in her handbag. 'He's gone upstairs. How can he have got in, Bert? I shut this door behind me, and I shut . . . Oh, well, I suppose I left the door to this apartment open while I went down to the basement, but only for a second. I don't understand how he could have got into the building, though.'

'You wait on the pavement outside, miss,' he commanded, 'I'll search the house.'

She looked appalled. 'You can't do that, Bert. He may be armed!'

'No, not if it's the old bloke I saw through the window, he'd hardly be able to swat a fly. The number of times these homeless beggars get into buildings where they can doss down drives me mad! They're mostly old drunks or druggies, anyway. You get on to the police, miss. I'll soon sort him out.'

Dialling 999, she stood at the bottom of the front steps, watching as Bert mounted the stairs to the first floor, taking them two at a time on his strong stocky legs.

Shocked by how shaken she felt, she reported the intruder to the Chelsea police, and then waited. Bert seemed a long time coming back, and the house fell uncannily silent. Realizing she should never have let him go after whoever had entered the house, she had terrible visions of him being stabbed to death in one of the upstairs rooms, or hit over the head with a weapon. When the lift doors glided open, she thought her heart would stop, but there was Bert, looking unperturbed and shaking his head.

'The bleeder's got away,' he said in disgust. 'Same way as he got in.'

'How did he get in?'

'The window on the landing's been forced. The one by the fire escape. He must have gone round the back, climbed the fire escape to the second floor and got in that way. Pretty nifty for an old geezer like that,' he added, half in admiration.

'What a scary thing to happen,' Linda said, as she and Antonia walked back to Cadogan Square after the reception that evening. 'I wonder what he wanted? There was nothing to steal, was there?'

'Not a thing, but of course he may not have realized that,' Antonia replied.

'But he must have seen, through the ground-floor windows, that the place hasn't a stick of furniture, or even any curtains, at present.'

'I know.' Antonia wasn't admitting it, but she felt deeply disquieted by the incident. The very fact that there'd been nothing to steal made it all the more sinister. 'I've ordered Bert to make all the windows more secure,' she continued, 'although, as he pointed out, it defeats the object if we put locks on the fire-escape windows.'

'I can see that,' Linda replied drily. 'It would be a choice of being burned to death or having all your valuables stolen, wouldn't it?'

When they entered the flat, Crash welcomed Antonia with mews of delight, rubbing himself against her legs, and then trotting off to the kitchen where he sat looking at the fridge in a very pointed way.

'He is a character, isn't he?' Linda remarked.

'Quite what *sort* of a character I'm not sure,' Antonia agreed, taking out a cooked leg of chicken. 'I'll just cut this up for him, and then we'll have a drink.'

'Chicken? When I used to have a cat he only had tinned cat food; filthy it smelled, too,' Linda observed, sitting herself down at the kitchen table.

'I spoiled him when he was a kitten,' Antonia admitted, 'and now of course he only wants the best: calf's liver, turkey, salmon . . .'

'*Salmon?*'

'He only likes salmon. I have the cod for dinner; he has the salmon.'

Linda laughed for the first time in days. 'Now I've heard everything.'

'I'm not completely deprived,' Antonia joked. 'I feel like a glass of champagne right now. How about you?'

'I can't think of anything more blissful.'

When they strolled into the drawing room a few minutes later with a bottle of Bollinger and two glasses, Antonia suggested they catch the news on the TV.

'I just like to know what's happening in the world before I do anything else,' she explained, flipping the switch on the remote control.

They'd missed the headlines but they were in time for the main news.

'. . . The body of Roxana Birch, the third victim to be found strangled in central London in the past two months, was found in the basement area of the house where she lived. It is thought her body may have gone undetected for several days because it was partially covered by a tarpaulin left by builders . . .'

Linda's brow wrinkled in distress. 'That's the murder I

was telling you about this morning.'

'I know.' They both listened, and then blinked as the screen was filled with the picture of a very pretty dark-haired young woman.

'. . . Roxana Birch, who was thirty-two, had recently been appointed Overseas Manager of Jupiter Pharmaceuticals . . .'

It was a repeat of what Linda had read aloud earlier in the day. After a few seconds, in which shots of the house in Pimlico where she'd lived were shown, the faces of two other young women were shown.

'. . . Both Pauline Ashford, who was thirty-four, and Valerie Martin, thirty-three, had also been recently promoted . . .'

'Sick, isn't it?' Linda remarked. 'Obviously someone with a grudge against upwardly mobile successful young women.'

'Yes.' For some reason she couldn't explain, Antonia felt uneasy. The incident in the house today had shocked her. Then she remembered the taxi which had practically rammed the back of her car; what had that been all about? She said nothing for fear of sounding foolish; in any case, Linda had enough on her plate right now, *and* she was staying alone in a large semi-empty house; no point in making her nervous, too.

At the end of the weather forecast, Antonia picked up the remote control. 'OK? Seen enough? Shall we switch off?'

'Yes, let's. Watch enough news and you could die of depression,' Linda replied, sipping her drink.

Later, Antonia made mushroom omelettes and a salad, and listened to Linda as she told her all about the man she'd been in love with, and Robin who was still determined to divorce her. It seemed to help her to talk and talk, and go over all the details again and again, until Antonia knew the story by heart; but she remained attentive, offering words of comfort when they were appropriate, and morale-boosting support when Linda became tearful.

'I'm afraid I'm being a terrible bore,' Linda said finally, blowing her nose on an already damp handkerchief.

'No, you're not,' Antonia told her firmly. 'Talk as much as you like. It's therapeutic.' There didn't seem to be anything else to say. Linda had made a grave mistake in falling in love with a man who had no intention of leaving his wife and children, and right now Robin, sadly, was being unforgiving.

'Sit tight and do nothing,' was the only advice she could give. 'Robin may change his mind when he realizes what a final severance divorce is. He may regret having been so hasty. You'd like to go back to him if you could, wouldn't you?'

'I'd like to go back for the security,' Linda replied with honesty, 'but that wouldn't be right. It wouldn't be fair to Robin. The trouble is, I'm still in love with Angus and I think I always will be.'

'Oh, Linda, I'm so sorry,' Antonia sympathized. She'd never been in love like that herself, and found it hard to understand how Linda, who had always said she was happily married to Robin, could have possibly let it happen. If you loved one person, how could you fall in love with another? And was it love that Linda felt, or lust? As if she knew what Antonia was thinking, she said:

'This must all seem crazy to you. You must wonder why

the hell I left Robin in the first place.'

'I'm not being judgemental, Linda. It's just that I've never fallen passionately in love with anyone, so I find it hard to understand how it can happen.' She sounded almost wistful.

Linda gave a tired smile. 'I used to be exactly like that. Even a year ago I had no patience with people who messed up everyone else's life because they'd fallen in love. I remember thinking, why can't they control themselves? Why are they being so selfish?' She was silent for a moment, lost in thought, her eyes filled with the pain she felt.

'I can only tell you that when it happens, it's like being hit with a sledgehammer. It's like being caught up in a tornado. It's like being *drugged*! You're on this perpetual high and you're completely out of control. I don't know whether it would have made any difference if I'd had children but I have the awful feeling it wouldn't. I was obsessed with Angus. All I could think of was being with him. I couldn't . . . still can't . . . sleep. I couldn't eat. Hour after hour, day after day, this compulsion to be with him overwhelmed me and everything I did.'

Antonia looked mystified. 'How come I didn't notice anything? You always seemed to be your usual happy and efficient self.'

'I don't say this as a criticism, Antonia, but you're always so focused on your work, you simply didn't notice. I was thankful, actually. I didn't want anyone to know in case it got back to Robin, and I did my best to be professional about my work, so the business didn't suffer.'

'Oh, that's awful, Linda. I'd no idea I was so . . . so *blinkered* about what was happening around me. You're right, of course. I put everything into the business. It's *my* obsession, and the price I'm paying is that I now have no private life. No boyfriend. No husband or children.' She leaned back against the cushions on the sofa and gazed up at the dove-grey ceiling and the richly ornamental white cornicing, which looked as if it had been made of icing sugar.

'I should have noticed something was happening in your life, although, as you know, none of us brings our personal affairs to work,' she continued. 'It makes me feel very self-centred to realize I had no idea what was happening to you.'

'There's nothing you could have done, and I wouldn't have listened to you, you know, if you *had* talked to me. My mother tried to persuade me to give up Angus. She warned me I was doing the wrong thing; but would I listen? Even when she said it wasn't fair on Robin. Even when she told me I would ruin my life, because Angus would never leave his wife.' Linda shook her head slowly in disbelief. 'I was out of my mind. The terrible thing is, I still am. If Angus came back tomorrow, wanting to start the affair up again, I'd go back to him.'

'It must be quite scaring to be in the grip of such a strong emotion.'

'It's frightening, it's marvellous, it's exciting, it's unlike anything else, and the most scaring part of all is that you're convinced you're in the right and everyone else is wrong. The only good thing to have come out of this hideous nightmare is that it's made me more compassionate and understanding of other people's feelings. I don't think I'll ever be judgemental again, at least I hope I won't. I really hope this has taught me something. Otherwise it will all have been for nothing, won't it?'

'What a dreadful way to have to learn anything.' Antonia felt quite shaken to see Linda, who had always been so in control of everything, suffering now as she talked about her affair. Of all people, she would never have thought it would be Linda who would make a mess of her life.

Jane, Emma, Barbara, Denise . . . yes. It wouldn't have surprised her if any one of them had chosen the wrong man, or got entangled with someone who was already married. But not Linda. Always so sensible. Always matter-of-fact, and with her feet on the ground and her mind concentrated on her work.

'I'm thankful I never had children,' Linda continued. 'I don't know what the hell I'd have done if I had.'

'That must be the worst predicament for any woman,' Antonia agreed. 'I don't think I could ever leave a child, for a lover.'

Linda looked at her steadily. 'You can't be sure; you don't know *what* you'd do if you've never fallen hopelessly in love. I used to think like you; now I'm not so sure. It's like a sickness, Antonia. You're caught up in something so powerful you'd *die* for it.'

'I've never felt like that,' Antonia agreed, thoughtfully. Would she ever feel like that? Would Colin Holbrook, when she met him, cause her to lose her head and risk everything? She simply couldn't imagine it happening.

'Listen, Linda. It's getting late and you're tired. Why don't you stay the night? This is a sofa bed – it's so comfortable. I sleep on it myself when my parents come to stay, so they can have my room.'

Linda shot her a grateful look, through eyes swollen from days of crying. 'That would be lovely,' she admitted. 'Thanks, Antonia. I do appreciate all you're doing for me and I promise I'll have pulled myself together by the end of the week. I feel I'm letting you down at the moment.'

'Of course you're not,' Antonia assured her firmly. 'I just wish there was something I could do to make you feel better.'

Linda gave her a watery smile. 'Having someone to talk to is the best help of all.'

'I'm always here to listen.'

At last it was Thursday and Antonia awoke early, a frisson of excitement making her instantly alert, much to the annoyance of Crash, who liked to have a morning cuddle before she got out of bed. This morning, however, Antonia bounded into her adjoining bathroom and turned on the shower before he'd had time to uncoil himself from the foot of her bed.

She chose her clothes with care; a navy-blue designer suit with touches of white and navy-blue tights and shoes. If she felt nervous now, she wondered, as she brushed her newly washed hair until it shone, what on earth was she going to be like by this evening?

At the office, the day seemed to drag and Linda, who was in better form, kept looking at her in perplexity, wondering why her boss seemed so distracted. For the first time ever Antonia felt bored with her work, so much so that she suddenly longed for the day when she could stay at home and do all those domestic chores she normally found repetitious and uninteresting. It was quite a startling discovery.

By seven o'clock, everyone else had left the office, including Linda, who had gone to meet Robin to discuss the divorce settlement. He wanted the whole thing to be cleared up as speedily and cleanly as possible, he'd said, and if they could agree on the terms and avoid calling in lawyers, they could save thousands of pounds.

Once alone, Antonia redid her make-up, added a spray of Pleasures, and brushed her hair. Her hands shook as she locked the main street doors and there was a mixture of fear and excitement coursing through her veins. It would be difficult to park her car near the Grosvenor House Hotel, so she hailed a taxi. As it rattled up to Hyde Park Corner she sat in the back feeling quite breathless. My God, this is a nerve-racking experience, she said to herself, wishing it was over, wishing she'd already met Colin Holbrook and they were on their way to a restaurant for dinner.

There were not many people in the hotel lobby as she crossed it to get to the bar, which was in a softly lit room with small tables covered with white cloths, and small but comfortable armchairs.

A middle-aged man in a dark blue suit was standing at the entrance, his head turning this way and that as if he were looking for someone. Antonia recognized him immediately, and swore under her breath. The last thing she wanted, as she waited to meet a blind date, was a client hovering in the vicinity. What on earth would he think? It would be obvious to anyone that Colin Holbrook, not knowing what she looked like, would be casting an eye over all the young women sitting on their own; he might even go up to someone else and ask if she were 'Susan'.

Antonia averted her face, and decided to walk briskly past him, into the bar, hoping he wouldn't recognize her. She'd taken half a dozen steps when he caught sight of her, and he raised his grey eyebrows in surprise.

'Miss Murray, isn't it?' he said, peering down at her through his thick glasses.

Antonia looked up, noting that his skin still had that strange grey phosopherescent look. For a moment his name eluded her.

'I'm Alec Preedy; your assistant, Mark Gillingham, has been showing me over some of your properties,' he said as if he knew she'd forgotten who he was.

'Yes, of course, Mr Preedy,' Antonia replied smoothly, shaking his hand. 'I remember you very well. You were shown around the house in Wilton Place, weren't you? I believe you rather liked it.'

The grey eyebrows rose again, and the tired folds of his face twitched very slightly into a smile.

'My word, you are efficient. Fancy you remembering all that. I was actually talking to your colleague – or perhaps I should say employee – earlier today, and I'm going to look at another of your properties in Victoria Road.'

'Good. It's going to be fabulous when it's finished.' As she spoke, she too glanced around the lobby, hoping that Colin Holbrook would be late. What an impossible situation it would be if he arrived, just as she was talking business to someone else. She couldn't be brusque with Mr Preedy, either, as he was obviously a rich client.

'When do you think it will be ready?' he asked.

'Within six weeks.'

'You seem very sure of that, Miss Murray.'

Antonia nodded. 'I am. I have a first-rate team of builders and decorators working on that property, and I have a penalty clause in the contract, if they don't keep to the deadline.'

'I'm sure you do, Miss Murray.'

Was that a hint of sarcasm in his voice? she wondered, not liking him at all and wishing he'd go. Where was Colin Holbrook? Now she began to wish he would arrive so she could get away from this strange man.

Mr Preedy continued, 'It's quite expensive for my wife and I to stay here, so we obviously want to find a place of our own as soon as we can. I'm waiting for her now, actually.' His eyes scanned the lobby, his expression lugubrious. 'She's gone shopping; something women seem to enjoy doing.'

'Right. Well, I hope we'll be able to find you somewhere to live very quickly . . .' As she spoke she edged her way past him.

He looked at his watch, a slender, old-fashioned gold one on a thin brown leather strap. 'Oh dear, she's nearly half an hour late.'

'If you'll excuse me, I'm meeting . . . er . . . a client,' Antonia said in desperation.

'Why don't we have a drink while we're both waiting?' Mr Preedy suggested. 'If we take a table near the door, I can watch out for my wife and you can keep an eye out for your client. How would that be?' As he spoke he was firmly but gently steering her in the direction of a table with two chairs. God, she thought, I'd forgotten he'd told Mark that he and his wife were staying at Grosvenor House. And of all the places in London, what on earth had made her choose to come here to meet Colin Holbrook?

There was nothing for it. She'd have to have a drink with Alec Preedy, and when Colin arrived, she'd excuse herself and they'd go to another table. Antonia felt exasperated. Just when she wanted to be composed and at her best, Colin was going to arrive and find her in top-gear business mode, discussing million-pound properties with an older gentleman. Not the best of situations for the start of what she hoped was going to be a meeting with the love of her life.

Mr Preedy ordered gin and tonic for both of them. The waiter placed nuts and olives in little white china dishes on the table. Antonia bit into a large black olive and encountered a very hard stone in its middle, which nearly broke a tooth in its unexpectedness. And all the time she had to concentrate on the people who were drifting in and out of the bar area, hoping she'd be easily able to recognize Colin Holbrook by his photograph.

'Relax and enjoy your drink, Miss Murray,' Mr Preedy said, as he tried to engage her in conversation. Antonia gave a thin smile. She couldn't tell him the 'client' she was meeting was very important, because that would infer *he* wasn't. Gritting her aching tooth, she sipped her drink. It was so well iced it had very little taste. Surreptitiously she sneaked a quick look at her wristwatch. The hands pointed to a quarter to eight. Colin Holbrook was late again. With a horrible sinking feeling she wondered what had gone wrong this time. Of course the traffic might be heavy; or he might have been kept late by his boss. Could he have gone to the other

Grosvenor Hotel, by Victoria station? No, that was unlikely. She tried to remember whether or not she'd said 'in Park Lane'. Please God, let him come soon, she prayed, refusing to believe the awful thought that lurked at the back of her mind that he might not come at all.

Mr Preedy was droning on about the advantages of living in London, and how he was looking forward to it, and he seemed to have forgotten all about his wife. He listed the museums and galleries, the concert halls and theatres that he frequented, and said what wonderful value for money it all was. Antonia listened, or appeared to listen, nodding from time to time and agreeing to everything he said, but all the time her gaze kept flicking to the doorway. It was eight o'clock, and still there was no sign of Colin Holbrook.

After a while, Mr Preedy seemed to realize they were both waiting for people who hadn't turned up.

'I hope my wife's all right,' he said, showing concern for the first time. Then he looked at Antonia, his small eyes beady through his glasses. 'Your appointment is late, too, isn't he? Dear, dear, people seem to have no sense of time these days. I do so hate unpunctuality, don't you?'

It was now eight-twenty, and Antonia had had enough. Her disappointment was so great she could have cried, but instead, she rose to her feet and announced she was leaving.

'He must have got held up,' she remarked, gathering up her things. 'Thank you for the drink, Mr Preedy, and I hope we can find you something suitable in the way of a house or flat.' She shook his hand. 'I hope your wife turns up soon, too.'

'Thank you. It's been most interesting meeting you. Before

this evening you were a remote figure behind your desk. You're a very clever young woman, aren't you? Heading up your own prestigious property empire.'

'I'd hardly call it an empire yet, but I'm working on it,' she replied with a wry smile.

'I'm sure you are, Miss Murray, I'm sure you are.'

Antonia took a last look round the lobby, and then walked through the central part of the hotel to the other entrance, on the far side, just in case Colin had gone there to meet her. There was no sign of him. People were now dining in the glittering glass restaurant, and the drinking hour was over. Dispiritedly she hailed another taxi, although she could have easily walked, and told the driver to take her to Cadogan Square. All she wanted now was a hot bath and bed. Depression wrapped itself around her like a listless torpor and she wished she'd never put an advertisement in the newspapers in the first place. Never heard from Colin Holbrook, either. Roland's warning to have nothing to do with men who answered a lonely hearts advertisement had been right. It had been a stupid thing to do and a waste of time. Her hopes had been foolishly raised and now she felt greatly downcast. When she got home, she'd tear up Colin's photograph and his two letters, which she'd kept in the drawer of her bedside table, and she'd forget about the whole thing. Maybe she wasn't meant to get married. Or have children. By the time she got back to her flat, her mascara was streaked down her cheeks and she was sniffing because she couldn't find her handkerchief.

Crash, who had been waiting for her, rushed to meet her when she let herself into her flat, but she wasn't in the mood to pay him any attention tonight. Going straight to her bedroom, she was in the middle of getting undressed when the phone rang. Automatically she went over to her bedside table and picked up the receiver.

'Hello?' There was no answer. 'Hel*lo*?' she said again, angry now. The last thing she needed were silent callers when she was already so rattled. There was a click, and the dialling tone purred into her ear. Shrugging, she put on her towelling bath robe and was just about to turn on the shower, when the phone rang again. For a moment she looked at it suspiciously. Would she let it ring? Better not, she decided, in case it was one of her family.

'Hello?' Again the silence. Again no response. 'Hello?' she almost shouted. A moment later the familiar click told her the caller had hung up. This time, Antonia dialled 1471; a sure way of finding out the phone number of the caller.

'Dammit!' she exclaimed a moment later. Whoever had called had intended to remain anonymous by blocking their own number and dialling 141 first. Because she felt tired, dispirited and utterly fed up, she decided to leave the phone off the hook. If it was really urgent her parents and brothers had her mobile number. Meanwhile the rest of the world could stuff itself, she muttered under her breath as she went to have a bath.

Half an hour later, refreshed and feeling more relaxed, she shared some cold chicken with Crash, poured herself a glass of wine and settled down to watch a soothing nature programme on television, with Crash curled up on her lap. The evening had been a disaster but she decided to put it out of her mind. When she went to bed, she reminded herself that she must remove Colin Holbrook's photograph from the drawer in her bedside table. As far as she was concerned he didn't exist any more. That sort of aggravation she could do without.

Just as she began to switch off the drawing room lights, her front doorbell rang loudly, startling her.

'Who *is* it?' she asked through the intercom system.

'Is that you, Antonia?' The man's voice sounded thick and anxious.

'Who is that?' she repeated.

'It's me. Robin . . . Robin Dunn. I was passing and I wondered if I could drop in to see you for a few minutes.'

'Yes, OK, Robin. Come on up.' It was eleven o'clock, but Linda's husband sounded distraught. Their meeting earlier in the evening must have gone badly. A moment later she opened the door of her flat and Robin came bounding in, his face red and his blue eyes seeming to pop from their sockets.

'I tried to phone you but I couldn't get through . . . I'm sorry it's so late . . .' he gabbled, waving his arms about expansively. He was a big, shambling man, inclined to be charmingly gung-ho. Tonight he looked as if he'd run a marathon. He was sweating profusely and his dark pinstripe suit was crumpled. His shirt collar was unbuttoned and he looked as if he'd had a tussle with his tie, which flapped loosely.

'Are you all right, Robin?' Antonia asked. His presence seemed to fill the flat; his bellicosity made her shrink back.

'All right? I'm going out of my mind, Antonia,' he replied, kissing her on the cheek. His breath smelled of whisky and tobacco. His skin was coldly damp. 'I think Linda's lost the plot! I *cannot* make her see sense!' Without waiting to be asked, he stomped ahead of her into the drawing room and dropped in a dejected heap on to one of her sofas.

'Would you like some coffee, Robin?'

He looked searchingly round the room, his eyes blinking sadly, and she was reminded of Winnie the Pooh wondering where the honey pot was kept.

'I don't suppose you've got a drop of whisky, have you? I'm most frightfully sorry to come barging round like this, in the middle of the night, but I really am desperate, you know.'

He sounds desperate, she thought, relenting.

'Yes, I've got some whisky,' she replied, smiling. 'With a little water, I think, don't you?'

He didn't answer but continued to look doleful. When she handed him the purposely weak drink he looked up at her with pathetic gratitude.

'Thanks Antonia. You're a star. Did you know Linda was playing around with someone else?'

'I've only just heard about it,' she replied carefully, not wanting to get involved in this marital split.

Robin shook his head slowly from side to side. 'I thought that if I took a strong line it would give her a shock and bring her to her senses. I kicked her out and said I wanted a divorce, you know.'

'Yes. I know.'

'It didn't work.' He sounded perplexed.

'I know,' said Antonia again.

Robin smoothed his glistening brow with the palm of his hand and then absent-mindedly wiped it on his trouser leg.

'She says she still wants a divorce although I gather she's split up from this fellow. Does that make sense to you?'

'I've never been married, Robin, so I don't know. Maybe if you let the dust settle, things will change.'

He'd emptied his glass and was looking longingly at the whisky decanter again. 'Could I possibly . . .?'

Anxiously, she refilled it, with so little whisky it was straw-coloured.

'What am I going to do, Antonia?' It was a cry from the heart.

'Maybe if you give her time . . .' she suggested. She seated herself on the sofa beside him. He reminded her of a big sad child, confused and lost. 'Linda's a very intelligent woman. I'm sure she'll do the right thing for both of you.'

'She *is* intelligent,' he agreed. 'Like you. And strong too.' He turned to look into her eyes. 'And the fact that you're devastatingly sexy as well makes you very special, Antonia.'

She blushed, embarrassed. 'I don't know about that,' she said dismissively.

'Oh, but you are. I've always thought so.' He reached for her hand and gripped it, clammily. 'You should be married, Antonia. A beautiful girl like you would make someone a wonderful wife.'

She tried to pull her hand away but he held it tighter. 'In the meantime, Robin, I think it's time you went home,' she said briskly. 'It's getting very late—'

'Oh, please don't throw me out!' His eyes filled with tears. He put his glass down on the floor by his feet. 'You're so understanding. If only I'd met you first, I wouldn't be in this terrible mess now. I've always fancied you, you know.'

Antonia drew back in alarm. This was the last thing she'd expected from Linda's husband, who she only knew very slightly. She made a determined effort to stand up, but he released her hand only to grab her around the waist and pull her down beside him again.

'Darling . . .' he said thickly. 'You've no idea how much I want you . . . you won't send me away, will you?' He put his leg over her knees and pushing her back, tried to kiss her. His rotund body was heavy. The strong muscles of his leg held hers in a pinion-like grip. His breath was hot and fetid. Antonia turned her head sharply away and swung her body sideways, so they both rolled off the sofa on to the floor. Thanking God she'd landed on top of him, she jumped up before he could recover his befuddled wits and strode over to the phone.

'I'm calling a taxi for you, Robin,' she said icily, as she rang Dial-a-Cab. 'You're in no fit state to be out.'

He lay on the floor staring up at the ceiling for several minutes before he got lumberingly to his feet. Then he sat on the edge of the sofa with his head in his hands.

'I'm sorry, Antonia,' he murmured in a muffled voice. 'I shouldn't have done that. You *are* terribly sexy, though,' he added after a pause.

She said nothing. Her disgust at what he'd done was mixed up in her mind with the dreadful realization that for just one second she'd actually enjoyed being held close, wanted, needed. His desire, though drunken, had been a momentary turn-on, making her realize, perhaps, what she was missing in life. If only he had been someone else, she thought. And how ironic it was that just when she was looking for love and desperately wanting a man in her life, it was her assistant's husband, of all people, who had come on to her.

After Robin had bundled himself into the taxi, still murmuring his apologies, she went to her bedroom and picked up Colin Holbrook's photograph. He was looking straight at her and he was smiling. God, he *was* attractive, she thought, as her heart gave a little lurch. And he looked witty, and kind, and fun to be with . . . and, Oh God, was it possible to fall in love with someone one had never met? Antonia sat slumped on the edge of the bed, gazing at his picture and wishing she could forget all about him. She picked up his letters and read them again and was filled with regret. If only it had worked out, it could have been perfect. Instead he was obviously someone who was utterly unreliable. Maybe, for him, it was just a game; reply to a few lonely hearts advertisements, promise to meet them and then amuse himself by thinking of them waiting in vain in various hotel lounge bars.

Suddenly she was gripped with anger. What a louse he was! How *dare* he mess her about like this? Being stood up once, she was prepared to be understanding about, but *twice*! It's not on, she fumed, grabbing the phone beside her bed. It's time someone disrupted *his* life. Although it was midnight, she dialled the Islington number.

The phone rang only twice and she heard a cautious voice say, 'Hello?'

'Is that Colin Holbrook?'

'Oh, Susan! Oh my God, if only I'd taken your phone number. I've been desperate, trying to get hold of you, but I don't even know where you live, or I'd have sent a courier round with my apologies.'

'So what kept you?' She was not going to relent.

'I can't tell you how sorry I am.' He sounded downcast and subdued. 'God knows what you must think of me. It happened again! Can you believe my bad luck? Just as I was leaving the office, my boss called me into a meeting . . . all to do with a fall in value of the Japanese yen . . . and of course the time difference between us and Japan didn't help, and I couldn't do anything to get a message to you. I didn't get away from the office until nearly nine-thirty. I was going out of my mind! I knew it was no good going to Grosvenor House then, I knew you'd have left in disgust. Oh, Susan, what on earth do you think of me?'

'I think we should forget the whole thing,' she replied coldly.

'Oh!' His voice dropped and he sounded crushed. 'Really? I promise you I wouldn't have let this happen in a thousand years if I could have helped it. Oh, Christ, what a mess. I so wanted to meet you.'

'Perhaps we're destined not to meet.'

'Don't say that. I really couldn't get away, you know. I couldn't even get to a phone. One doesn't seem to be allowed to *have* a private life where I work. And I wasn't the only one, tonight. One of the chaps in my division was supposed to get home in time for a dinner party for his wife's birthday . . . can you imagine? I was so looking forward to meeting you, too.'

'Really?' she replied crisply, although she could feel herself weakening. If all he said was true, then it really wasn't his fault. And he sounded so sincere, distraught even; perhaps she ought to give him another chance? Except, of course, this was exactly what had happened last time, and she wasn't prepared to be stood up again. How could she be sure he was speaking the truth? Maybe he'd gone to the pub after work, with some of his colleagues. Maybe he'd had another date with another lonely hearts . . . no, she couldn't bear to think of that. Maybe he was just one of those disorganized people who were incapable of keeping to arrangements, and if that was the case, he was the last person on earth she wanted to know. People like that did not figure on her agenda.

'Please, Susan. Next time, let's make it anything you want: breakfast on the way to work? Drinks before lunch? Lunch? Afternoon tea? If I have to get rid of my boss, I promise it won't happen again.'

'I don't want to be unreasonable,' she said, 'but I am a very busy person. I simply haven't the time to be messed about like this.'

'I understand that, Susan. I hate unreliable people, too. But can't you give me another chance? Please?'

'Why don't we leave it for the time being, Colin? I have your number. I can always give you a call . . .'

'I wish I could call you,' he cut in with boyish eagerness. 'If we could just forget these two appalling gaffes on my part and start all over again . . .'

As he spoke, she was looking at his photograph again, propped up on her pillow; for a moment she had a wild impulse to tell him where she lived and invite him round for a drink the following evening. A voice in her head was saying, *You're crazy to turn someone like this away just because he was kept late at work and couldn't meet you.*

'Maybe we could meet at some point,' she heard herself say with applaudable casualness, 'but I'm rather busy for the next week or so . . .'

'Right. Good. I mean good that you think we could still meet. I could kick myself for tonight. Tell me about yourself, Susan. I know nothing about you. Except that you've got a wonderfully husky voice. Very sexy.'

Antonia blushed for the second time that evening, but said nothing.

'What do you do? I know you're a dedicated career girl but what do you actually do?'

'I work in the property field,' she replied cautiously.

'Have you always done that?'

'Yes. Ever since I left university.'

'Which one?'

'Edinburgh.'

'What did you read?'

'Economics.'

'Wow! You *are* bright.' His tone was full of admiration.

Antonia laughed, feeling more relaxed, feeling that she was beginning to get to know him. 'What about you? Which university did you go to?'

'Oxford. Magdalen, actually. I read politics, for some extraordinary reason. Anyway, I left for Canada soon after I graduated and . . . well, you know the rest. Now I'm back in this country; being worked to death and tired and alone in a rented flat, and desperate to meet the girl of my dreams.' His joky voice was in contrast to his gloomy observations. Then he chuckled.

'Please put me out of my misery, Susan! Say you'll let me buy you a drink, or dinner, or breakfast, or a *cup of tea* before I go completely stark staring bonkers!'

Antonia found herself laughing in spite of herself, liking him for his zany wit and lightly flirtatious manner. He sounded as good-tempered and humorous as his photograph suggested and she decided that she probably would contact him again. But not for a while. She was determined not to appear too keen.

'Yes, well I'll give you a ring when I'm less frantic at the office,' she said.

'You haven't got your diary with you now?'

'No.'

'Have you got a mobile number, if you don't want to give me your home number?'

Why not? she thought recklessly. She was always so damned careful . . . go for it! she told herself. He's obviously on the level and I'm just being paranoid.

'That's great,' he said, repeating it after her. 'Let's fix to meet very soon.'

'Yes. OK.'

After she'd bid him a brisk goodbye, Antonia got into bed, and lying on her back with Crash snuggled into her side, thought about their conversation. The more she knew, the more she liked the sound of Colin. In fact, everything seemed right. His age, his occupation, his background, and, most important of all, his sense of humour. It still rankled that he hadn't turned up tonight, but she had enough experience of the business world to know that sometimes urgent business meetings, called at all hours, were inevitable.

It was just so unfortunate that it had happened to Colin on both occasions they'd been going to meet. How long should she leave it before fixing another meeting? Two or three days? Or a couple of weeks? In her position it was silly to play hard to get, of course. A woman who played hard to get was a woman who was being pursued by lots of men, not a slightly desperate thirty-two-year-old who was advertising for a husband in a national newspaper. Nevertheless . . . Antonia rolled on to her side and turned off the light. Maybe it was all going to turn out all right. Maybe, when she met Colin Holbrook, it would be love at first sight.

Crash gave a squawk of protest as she nearly squashed him with her knees.

'I'm sorry, sweetheart,' she said, rolling on to her back again as she stroked his head. He was not, she realized with amusement, going to like sharing her bed with another male.

'Darling, I'm upset because I think it's my fault,' Hilary said in distress, when she phoned Antonia at the office the next morning.

'Mum, it's not your fault at all,' Antonia replied stoutly. She was shocked, though, to be told that Jinny and Roland had broken off their engagement. 'How can it be your fault?'

'Because of the fuss over the reception. Perhaps I should have gone along with what Jinny wanted . . .'

'Mum, you bent over backwards to please her!' Antonia exploded. 'She's a spoiled brat, and she should be grateful to you for offering to give them a big reception in the first place.'

'Yes, but that wasn't what she wanted, was it? She wanted

her own sort of party, a discotheque for her friends.'

'So? She and Ro were going to have that, in the evening, weren't they? In a club in St Albans. So what's the problem?'

Hilary's voice quivered. 'Jinny's furious with Ro for saying that if I gave a little wedding party here, they'd pay for the party at night. She says they can't afford it. Now they've had a terrible bust-up and she's walked out.'

'What does Ro say?'

'He thinks she's being selfish and childish. She hasn't any parents, though, and that's why I feel bad about it. I should be a mother to her as well as to Ro.'

'That's fine, as long as she behaves like a daughter to you,' Antonia pointed out. 'Where's she gone?'

'To stay with an old school friend.'

'I hope he doesn't go after her. And Mum . . . you mustn't back down now. She's probably hoping she can emotionally blackmail the family into letting her have her own way, but you must stand firm.'

'But I feel I ought to offer to pay for everything now; that's been the cause of the break-up and I can't help feeling guilty,' said Hilary.

'Mum. Listen to me. For the first time in his life Ro has shown a streak of maturity. Don't deny him this new-found independence. He'll thank you in the long run for allowing him to take some responsibility and, frankly, if Jinny is going to be such a selfish little bitch, he's better off without her,' Antonia added hotly.

'You've never liked her, have you, darling?'

'Not much.'

'But then you're so close to Ro. I have a feeling you'd

think no one was good enough for your little brother.'

'Nonsense, Mum! Personally, I think Ro's always been far too dependent on the rest of us. I was really pleased when he showed he was growing up at last, by saying he'd pay for their evening party. It's what he *should* do. For goodness' sake, he's twenty-five, able-bodied and he has a good job. It's about time he stopped leaning on you and Dad, especially financially.'

Antonia knew that Hilary secretly slipped him a few hundred pounds from time to time, when he couldn't meet the bills for his flat.

'I suppose you're right, but I still feel dreadful,' Hilary lamented.

'Mum, don't,' said Antonia, trying to sound comforting. 'It really isn't your fault, and I'm sure Ro will survive. Why don't you get away for the day? Come up to town and do some shopping and we can have lunch.'

'I'll think about it, sweetheart. It would certainly be lovely to see you again.'

'Then let me know when you're coming, and I'll book a table at the glitziest place in town.' Antonia was pleased to hear her mother laugh. 'That's better, Mum! Your baby's a big boy now.'

'I expect he'll phone you and tell you all about it.'

'I've no doubt he will. Mum, I've got to go now. I'm supposed to be doing a whistle-stop tour of all the properties today, as it's Friday, to see how the work's progressing before the builders clock off for the weekend. I'll be in this evening if you want to call me.'

'All right, my darling. Lots of love.'

'Bye, Mum. Lots of love to you and Daddy.'

Antonia gathered up her papers and slipped them into her briefcase. 'I'm off now, Linda. You can get me on my mobile if you need me, but I should be back by late afternoon.' She decided not to mention Robin's late-night visit. There was no point making things worse between them, and the incident was best forgotten. 'I'm looking at various properties today and I might pop into the warehouse in Chelsea. I've got to do a feasibility study before we can put in a bid.'

Linda nodded. 'OK. By the way, a Lebanese couple are interested in seeing over Wilton Place. I cleaned up this morning before I left, and Mark is going to show them round this afternoon.'

'Good.' Antonia turned to Mark. 'That reminds me, I bumped into Mr Preedy last night; I think he's quite interested in Victoria Road now. Have you heard from him about it?'

'I tried to get hold of him this morning but I had no luck. I left a message for him, though, to phone me as soon as he got back but I haven't heard from him yet,' Mark replied.

'We don't want to let him slip through our fingers and go somewhere else,' Antonia pointed out. 'The money from the sale of his country house is burning a hole in his pocket, from what I can gather. Let's get him fixed up as soon as possible.'

'Will do. I've got the situation in hand, but he's a man who can't be pushed. He knows exactly what he wants and no sales talk in the world is going to make any difference.'

Antonia paused as she walked across the office, stopping in front of Mark's desk. 'But *does* he know what he wants? First it was a house, then it was a flat. He didn't seem set on anything in particular last night, except to settle on somewhere quickly because he was finding Grosvenor House expensive.'

'I'm not surprised,' Linda observed.

Mark shrugged. 'I can't make him out, actually,' he admitted. 'He's a strange fellow. I wouldn't be surprised if his wife's a bit of a dragon. He looks decidedly henpecked to me.'

Antonia decided to walk to the nearby Eaton Place and Belgrave Square houses, then to pick up her car from outside her flat to go to Marble Arch and Victoria Road. Several times, as she hurried along Cliveden Place, she had the sensation of being followed but although she turned round sharply and looked back the way she'd come, she couldn't see anyone in particular who might be stalking her. At this time of day, the residents of Chelsea and Belgravia were going about their usual business. A smart young woman in jeans and a blazer walked slowly, laden with Peter Jones shopping bags; an elderly man walked his dog; two teenagers chattered and giggled as they headed for Sloane Square tube station; a nanny pushed a child in an expensive-looking pram. Taxis and cars whizzed past, or cruised very slowly looking for a parking space. Antonia walked on, but the strange feeling persisted; and the feeling of being watched made her uneasy. When she got to Eaton Place she was pleased to see the comforting shape of Bert, standing on the doorstep.

'Good Morning, Bert . . . or is it afternoon? How's it all going?'

'Good afternoon, Miss Murray. Everything's fine. I've been fixing locks on the windows, and the carpets are being laid right now.'

'That's great.' She climbed the steps and looked up and down the street. 'D'you know something, Bert? I had the strangest feeling I was being followed just now, when I came along Cliveden Place.'

Bert's kindly pink face creased into a frown. 'That's not very nice, Miss Murray. Did you see anyone?'

She shook her head. 'No. At least no one who looked likely, or seemed interested in me. Yet I had the distinct feeling someone was watching my every move.'

'Could it have been someone in a car?'

Antonia hadn't thought of that. 'I suppose it could,' she said slowly. 'But where is it now?'

'There's so much traffic about, a car could quickly get lost. Nasty that, coming on top of there being an intruder when you were in this house last week.'

'I know. Well, anyway, I'll have a quick word with the carpet people and then I'll be off.'

'Can I give you a lift, Miss Murray? I'm finished here; thought I'd go over to Marble Arch and see how they're getting on there. They're laying new floorboards in the basement today.'

'I'm going over there myself, later on,' Antonia said, 'but you could drop me off at Belgrave Square.'

'No probs.' He stuck his pudgy hand into his jacket pocket and withdrew his car keys. 'I was there yesterday. It's near completion. They've finished the cornice in the main lounge area, and the doors are going in tomorrow.' He looked at her out of the corner of his eye. 'Don't worry, Miss Murray. We'll be finished on time.'

Antonia grinned. 'You must be the only builder in creation who's ever said that and meant it.'

He smiled back. 'Can't afford your penalties if we run over time.'

'Too right you can't,' she quipped.

When she got to Belgrave Square and Bert had zoomed off in his rather smart BMW, she did a thorough tour of the house with its six reception rooms, ten bedrooms with bathrooms en suite, and six other rooms which would originally have been for the servants but which would now make a suite of offices, and large kitchen quarters in the basement, which included a staff flat. Bert had not exaggerated. The place looked as if it could even be ready to put on the market ahead of schedule.

The builders were fixing the double mahogany doors in the main ground-floor rooms when she arrived, and a craftsman was standing by, ready to give them a final polish before fixing the gilt door handles.

Antonia felt really proud of what had been achieved. When she'd bought the house, it had previously been used as the London headquarters of the Institute of the National Pension Fund for Transport Workers. The beautiful old rooms had been divided up into ten or fifteen poky little offices with hardboard partitions; leaflets and posters were sellotaped to all the walls. A green-baize screen served as a noticeboard in the marble-floored hall. The battered desks and chairs looked as if they had been through two world wars; which, as her father pointed out, they probably had. But Antonia immediately visualized it as it must have been a hundred years ago, when it would have been the town house of some noble aristocrat, and filled with fine antiques, crystal chandeliers, tapestries and old masters, silk curtains and Persian rugs on the polished parquet floors; a setting for elegant living. In this day and age there were few private individuals who could afford to run a house on that scale, but she realized it would be perfect for an embassy or an ambassadorial residence. Now it was near completion, and it would be the finest property she had ever handled.

An hour and a half later she was hurrying along Chesham Place, towards Pont Street and Sloane Street. She still had two more buildings to look at, and at this rate she'd never get to see the warehouse on the Embankment. As she approached Cadogan Square she realized there wasn't even time to drop in at her flat for a cup of coffee.

Then it happened again. That uneasy feeling of being followed, of being watched. Antonia stopped very deliberately, and stood in the middle of the pavement, looking around. At that time of day there weren't many people about in the square. A taxi shuddered to a stop in front of a house several doors away from her flat, and a very old lady with a stick crawled out. A well-dressed, middle-aged woman came down the front steps of another house and set off in her high heels in the direction of Pont Street. A young man in a suit carrying a briefcase crossed the road to the other side and did not even look in her direction. And yet she had been so sure there was someone trailing her, as she'd been about to unlock her car. Antonia shrugged, telling herself she must have imagined it, and yet the feeling of deep misgiving persisted. Something was wrong. She could feel it in her bones and it made her flesh creep. But why would anyone follow her? Even to breaking and entering an empty house as she looked around it? Stalkers usually made their presence felt by pestering their victims, trying to engage them in conversation in the street, writing them letters, making silent phone calls . . . She froze, remembering the calls the other night, remembering that whoever had made them had deliberately blocked their own number so they could not be traced. Robin had said he'd phoned but couldn't get through; had there been another caller?

She sat in her car for several minutes, wondering what she should do. What *did* people do when they were being stalked? Call the police? Find out who the stalker was, and threaten them with a lawyer's letter if they didn't stop? Face the stalker personally, and then tell them to leave you alone? But how did one find out who it was if they didn't reveal themselves?

Feeling a mixture of anger and disquiet, Antonia started the car and shot off at high speed down Cadogan Square, her one desire to get away. It was absurd, of course, she told herself, because there was no hiding place if some crank was deliberately trying to stalk her.

As she parked the car outside the Marble Arch property, she remembered again the taxi that had nearly run into the back of her. She remembered seeing the back view of the passenger, as he'd slid out of the cab on the far side, before hurrying away to get lost among the crowds without even paying his fare. Was that *him*?

After she'd spent some time talking to the builders and

inspecting the newly laid floors, she drove across Hyde Park to Kensington, to look over the house in Victoria Road. It had started to rain and a damp greyness was closing in, making the atmosphere depressingly clammy. Getting out of the car she looked around before entering the house, but there was no one about, and she had the feeling that whoever had followed her earlier had given up. Another team of builders was putting a new kitchen into this charming family home which, being in a backwater off Kensington High Street, had an almost countrified air, with rose bushes in the paved front garden, and a laburnum tree which dripped with golden blooms in spring.

Having inspected the progress of the redecorating from the attics to the basement, she looked at her wristwatch. The time had flown. It was already a quarter to five. She contemplated driving down to Chelsea, but somehow the idea of wandering around an empty warehouse on a dark, wet afternoon had lost its appeal. Nothing would induce her to admit that her earlier feelings of being followed had left her nervy, but she now decided it would be sensible to take someone from the office when she did decide to go. After all, Guy had a flair for judging the viability of a project, and Carina was in overall charge of building, so it was only sensible to ask one of them to accompany her on what was going to amount to a fact-finding mission.

Antonia phoned the office on her mobile to see if there were any messages. Linda answered.

'Everything's under control,' she said, sounding more cheerful. 'The furniture you chose from Bevan Funnell is being delivered to Eaton Place at the end of the week, and the curtains are being hung tomorrow.'

'Fantastic. Then we can start the fun bit on Monday.'

Annabel Hall of Private Lives had done a brilliant job designing the interior and now the 'fun bit', as far as Antonia was concerned, was putting the finishing touches that instantly transformed the place into a fully equipped home of the highest standard. The beds were made up with Porthault linen and the country-style kitchen designed by John Lewis of Hungerford was stocked with Waterford glass and Royal Doulton china. Rugs and kelims from the Odiham Gallery harmonized with soft furnishings from Thomas Dare. Stacks of soft towels from The White House graced the Max Pike bathrooms. Objets d'art from Thomas Goode and the various antique shops she frequented completed the lived-in look, and as a final flourish, she always ordered plants from John Plested at Town and County Flowers, and fresh flowers when she was showing an important accountant around. Her address book read more like a list of top suppliers than anything else, and *that*, she reflected wryly, was why she was still with only a handful of friends and no husband.

Once everything had been delivered, Antonia would spend days unpacking and setting out all the things she'd chosen with care, taking delight in 'playing house', as her brothers teasingly called it. And once an interest was shown by prospective clients and they'd made an appointment to view, she'd rush along with a crusty loaf to put in the oven and freshly ground coffee for the percolator, so that the mingled fragrances infiltrated the rooms with a tantalizing aroma.

'Your brother also rang,' Linda continued, breaking into her thoughts.

'Which one?' Antonia was still totting up in her head the amount she'd spent on Eaton Place, and wondering if she could push the asking price to three million pounds.

'Roland. He asked if you could call him back.'

'OK. I'm going to go back to the flat and do some work there, so if you need me, I'll be home in twenty minutes.'

'Are you all right, Antonia?'

'I'm fine. Why?'

'You sound tired. Has it been a hell of a day? Any problems?'

Antonia decided not to mention the fact that she believed she had been followed earlier. 'None,' she replied robustly. 'But there's little point in my coming back to the office now. I can just as easily do my phoning from home.'

'You're not going to look at the Embankment warehouse? The owners phoned earlier and asked if you could return the keys if you'd finished with them.'

'If we go ahead it's going to be such a huge project, so I thought I'd take Guy or Carina with me, to see what they think. Tell the owners I'll have a look at it within the next couple of days.'

Five

Antonia phoned Roland as soon as she got home.

'You've heard what's happened?' he asked immediately.

'Yes, Mum told me, Ro. Are you all right?' She thought he sounded fraught and upset.

'Jinny's walked out, Antonia. What am I going to do?'

'That depends, Ro,' she replied carefully. 'I gather you had a fight.'

'She's furious because I said we'd pay for the nightclub party. I was right, though, wasn't I?'

'You were quite right. What's the problem, exactly? Can't you afford it?'

Roland hedged. 'It would mean running up a bit of an overdraft, but we could have paid it off gradually. Jinny seems to think, though, that Mum and Dad should foot the bill for everything. She's suddenly got awfully ambitious,' he added dejectedly.

'In what way?'

'Oh, God, she wants us to buy a big house, and a new car; I don't know how she thinks we're going to be able to afford everything, but there you go. She says why should you live in a luxurious flat in the best part of town, while she has to make do with a country cottage.'

There was a stunned silence. 'But I worked for everything I've got!' Antonia protested. 'And I did it on my own.'

'I pointed that out to her, but it didn't make much difference. D'you know what I think?'

'Tell me.'

'I'm afraid she thought she was on to a good thing by marrying me. I think she imagined the parents were seriously rich, and that they'd set us up in a house and that our lifestyle would be like theirs . . . you know, servants and everything.'

'How could she think that, Ro?' Antonia asked in genuine amazement.

'Don't ask me. Anyway, she says she's fed up with the lot of us, and she's gone off in a huff.'

'Maybe it's for the better,' she said gently. 'Wouldn't you rather find out all this before you get married, than after?'

'But I'm in love with her, Antonia,' he said wretchedly. 'And I thought she was in love with me. Not with my prospects.'

'I know, Ro. It's tough and I'm really sorry. Why not let things drift for a little while and see what happens? Maybe she'll realize in a few days that she's been very stupid and she'll come back.'

'I suppose I could do that.'

'I would if I were you. Play it cool, Ro. You deserve better than this.'

'I'm sorry to burden you with all my woes. How's everything with you? Are you OK?'

She knew by the tone of his voice that he was referring to her attempt to alter her single status.

'Everything's fine,' she replied brightly. 'I've been going around my little empire all day, and now I'm about to feed Crash.'

'Take care, love,' he said, not fooled by her breeziness. 'And I'll let you know what happens with Jinny.'

'Yes, do. And remember, don't let her mess you about.'

After they'd said goodbye, Antonia went to the kitchen where Crash was stampeding around, demanding his dinner, and managing to knock over a bottle of walnut oil in the process. Luckily the lid was screwed on. She flipped on the switch of the small TV set which sat on the kitchen counter, in time to catch the six o'clock news.

A moment later she was frozen to the spot, transfixed by the announcer's words, as once again pictures of the three murdered women were flashed up on the screen.

The announcer spoke with the suppressed excitement of someone who knows they are about to impart startling information.

'Police investigating the murders of three London women, Pauline Ashford, Valerie Martin and Roxana Birch, who were found strangled and their bodies dumped near their places of work during the past month, have turned up new evidence that points to these killings having been committed by a man who may have answered their advertisements for a partner, in a lonely hearts column. In each case it seems that initially the man in question arranged to meet them, but each time failed to turn up, making excuses about being kept late at work. He is thought to be six foot tall, well spoken and to have put forward a highly plausible story . . .'

Antonia sat down heavily on a kitchen chair and stared at

the television screen. She was bathed in cold sweat, and for a moment she thought she was going to faint.

Colin Holbrook! It all added up now, she thought in a wave of breathless panic. He was playing a game of cat and mouse before he finally struck. That would explain his failure to turn up for their two arranged dates, while at the same time making silent phone calls . . . breaking into an empty house she was looking at . . . and why finally, today, she'd had the sensation of being followed. He was probably also the man who'd followed her in a taxi.

But he'd seemed so *right*. He'd sounded so nice. And from his picture he looked so attractive. Deep disappointment fought with fear for prominence in her mind. She should have known something was wrong when he hadn't shown, not once but twice. His excuses may have been plausible, but if she hadn't been so desperate for everything to be right, she'd have smelled a rat from the beginning. As it was, she'd foolishly gone along with what he'd said and . . .! For a moment her mind went into free fall, leaving her dizzy. *She'd given him her mobile number.* God! What a fool! How could she have been so stupid? But he'd seemed so genuine, and she knew what it was to be kept late at work and . . . *what was Roland going to say?* At least, thank heavens, she hadn't told her parents what she'd been doing. And there was one other lucky thing. The mobile number was ex-directory, something she'd arranged to stop clients ringing her at home at all times of the night and day from around the world. Colin Holbrook wouldn't be able to find out where she lived. He also thought her name was Susan. She felt safer.

Almost immediately, she clapped her forehead with the heel of her hand, shocked at her own incredible stupidity. Of *course* he knew where she lived and what she looked like, or he wouldn't have been able to stalk her!

Switching off the television, she wandered around her flat in a state of panic. What was she going to do? Who could she talk to? Should she hire a bodyguard? Then her worry about her personal safety became overshadowed for the moment by the humiliation she knew she'd suffer if it got out how Colin Holbrook had contacted her. How undignified and desperate it would look! She could just imagine the tabloid headlines: Antonia Murray, millionairess owner of Murray Properties Ltd, seeks husband in lonely hearts ad!

For the first time she understood Roland's horror when he discovered what she'd done, and she realized she should have gone to a discreet and reputable agency who would have screened the applicants first. Now, whatever happened, she knew she must somehow keep this whole thing under wraps. She wouldn't tell a soul; after all, she had no *proof* Colin Holbrook was the man they were looking for. It was possible she was getting in a state over nothing. Possible but unlikely.

After a restless night, during which she planned what evasive action she could take without her office realizing anything was wrong, she got up at seven o'clock, had a quick shower, fed Crash who was getting miffed by her lack of attention to him, and phoned A1 Cars. She'd had an account with them for several years, hiring their chauffeur-driven cars for such things as going to the theatre, when parking her own car would be impossible, or going to a late party where she'd want to drink.

'Good morning, Miss Murray,' the head telephonist greeted her when she got through. 'What can we do for you?'

'I'd like to arrange for a driver to collect me from my home address at eight-thirty every morning, to take me to my office,' . . . *All of five minutes' walk away, she reflected ironically* . . . 'and I'd like him to park nearby and be at my disposal all day, taking me to various properties, etcetera, and then take me back to my flat at seven o'clock in the evening.'

'Certainly, Miss Murray. And that's *every* day?'

'Every day until further notice. And there's something else.'

'Yes, madam?'

'I want the same driver every day. I'd like you to tell me the name of the one you'll assign to me, and I'd like him to announce himself over the entryphone when he arrives every morning.'

'Very well. Please hold on a moment.' There was a click and Antonia listened to the strains of The Blue Danube.

The telephonist came back on the line. 'Miss Murray? We'll assign Donald to you. He's driven you several times in the past and he's a very good, steady driver.'

'That's fine.' Antonia remembered him, a burly man in his fifties; someone who would not be easily scared.

'If, by any chance,' she continued, 'Donald is unable to drive me at any time, will you please phone me in the morning to warn me that it'll be someone else?'

'Yes, of course, Miss Murray. We have your home number and your office number—'

'Please only use my mobile number or my office number for the time being,' Antonia cut in. 'I'll let you know my new home number in due course.'

When the telephonist had thanked her, and so he should, she thought, for a job worth a hundred and fifty pounds a day, every day, for the foreseeable future, she hung up. Her coffee was getting cold. She picked up the mug and was just about to take a sip, when Crash nudged her exuberantly, delighted to find her sitting and doing nothing for a moment. The coffee splashed all over her lap, staining her white lawn nightdress.

'Crash! Will you be careful?' she yelled, springing to her feet. She ripped it off, and was about to dash to the bathroom to soak it in cold water when the mobile rang.

'Oh, damn!' she swore, automatically picking it up without thinking. 'Hello?'

'Hi! At last I've got hold of you, Susan. You know, there must be something wrong with your phone. I tried for hours to get through to you last night, but the line was always busy, so I thought I'd try and catch you before you went to work. How are you?'

Antonia's involuntary gasp was audible and before she could say anything, Colin Holbrook spoke again.

'I couldn't wait for you to phone me to suggest a date, so I'm phoning *you*. What about dinner tonight? I know I can get away early because my boss is in Washington so how about—'

She gripped the phone tightly. 'I . . . I've changed my

mind. I don't want us to meet,' she said coldly, hoping her voice wasn't quavering.

He sounded shocked. 'Why, Susan? What's made you change your mind? You haven't even met me; please give me a chance.'

'I've decided not to go ahead with . . . with this lonely hearts business.' She spoke haltingly.

'That's a great shame,' he said, sounding genuinely disappointed. 'What's your reason?'

'I don't have to have a reason.'

'Well, no, of course you don't. I understand that. I just wonder what's gone wrong? When we spoke the other evening you were willing to meet me, as soon as you had a free moment.' There was no denying the regret in his voice, she thought, wondering if she wasn't making a terrible mistake. Colin sounded so *normal*. Such a genuine guy. Polite. Concerned. Respectful. Supposing she'd let her imagination run away with her, and he had nothing to do with the murders? She'd nothing to go on except a hunch. For all she knew he could be the type of young man her mother would welcome into their home with open arms.

Caution came to her rescue. 'I've changed my mind,' she said briefly. 'I must go now. Goodbye.' She put down the phone quickly, before he had time to say anything else.

Then she stood there for several moments, shaking all over, realizing she was cold and also naked.

Switching off the phone, she decided to continue taking precautions. Something wasn't right. She could feel it in her bones. Even if Colin Holbrook wasn't the serial killer who found his prey in the lonely hearts column, something was wrong. The whole situation just didn't ring true. It wasn't his face; she still had his photograph propped up on her bedside table, and it was the face of an open, honest-looking man. It was something in his manner that was confusing her. Something terribly wrong.

As soon as she'd dressed, she phoned her mobile phone company and asked them to cancel the ex-directory number of her mobile and give her a new one. Now Colin would have no way of getting in touch with her except by writing to her PO box number.

At eight-thirty on the dot, the bell on the entryphone on the street door rang.

'Miss Murray? This is Donald. The car's waiting for you when you're ready.'

'Thank you, Donald. I'll be right down.'

Antonia checked her appearance in her long bedroom mirror. She looked more serene and in charge of her life than she felt. But she did feel safer as a result of the precautions she'd taken. Maybe, if she carried on as usual, with the protection of Donald during the day wherever she went, Colin Holbrook would lose interest.

'Where are you off to?' were Linda's first words when Antonia sailed into the office, having alighted from the chauffeur-driven car, watched by all her staff through the plate-glass office windows. Mark Gillingham and Carina Knight looked up at her with interest.

'Swish car, Antonia,' Mark observed, grinning. 'Who are you out to impress today?'

'Perhaps Antonia's off to meet the Sultan of Brunei; you're looking for a rich buyer for Belgrave Square, aren't you?' Carina joked.

Antonia flashed them all a brilliant smile. 'Oh, didn't you know? I always take a chauffeur-driven limousine to do my shopping at Marks & Spencer!' She laid her briefcase on her desk and opened it. 'Actually, the real reason is I'm tired of driving my own car in London. I spend more time trying to find somewhere to park than I do looking over a property. Anyway, my accountant tells me it's tax deductible.' Then she sat down in her leather swivel chair and started going through her mail. 'Anything exciting happening, Linda?' she asked.

Linda looked at her curiously, but made no comment about the car. 'Nothing special. Bert has sent in an invoice for building materials, and needs the money up front—'

'—Get Carina to go through it, will you, and then make out a cheque for him,' Antonia cut in.

'OK.'

For the next hour Antonia and Linda worked together until her desk was cleared. She made it a rule that there should be no loose ends left at the end of the day, and that everything must be attended to on the spot. Then she asked them all to gather round the large central table in the middle of the office, so that they could brief her on exactly how things were progressing in each of their departments. Sally Adamson and Guy Ramsay, both negotiators, gave their reports on prospective clients and the progress of sales, while Carina Knight reported on the building works. Then Mark Gillingham had something interesting to report.

'Mr Preedy has decided he wants the house in Wilton Place after all,' he told them.

Antonia looked at him in surprise. 'I thought he felt it was too big for him and his wife; it *is* far too big for an older couple. Why has he changed his mind?'

Mark shrugged, but looked pleased. 'I'm not exactly complaining, Antonia.' He was thinking of his commission. 'He said he'd come in later this morning, to finalize the details.'

'Well . . .!' Antonia looked at Linda with commiseration. 'We're going to have to find another place for you to house-sit.'

'Don't worry about it.' Linda spoke abruptly, as if she didn't want to talk about it. As they all knew she was staying at Wilton Place, having separated from her husband, Antonia wondered why she was being so curt.

'OK. Let's go and look at that warehouse,' Antonia announced as the meeting came to an end. 'Carina? Guy? Are you free to see over it with me?'

They both said yes, with alacrity. There was nothing more exciting than looking over a property, especially a derelict one, with a view to converting or restoring it. Imagination could take flight, wild schemes could be suggested and discarded, but the undercurrent of all their discussions had to be a long, hard look at the financial feasibility.

Antonia put a call through to Donald on the car phone. He told her he'd be parked up a side street and could be with her in a couple of minutes.

'Donald, we'd like to go to Chelsea Embankment right away,' she told him.

'Very well, Miss Murray. I'll come round now.'

When they arrived at the warehouse Antonia realized she'd been very sensible in not coming here alone the previous evening. If there was a place suitable for murder, this was it. Dark, damp and deserted, it stood by the water's edge with a brooding presence, and she disliked it instantly. The thought of being followed, watched and pursued in a place like this made her shudder. It could be turned into four or five luxury flats, but she wanted nothing to do with it.

After going all over it, inspecting every nook and cranny, she turned to the others and they knew by her expression what she was going to say.

'This is a no-no. The only good thing is the view of the river. Otherwise you've got rising damp, wood rot, that outside wall looks bowed, and I'm sure a surveyor's report would stink! Let's not waste any more time. Apart from anything else, the atmosphere is from hell. No one would be happy living here, even if we turned it into Buckingham Palace.'

Carina and Guy nodded, but said nothing. The success of Murray Properties Ltd had sprung from Antonia's gut instinct about properties. And she was never wrong. She sensed exactly what would work and what, in terms of good vibrations, wouldn't. To her, the prevailing mood of a place was what mattered. She'd often referred to 'happy houses' and 'unhappy houses'.

Back at the office, she handed the warehouse keys to Linda.

'Will you return these to the owners,' she asked, 'and tell

them it's not quite what we're looking for?'

Linda nodded. 'Can I have a word with you?' she asked in a low voice.

'Of course. What is it?' Antonia was instantly off duty, concerned that something was wrong.

'Robin has asked me to go back to him,' she said quietly.

Antonia's face lit up, while she remained careful to keep her back to the room, so the others wouldn't see.

'That's marvellous, Linda! Aren't you thrilled?'

Linda shook her head. 'I don't know what I feel. Part of me is glad I haven't messed up everything; Robin says we must forget what's happened and start again. But another part of me wonders if I care for him enough to even want to make a go of it. I'm still in love with Angus, you know. I don't think I'll ever get over him.'

Antonia, who had never known great love, or fatal passion for that matter, found it hard to understand how Linda could be, in her opinion, so stupid. With a kind, generous and obviously forgiving husband like Robin wanting them to get together again, why on earth was Linda hesitating?

'It's up to you, of course, Linda,' she whispered, 'but surely it's worth a try, isn't it?'

'I don't know. There's no point in living with one man when all the time you're longing for someone else, is there?'

'I'm sure it'll pass . . . your wanting Angus, I mean. People do get over these things, Linda. Like they get over a death. Give yourself a chance with Robin. You don't want to spend the rest of your life alone, do you?'

Linda looked obstinate. 'It's better to be alone than with

the wrong person,' she asserted. 'But it would solve my housing problem. I know I have to get out of Wilton Place now that it's been sold.' Suddenly she stopped and looked beyond Antonia to the office entrance. 'Talk of the devil,' she said quietly.

Antonia turned round, and there was Mr Preedy, carrying a rolled umbrella and a grey mackintosh which he'd hung over one arm, coming through the glass doors.

'Good afternoon, Mr Preedy,' Antonia said, striding forward to shake his hand. 'How nice to see you. I gather from my colleague, Mark, that you're interested in the Wilton Place house after all.'

'I am indeed, Miss Murray.' He returned her handshake gravely as he peered at her through his brass-framed glasses. 'Very interested indeed.'

Mark had come forward too, in greeting. After they'd shaken hands, Mr Preedy was guided to the chair by Mark's desk.

'Although it's a bigger house than I at first wanted,' he began, running the palm of his hand over his domed bald head as if he were smoothing imaginary hair, 'I prefer a house to a flat, so I've come to give you a deposit, and also the name of my solicitors, so we can get on with it.'

'Certainly,' Mark beamed, getting out the Wilton Place file, while Antonia drew up a chair. This was Mark's sale and he'd be getting a good commission, but she always liked to be in on the close of a deal to smooth out any problems that might arise.

'Right, then.' Mr Preedy gave them both a pale smile and at the same time withdrew a chequebook from his inside coat pocket. Antonia noticed he banked with Coutts and Co, the Queen's bankers.

'And your wife likes the house, too?' she asked conversationally.

Mark looked up in surprise as if he'd just thought of something. Antonia glanced from him to Mr Preedy, and back to Mark again.

'Very much indeed,' Mr Preedy replied. 'It will be so nice to be near Hyde Park, too. And a great relief not to be living in a hotel any more.'

'Absolutely,' Antonia agreed. Mark was writing down some figures now, working out the amount required for the deposit.

'How soon do you think I can move in?' Mr Preedy asked, taking an old-fashioned gold fountain pen out of his breast pocket.

'The house is ready for occupation now,' Mark said, looking up. 'You could move in as soon as the contracts have been exchanged.'

'Good. Good.'

Antonia watched as Mr Preedy wrote out the cheque, and told Mark the name and address of his solicitors, and she wished all the transactions they carried out were as smooth and easy. She was making an excellent profit on Wilton Place, and it was a house she'd enjoyed working on from the beginning. At moments like this her sense of achievement was enormous.

Donald collected her from the office when she phoned him in the car at half past six. The short journey to Cadogan

Square took seven minutes, because the traffic in Sloane Street was heavy, and she wondered if he thought she was mad, crippled or just plain lazy.

'I'll see you in the morning,' she told him, looking up and down the street before she got out of the car.

'Yes, Miss Murray. I'll be here.'

There was no one about. Jumping out of the car she hurried up the front steps and let herself in, shutting the door carefully behind her. She knew she was overreacting, and probably being hysterical, but she wasn't going to take any risks.

Hurrying up the stairs to the first floor, she suddenly heard loud miaowing.

'Crash?' she shouted, alarmed. What was he doing outside her flat? Surely her neighbour, Mrs Miller, wouldn't have allowed Crash to get out?

As she turned round the bend in the stairs, Crash came bounding to meet her, like a dog, miaowing and chirruping and in a very agitated state.

Antonia gathered him up in her arms. 'What is it, sweetheart? Are you all right?' She spoke to him as if he were a child, stroking him to see if he was hurt.

Crash seemed perfectly all right, but her front door wasn't. The lock had been forced, damaging the door, and it was ajar.

Mark and Guy, having a beer at the pub on the corner of Sloane Square after they'd left work, toasted each other on having had a successful day.

'What with you selling Wilton Place,' Guy remarked jovially.

'. . . And you, selling one of the flats at Marble Arch,' Mark rejoined, in high spirits.

'. . . Why are we drinking this stuff when we ought to be drinking champagne?' Guy demanded.

They both laughed. Life was great. The pennies kept rolling in now there was a bit of a boom in property, and Antonia knew how to keep them happy and keen, with generous commission and a fat bonus at Christmas. Suddenly Mark frowned, remembering something.

'What is it?' Guy asked.

'That old cove . . . Preedy. He said his wife liked the house very much.'

'Well, I hope she does, old chap! It's costing him a fortune. It wouldn't be much good if she hated the place!'

Mark shook his head. 'No. No, I mean I thought it was a strange remark for him to make.'

Guy looked at him blankly. 'Why?'

'Because I never showed the place to his wife, and I don't think anyone in the office did, either. I don't think any of us have even seen his wife.'

Six

For a moment Antonia paused, uncertain what to do. The thought that someone might still be lurking in her flat made her hesitate to rush in, yet her indignation that anyone should dare to break and enter her private property angered her deeply. Then, through the solid wall of shock that had blocked off her initial reaction, came fear. Colin Holbrook obviously *did* know where she lived. For all she knew, he might be hiding in her flat right now.

Still clutching Crash, she ran up the stairs to the landing above and getting her mobile phone out of her shoulder bag, dialled 999. Her hands were shaking. Supposing Colin Holbrook was still in her flat? Suppose he heard her phoning the police? To be on the safe side, Antonia ran up another flight.

'Which services do you want, please?' asked the operator.

She kept her voice low. 'Police. Quickly, please.'

'I'll put you through.'

Seconds later, Antonia was connected with the local police station. 'How can I help you?' asked an impersonal male voice.

As calmly as she could, Antonia gave her name and address.

'I've just come back from my office to find my flat's been broken into,' she continued.

'Where are you now, madam?'

'I'm on the landing two floors above.'

'You think there's an intruder still in the premises?'

'I don't know. The door to my flat has been forced open. It's still open. I found my cat on the landing outside.'

'Stay there. We'll be right with you.'

Antonia switched off her phone with one hand, while hanging on to Crash with the other as he wriggled to get down.

Suddenly, two yards away from where she was standing, one of the two doors on the landing, leading to two other flats, was flung open with a flourish. Antonia thought for a moment her heart was going to stop with fright. Then she saw the familiar figure of Mrs Miller.

'What's happening?' Mrs Miller asked in alarm.

Antonia put her finger to her pursed lips. 'I think there's a . . . a burglar in my flat,' she whispered. 'I've phoned the police. They're on their way.'

Mrs Miller's faded eyes grew round with horror.

'Oh! Oh!' she repeated in a dazed fashion. 'How dreadful. My dear, how absolutely *awful*. Would you like to come into my flat? Until the police arrive?'

'I'd be very grateful if you could look after Crash for a few minutes, Mrs Miller. I'm going to have to go down to the main hall to let the police in.'

'Of course. Of course. Oh, my dear, what a terrible thing.

How do you know there's a burglar in your flat?'

'My door's been busted and it's still ajar.'

Mrs Miller gave a tiny thread of a scream, and then instantly clamped her gnarled hand over her mouth.

'You've heard nothing?' Antonia asked.

'Not a thing, but then I've been watching the news on television.' She reached out to take Crash. 'Is he all right? They haven't hurt him, have they?'

'He's a bit scared.'

'Poor boy. Poor boy,' Mrs Miller crooned quietly. 'I'll give him some milk. I may even have some cream.' She cradled him like a baby, and he instantly started to purr.

'You're an angel, Mrs Miller.'

In the distance, the wail of a police siren echoed with deafening resonance through the evening air.

'I must go and let them in,' Antonia whispered.

'Oh! My dear! *Do* be careful. You're going to have to pass your flat door to get to . . .' Her eyes widened so much it looked as if they might pop out.

Antonia nodded. There was a lift, though she never used it, preferring to walk up the one flight to her flat. Now she decided it would be safer than risking bumping into Colin Holbrook.

'Take care . . .' Mrs Miller said in a tone of doom, as Antonia pressed the button to summon the lift. When it arrived, she stepped into its tiny, plush interior and plummeted to the ground floor swiftly and silently. The hall was empty. Then she heard people coming up the front steps. A minute later she saw three uniformed policemen through the glass panels set into the door.

'Miss Murray?' They stood looking expectantly at her. One of them was talking into a mobile walkie-talkie.

'Yes. My flat's directly above here, on the first floor.'

'You've seen no one leave, since you phoned the station?' asked the senior officer, a sharp-faced, sharp-eyed man in his late thirties.

'I don't think so. I've been up on the third floor, but I think I'd have heard the front door close if anyone had left.'

As she spoke another police car, a white police van and two men on motorbikes drew up outside, their sirens blaring in a cacophony before cutting out abruptly with a wail and a whimper. Almost immediately a domestic-looking car screeched to a halt, and two plain-clothes policemen leaped out. They were all brandishing mobile phones, orders were being given, orders were being obeyed, 'Yes, sir.' 'Right, sir'; someone was asking her if there was a back exit to the building and where did it lead to? And then they were running up the stairs to her flat, jumping into the elevator, swarming around the hall and on the pavement outside.

Antonia moved to follow them, but a young cop, fresh-faced and eager-eyed, barred the way.

'You can't go up, miss, until we've made sure there's no one hiding in your flat. I'd appreciate it if you'd wait outside until we ascertain the position.'

Antonia was about to argue that it was her flat and that, now they were all here, she was quite safe, until he spoke.

'The intruder might be armed, miss.'

Outside in the street a surprising number of people were leaning out of windows and stepping on to the balconies of the red-brick Victorian houses to see what the commotion was all about. Antonia, impressed by the activity and the speed of the police, waited to see if they'd bring down Colin Holbrook.

She didn't even want to think about how humiliated she was going to feel when it got out that he'd broken into her flat as a result of her advertisement. Trust me, she said to herself, to go and pick a psychopath from all the letters of response she'd received.

A couple of minutes later, the officer in charge came out of the building and walked slowly down the front steps. She could sense the sharp drop in adrenalin among the others, who seconds before had looked keyed up as if for a shoot-out.

'The flat's empty,' he announced. 'Would you like to go up now, madam? The place is in a bit of a mess, but maybe you could tell us what's missing.'

Antonia's heart sank. How much of a mess was a mess? She was so proud of her flat. She'd taken such care in getting it right and it had cost her thousands of pounds.

Dispiritedly, she went back into the building and up to the first floor again.

Inside her doorway, she looked around her small square hall with dismay. Then she went into the drawing room, hardly able to believe what she saw. It was the same in the bedroom.

Everything that could be pulled out of cupboards and drawers had been pulled out and strewn around the floor, in what looked like a frenzied fashion. In the hall coats and umbrellas, wellingtons, the hoover, and, embarrassingly, all the photographs and letters she'd received in answer to her advertisement were scattered around. In the drawing room, her desk looked as if it had been almost dismantled, each drawer ripped out and the contents dumped on the carpet. The pigeon-holes had been emptied. The drawer of a table had been cleaned out. Even her stack of glossy magazines had been chucked around the room. And, as if in frustration, whoever had caused this mess had thrown a glass flower vase at the wall, scattering the flowers and soaking the carpet.

Antonia gazed around her in confusion. The scene that met her eyes looked like destruction for the sake of destruction.

The police officer followed her into her bedroom, where it looked as if a tornado had done its best to create chaos. There wasn't a stitch of clothing that hadn't been flung on the floor. Suits, shirts, sweaters, coats, dresses, underclothes and shoes were heaped all over the carpet, her bedclothes had been ripped off the bed, her box of costume jewellery had been thrown in the fireplace, and the strong smell, coupled with the sight of several empty bottles told her that the intruder had tipped out all her perfume.

'I don't believe it,' she whispered weakly. 'What did they *want*? This looks like a revenge attack.'

The police officer turned sharply to look at her.

'Do you know something about this?' he asked.

Antonia nodded. 'I think I do.'

'I'd like to take a statement from you, please. Is there somewhere we can sit . . .?'

'I don't suppose they've demolished the kitchen?' She made a wry grimace. 'We can go in there.'

Pots and saucepans had been pulled out of cupboards

and all the kitchen unit doors had been flung wide open, but it wasn't too bad. While she sank on to one of the pine chairs at the central table, the officer, joined by another policeman, sat in the other chairs. The police cars and vans and motorbike riders had departed as soon as they had ascertained the intruder had gone. They were now on their own, and Antonia knew she was going to have to tell them everything.

It didn't take long. Briefly, she told them about her advertisement in a reputable newspaper, the response she'd had, and how she'd eventually decided that a man called Colin Holbrook was what she was looking for. The officer wrote steadily in his small, neat handwriting as she described how Colin had failed to keep two dates with her, but how genuine he'd sounded on the phone as he explained and apologized for what had happened, and how she'd decided she would arrange another meeting at some future date. Until she'd realized she was being followed. Until there was a silent caller on her phone. And until she'd heard the news bulletin in which it was revealed that the three women who'd been murdered and dumped near their places of work, had all placed an advertisement in the lonely hearts column of a newspaper; the same newspaper she'd used.

'What makes you think this Colin Holbrook and the man wanted for the murder of the other women is one and the same person?'

Antonia shrugged. 'I don't know. I've nothing actually to go on, but I have a very strong feeling it's the same man.' She frowned, deep in thought. 'There are too many oddities about the whole situation. It's hard to explain, and certainly his behaviour doesn't match his face, which looks open and

189

honest and . . . well, very attractive,' she added lamely.

'Could you show us his photograph, please? He may already be known to us, and have a police record.'

'Yes. I can give you his picture and the two letters he wrote to me . . .' she paused. 'That is, if I can find them under all the mess in my bedroom.'

They went back into her bedroom, and Antonia walked straight to the table by her bed, on which stood a lamp and the telephone.

'It's here . . .' she began. Then they all realized at the same moment that there was no photograph on the table.

'You're sure you left it there?' the officer in charge asked, lifting handfuls of bedding off the floor, moving a pile of clothing, burrowing under several pillows that had been flung aside by the intruder.

'I *know* it was here,' Antonia said. She was blushing but she no longer cared. So what if the policemen realized she was half in love with a man she'd never met, but whose photograph stood on her bedside table?

'And his letters, miss?'

'They're in the drawer . . .'

But the drawer was empty.

The police officer straightened his back, casting his eyes around the room in a puzzled fashion. Antonia, standing forlornly in the middle of the mess, wondered what he was thinking.

'Is there anything else missing from your flat?' he asked.

'I don't know,' she replied, vague from shock. 'Apart from the usual things like video and hi-fi equipment, and a camcorder and a camera, I don't really *have* the usual sort of things burglars go after, like silver and valuable jewellery.'

'Ah, but are we talking about the usual type of burglar?'

They fell silent, all thinking the same thought.

Colin Holbrook had entered her flat and the only thing he'd wanted was the photograph of himself and his letters, so that when Antonia was eventually found dead, there'd be no evidence around to incriminate him.

'What shall I do?' Antonia asked in a small voice.

'Let us know if he contacts you again,' said the officer, scribbling away.

'But in the meantime . . .?' She felt really frightened now. She'd imagined she'd be safe in her flat. And in her office. Now, she didn't know where she'd be safe. Colin Holbrook was obviously intent on trying to terrorize her on one hand, while destroying evidence of his existence on the other.

'Can you give us a description of this man?' the officer asked, as he waded ankle-deep in her best fragile lace and satin lingerie that had been dropped by the side of her bed.

Antonia told them all she knew and did her best to describe the face she'd been so attracted to.

'I wish his photograph was still here,' she said at length. 'Then you'd see that he looks so honest. A straightforward person, who you'd think wouldn't hurt a fly.' Was she trying to justify getting involved with him? she asked herself. After all, she didn't want the police to think she'd encourage the advances of a murderer. She had to admit, though, that he *had* looked like a kind, compassionate person, with a sense of humour, and it was a blow, on several levels, to find she'd been so wrong.

'They all look like butter wouldn't melt in their mouth.'

'Who? Stalkers? Psychopaths?' she asked.

'All I can tell you is that if he's the same man who murdered those other women, you're up against a dangerous criminal with a grudge. Probably against career women.'

Antonia blanched. 'Really?'

'We reckon, from our study of these particular murders, that some women, perhaps in the same line of business as himself, stitched him up. Maybe she pipped him to the post for a promotion.' The officer shrugged and looked grave. 'Now he's out for blood.'

'What happens next?' Antonia asked, appalled. 'I'm already taking precautions. I've got a car and a driver to take me around during the day. I've had my mobile phone number changed. I'll get the locks to this flat changed right away.' She paused, looking from one to the other. 'I don't know what else I can do.'

'Why don't you get a friend to stay with you, here?'

Antonia paused, embarrassed. 'Frankly,' she said at last, 'I don't want either my family or my friends to know I put an advertisement in the lonely hearts column in the first place.'

The officer nodded as if he understood, but he avoided eye contact with her. 'You could say you were just nervous, after your flat had been broken into and you didn't want to be on your own.'

'Yes. Yes, I could.' She thought of Barbara or Emma. They were good friends and were likely to be more available and willing to stay for a few nights than Jane, who was now living with Percy.

When she'd signed her statement they rose to go, saying they were going to question the other residents in the building.

'As the main street door hasn't been tampered with, it's likely the intruder was let in by someone who lives here,' the officer observed. 'He probably said you were expecting him and they let him in. That's how they usually do it.'

Antonia gave a little shriek. 'Oh! Crash! I've forgotten all about him.'

They looked at her, mystified. Quickly she explained. 'I must go and fetch him. Poor Mrs Miller, she's probably wondering what on earth has happened.'

'We'll go up to her flat with you. Then we can ascertain whether she let someone into the building earlier or not.'

Antonia wanted to straighten up the flat, but the police had warned her not to touch more than she had to, because they'd be sending the fingerprint expert along in the morning.

'The drawers of your desk and the cupboard doors in particular may have prints on them,' the officer said. 'Best to leave everything as it is for the moment.'

Grudgingly she'd agreed. In the morning, she'd cancel Donald and the car, phone Linda and say the flat had been broken into but no more; meanwhile she'd phone Barbara and tell her the same but ask if she could stay with her for a few days because she felt nervous, then call Banham's Central Service System, which operates at night, and get them to come and change the locks.

But was she safe from Colin Holbrook? It felt like her life was more in danger than ever.

It was late afternoon the following day when Antonia decided to go home for the weekend. She'd already phoned her family

193

to tell them that her flat had been broken into, and they, like everyone in her office, had sympathized. But that was all she'd told them. Burglaries happened all the time, especially in the area she lived in, where most of the homes contained valuable silver and paintings and jewellery, so everyone took what had happened at face value. Providing the police could trace Colin Holbrook, and charge him for the murder of the three other women, her involvement with him need never come out. There was only one problem. They'd no idea where to find him. It transpired that the Islington address and phone number Colin Holbrook had given her belonged to an Italian businessman who had sub-let his flat to someone calling themselves James Maxwell. The letting had been arranged through an agency, and there was a lot of vagueness and confusion as to where James Maxwell had come from and what he looked like. The young women who ran the agency were a giggly bunch and not very helpful. They were able to say, though, that James Maxwell had paid three months' rent in advance, in cash.

The neighbours could only tell the police that they thought the flat was empty, as they never saw anyone go in or come out. Except for the woman in the flat below. She'd never seen James Maxwell either, but she'd heard him on several occasions walking around in the early evening. She'd heard nothing, though, for the past twenty-four hours.

Antonia finished hanging up the last of her clothes, putting all her papers back in her desk, trying to wipe off the silver powder the fingerprint expert had brushed so lavishly over the woodwork, and generally straightened up the flat again. The photographs and letters she'd received from other applicants were torn up and binned in a big black plastic bag.

Barbara, who'd promised to stay the night, but had to leave the next day to stay with her sister in Shropshire, was due in a couple of hours. Meanwhile, the ever-faithful Linda had gone to Harrods to buy food for Antonia and Barbara's dinner and was bringing it round after work.

'You're so kind,' Antonia told her. Linda had absolutely believed her when she'd explained that she wasn't able to get out herself because she had to wait in for the fingerprint expert, and various phone calls she was expecting.

For the first time for many years Antonia had a great longing to be with her family, in the safety of her old home again. Not that she intended telling them, not even Roland, the truth behind the burglary. It would only worry and upset them, and they'd be nervous at the thought of her returning to an empty flat when the weekend was over.

Quentin greeted her with delight when she phoned Clifton Hall.

'My darling girl! How wonderful to hear from you. When are you coming down to see us?'

It was just what she needed, a balm to her soul, and such a comfort at a moment when she felt scared and alone. She found herself fighting back tears at the realization that she was so loved and so welcome at home.

'How about tomorrow evening?' she asked, forcing herself to sound lightly casual.

'Splendid! Oh, Mummy will be thrilled. Are you all right after your terrible burglary, darling?'

'Yes, I'm fine. Barbara is staying with me tonight, as I'm not crazy about sleeping here alone, but everything's under control, Daddy. It's one of the hazards of living in this area. I've been lucky up to now.'

'You didn't tell your mother earlier if they'd taken much? Anything of any value?'

'Nothing of value,' she replied with honesty. *Just a photograph and a couple of letters*, she reflected, of no value to me, but maybe the difference between freedom or a life sentence to Colin Holbrook. Aloud she said: 'I'll be down in time for dinner. Give my love to Mummy, and I'll see you then.'

'We'll look forward to it,' Quentin told her warmly.

Linda and Barbara arrived at the same time, full of commiseration and sympathy.

'What a shock you must have had when you got home,' Linda observed, carrying the shopping into the kitchen, where she unpacked a large bunch of tender green asparagus, two tournedos steaks, salad and fresh strawberries and cream, on to the pine table, where Antonia had already set out glasses and a bottle of wine.

'I think Crash was the one in a state,' Antonia quipped. 'He hasn't forgiven me yet for parking him upstairs with Mrs Miller while I called the police. You know how he loves meeting people.'

'Little angel,' murmured Barbara, following them into the kitchen, while Crash rubbed himself against her ankles, making little burbling noises of pleasure.

'You'll stay for some wine, won't you, Linda?' Antonia asked. She'd invited her for dinner, but Linda had said she was already meeting friends.

'Thanks awfully, but I must fly. I've got a taxi waiting. Will you be in the office tomorrow?'

Antonia nodded. 'I'll see you then. And thanks so much for doing all this shopping for me. Today's been crazy. I've only just finished tidying up the place.' After she'd seen Linda off, she returned to the kitchen where Barbara was still talking to Crash.

'Let's relax in the drawing room with a drink,' she suggested. 'I want to hear all *your* news, and the latest about Jane and Percy.'

Barbara beamed as they settled themselves on the big sofa facing the window. 'Jane's on cloud nine. They're getting married in October. Can you believe it? As usual Denise is saying it's a big mistake, and she doesn't know why Jane thinks a man is such a big deal. She told Jane she'd be much happier if she settled down with another woman.'

Antonia threw back her head and laughed. 'She really is keen to try and turn us against men, isn't she? Why does she think, just because she's gay, that we should all be, too?'

'I suppose she thinks hers is the best way to be happy. I can't say it's ever appealed to me,' Barbara replied. 'Emma is still heartbroken at losing Tom. He's getting married to someone else, you know. A girl who works in his office.'

'Poor Emma. I must give her a ring. She really did think she and Tom were going to get married, didn't she? Did I tell you that Roland and Jinny have broken off their engagement?'

Barbara looked stunned. 'What went wrong?'

Antonia smiled wryly. 'There were severe disagreements between them over the wedding. It was she who broke it off.'

'She *didn't*? But how could she? What a fool! I can't

understand anyone chucking Roland; he's divine.' Then Barbara blushed a deep shade of crimson, and bent down to talk to Crash again.

'Yeah. He is very sweet,' Antonia said, observing her friend's embarrassment. She'd never realized that Barbara found him attractive; was there a chance he might be interested, too? she wondered. Maybe, now that he was on his own again, she should invite Barbara for a weekend at home, when Roland was around.

Barbara sat up again, her face a normal colour once more. 'Did I tell you Sarah and Andrew are going to have a baby?'

'What? Already? My God, they haven't hung about, have they?'

Barbara giggled. 'Someone said they must have been shooting before the twelfth!'

The evening continued to be relaxed, as they gossiped about all their friends and Antonia tried to put the nightmare of Colin Holbrook to the back of her mind. By tomorrow night she'd be in Hertfordshire. Meanwhile they had their supper at the kitchen table, opened another bottle of wine . . . 'How wicked!' Barbara said, already slightly tiddly.

It was nearly midnight, and she was getting undressed in her bedroom, when the phone by her bed rang. She eyed it suspiciously for a moment; then telling herself not to be ridiculous, she picked up the receiver and held it to her ear.

'Hello?'

A moment later a freezing wave of fear swept over her, leaving her skin covered in goose pimples and her legs weak. It was Colin Holbrook, and he wanted to know when they could meet.

Seven

Antonia felt she was probably overreacting but after the shock of Colin's phone call last night – she realised she must have forgotten to dial 141 the last time she'd called him – she made elaborate plans not to be alone for the time being. Waiting until Barbara had left after an early breakfast, Antonia packed some country clothes and shoes into a holdall, and then ran up the stairs above to tell Mrs Miller she was going away and to ask if she could feed Crash over the weekend.

'There's masses of food in the fridge for him,' Antonia assured the old lady, who luckily adored having someone to make a fuss over.

'Oh, I'd be delighted, my dear,' Mrs Miller exclaimed, her light blue eyes gleaming with surprised pleasure. 'I might bring him up here to watch television with me. He enjoyed that the other afternoon.'

Antonia kissed her on both cheeks. 'You're a saint, Mrs Miller, and we both love you.'

The widow grew pink with pleasure. 'My dear, you know how I love Crash. And he's never knocked over anything in *my* flat.'

Antonia cast her eyes to heaven. 'Don't speak too soon!' Handing over the new set of keys to her flat, she ran back downstairs again to await Donald with the car.

When he arrived, she took the holdall with her and asked him to put it in the boot of the car. 'I'm going straight down to the country for the weekend, Donald,' she told him.

'Am I driving you down, Miss Murray?' he asked.

'No, I'll be taking my own car,' she said briefly. She would tell him this evening, when he picked her up from the office, that she wanted him to drive to where her car was parked on the opposite side of Cadogan Square. Then she'd switch cars. So profound was her fear now, she didn't even want to risk walking alone around the square. And she kept recalling horror movies in which people hid in the backs of cars, ready to pounce on the unsuspecting driver. She no longer felt safe anywhere. And if this goes on much longer, she reflected, and the police don't pick Colin Holbrook up soon, she felt she could become seriously disturbed.

After his call she'd rung the police, while Barbara was still in the shower. She was not exactly sure what she'd expected, but the laid-back response she'd got was far from comforting.

'You didn't find out where he was calling from?' the police sergeant asked.

'No,' she replied in a small voice. She realized that of course she should have asked Colin Holbrook for his number, on the pretext of wanting to have it so she could get hold of him to fix another date, but her only thought had been to get him off the line, to get away from his cloyingly charming manner, and to escape the hypnotic power of his husky voice and the memory of his face.

'Do you think he'll phone you again?'

'I don't know. I'm going away for the weekend . . .'

'When will you be back?'

'Sometime on Sunday, late afternoon, probably. Why?'

'Let us know when you return, Miss Murray. We'll probably put a tracer on your line . . . you said he called you on your house phone?'

'Yes.'

He was all brisk efficiency. 'If he calls again, try and get as much out of him as you can. Right now we've no idea where he is, but we think he's in hiding in your area. We need a lead, though.'

'Right. Yes. Thank you.'

Barbara had come out of the bathroom at that moment and Antonia started almost guiltily, the phone still in her hand.

'Just making plans for the weekend,' she said, although there was no need to say anything at all.

'Give my love to your family,' Barbara said, and there was a tinge of longing in her voice.

'I will. We must arrange for you to come down for a weekend. It's ages since you've stayed, isn't it?'

'That would be lovely,' Barbara agreed, beaming. 'I'd love to see all your family again.'

Once in her office, she did her best to concentrate on work, but it wasn't easy and for once she was quite glad of the distraction of Linda talking about her private life in an intense whisper, while the others were out or on the phone.

'Robin really does want me back,' she hissed at one point. 'I don't understand it.'

'I wouldn't knock it,' Antonia pointed out. 'Why don't you see how it goes for a while. What have you got to lose?'

But Linda shook her head, and talked about 'to thine own self be true'.

'But you were happy with Robin until you met this other chap, weren't you?' Antonia pointed out.

'I think I only *thought* I was happy. Because I didn't know any better. Now I'm not sure what to do.' She leaned back in her upholstered swivel chair, limp and indecisive, and totally unlike herself. 'Maybe I should live on my own, without either Angus or Robin? After all, you like being on your own best, don't you?' She asked the question with the self-assurance of someone convinced they know what they are talking about.

Antonia looked up slowly, surprised while trying not to show it. 'Oh, I don't know,' she said lightly. 'I sometimes think it would be nice to be married.'

'You?' Linda said in amazement. 'I can see you with a lover; perhaps even a live-in lover, but you wouldn't want to get yourself tied down by a husband, would you? It would alter your whole lifestyle.'

'Yes. It would.' Antonia looked at her steadily. 'And that mightn't be a bad thing.'

'You'd hate it, Antonia,' Linda said laughingly. 'Your life wouldn't be your own any more. You know how you like your independence and being free to do what you want. Imagine having a man in your elegant flat, spreading his things all over the place and expecting you to cook dinner every evening whether you wanted to or not.' She shook her head. 'It would drive you mad.'

Antonia didn't argue. She wasn't feeling strong enough to get into a discussion about having a man in her life, and damnably she kept remembering the face of Colin Holbrook in the photograph. The man, she reflected ironically, she'd set her heart on. So much for her judgement of character!

At last the day was over. Linda summoned Donald for her, and having said goodbye to the rest of her staff, Antonia got into the hired car and told Donald to drive her back to Cadogan Square.

If he was surprised, he said nothing. When they arrived in the square a few minutes later, she directed him to where her car was parked, rather than to her flat.

'Everything all right, Miss Murray?' was all he said, as she looked in the boot of her car before he put her case in, and then in the back.

She smiled, grateful there was nothing. 'Yes, everything's fine, thank you. I'll see you on Monday, eight-thirty as usual.'

'Have a good weekend, Miss Murray.'

'You too, Donald.'

She glanced up and down the street before getting into her car. As far as she could tell there was no one about. She turned on the engine, slipped the gear into first, and with a final wave to Donald released the handbrake. The weekend had begun. In two hours she'd be home. And safe.

They were all there when she arrived at Clifton Hall, waiting for her in the library, and wanting to know about her 'burglary'.

Hilary greeted her first, and then her father, with a bear-hug, followed by Tristram and Leo and Roland. Everyone was talking at once, and offering her a glass of wine, and wanting to know exactly what had happened, and suddenly it was all too much. The strain of the past few days, and the knowledge that she mustn't tell them the truth, suddenly broke her resistance and she burst into tears.

'Oh, my darling . . .' Hilary murmured, taking her hand as if she were still a child. 'What you need is a break.'

'Why don't you take a holiday?' Tristram asked.

'Yeah!' Roland agreed, eagerly. 'Fly off to the Caribbean for ten days, love. Choose one of those really gorgeous islands with marvellous beaches . . .'

'I'm all *right*,' Antonia protested, as she wiped the sudden tears from her eyes. 'Just leave me alone. I'm going to have a bath before dinner.' She rose from her chair and Roland put his arm around her shoulders.

'It's all right, love. You're suffering from delayed reaction. It's only to be expected and you really should go away somewhere.'

Shrugging him off with an uncharacteristic gesture of impatience she fled the room and raced upstairs, crying as if her heart would break. Maybe I am suffering from delayed reaction, she thought, but she knew it was more than that. When Roland had suggested she take a holiday in some wonderful resort it struck her with agonizing force that, quite simply, she had no one to go with.

* * *

Down in the drawing room, Quentin poured himself another drink. 'She's had a bad shock,' he observed sadly.

'What happened, exactly?' Tristram asked, his bearded face anxious. 'Someone broke into her flat, but did they take much?'

'Nothing,' said Roland quietly, his own face pale and drawn since he'd broken up with Jinny.

Leo, still brushed with the bloom of youth and charged with eager interest in everything, spoke. 'Isn't that strange? Burglars don't usually break into a place and then take nothing. Perhaps they were *looking* for something?'

His father looked at him with mild astonishment. 'What could they be looking *for*?'

Leo shrugged, reddening. 'I don't know. Details of properties? Survey reports? Her tax figures?'

Tristram laughed unkindly. 'Get real, Leo! What do you think Antonia's doing? Working for MI5?'

'Perhaps they thought she was loaded, and had lots of jewellery and things?' Roland suggested.

'I don't understand why they didn't take her camcorder and video, though,' Hilary pointed out. She was concerned about Antonia. It wasn't like her to get upset. She also knew, instinctively, that her daughter was keeping something from them.

When Antonia rejoined them half an hour later, she appeared calm and in control again, but it was obvious she didn't want to talk about what had happened.

Dinner was announced and they all went into the oak-panelled dining room, seating themselves at the refectory table where everybody sat where they liked and Quentin and Hilary frequently sat together.

'What are you doing for your birthday next week, Mum?' Tristram asked, as they helped themselves to freshly made wafer-thin toast to go with the chicken-liver pâté.

'I hadn't planned to do anything.' Hilary put down her knife and looked at Quentin, resting her chin on her hand. 'We don't go in for birthdays in a big way, do we, darling?' she remarked.

'You can if you want to,' he replied, smiling, holding her gaze in such an intimate way, the others almost felt they were intruding on a private moment.

'It would be quite nice to do something this year,' Hilary said suddenly. 'It seems ages since we had a party.'

Roland looked down, embarrassed. He knew, that in spite of everything, his mother had been looking forward to organizing his and Jinny's wedding.

Tristram spoke. 'If we have a party it will mean extra work for Mum, in spite of Mrs Evans and the others. You shouldn't have to do anything on your own birthday, Mum,' he added.

'Why don't we all go out somewhere?' Leo exclaimed. 'Go up to London. Make a night of it.'

Antonia, who had been silent, exclaimed, 'That's a great idea! Would you like a night on the tiles, Mum?'

Hilary leaned back in the carved dining-room chair, and laughed until her eyes glittered with tears. Quentin watched her, amused.

'A night on the tiles!' she repeated, between bursts of mirth, 'My dear child, have you ever seen anyone more unsuited to a night on the tiles than me? With my muddy boots and gardening apron, and my big gloves?' She reached in the pocket of her long cardigan for a handkerchief, with which to dab her eyes. 'You're very sweet, but I think I might disgrace you all, by appearing with bits of twig stuck in my hair and the odour of weedkiller about my person!'

'What would you really *like* to do?' Roland asked.

Composed again, Hilary gave it some thought. 'I'd like to go to the theatre, to see something cheerful and amusing. And then a quiet dinner in a good restaurant would be lovely. Just us. Just the family.'

They all looked at each other.

'That's easy,' said Antonia immediately.

'Why don't you and Dad go to a matinée performance of a show, and we'll all join you for dinner,' Tristram suggested.

The three brothers all agreed that they could get off early from work and then drive up to town. 'What about you, Antonia? Can you give yourself the afternoon off?' Tristram asked.

Knowing how much it would mean to her mother, she nodded vigorously. 'Of course, and if you tell me what you want to see, Mum, I'll get the tickets.'

'Nothing sad,' Hilary affirmed. 'I refuse to spend good money to be made miserable, so I'll leave it to you, darling.'

'We'll all spend the night in town, won't we?' Leo asked. 'Otherwise none of us will be able to drink.'

'Can't have that,' Roland agreed.

'God, no!' Tristram said with serious purpose.

'I can put one of you up in my flat, or two, if you don't mind sharing the sofa bed.' Antonia offered.

Quentin, who had been listening with keen interest, spoke.

'As it's a rather special birthday . . .'

'Is it?' Hilary cut in, puzzled.

'Yes, my darling. To me you may still look twenty-five, but it will, in fact, be your sixtieth birthday.'

Hilary's hand flew to her mouth, her fingertips pressed to her lips, her eyes round with genuine astonishment, while the others made whooping noises of appreciation.

'Your sixtieth, Ma!'

'Wow! Six decades! Who'd believe it?'

'You certainly don't *look* sixty, Mum!'

'This we gotta celebrate,' from Leo.

'Am I really going to be sixty?' she said in a low voice, gazing down the table at Quentin. 'Oh, my dear, what a long time we've been together, haven't we?'

His expression was tender. 'Indeed we have, sweetheart.'

She gave her head a little shake. 'I'd truly forgotten. Most of the time I feel about forty . . . except for my back if I do too much heavy gardening . . . but sixty!'

'Which is why,' Quentin continued, refilling everyone's glasses with his favourite red Bordeaux, as Mrs Evans brought in a large dish of roast pheasant surrounded by fresh vegetables from the garden . . . 'Which is why I was going to suggest that as it's a special night, we have dinner at the Savoy Grill, and then stay the night in the hotel.'

'Stay at the Savoy?' Leo said, mouth gaping. 'Cool.'

'You'll have to wear a decent suit,' Tristram said. 'And have your hair cut.'

'And you must stay with us too, Antonia,' her father continued as if the others hadn't spoken. 'I'm not having you go off on your own at the end of the evening to an empty flat, when we can all be together at the Savoy, and have breakfast in the River Room the next morning.'

Antonia smiled at him, not trusting herself to speak.

Hilary clapped her hands together as if she were still a young girl. 'Oh, it will be such fun! Thank you, Quentin darling, for having such wonderful ideas. Will you make the reservations in the morning? It would be too sad if they were all booked up. And Antonia, will you book seats for a show? There *must* be a comedy on in the West End, mustn't there?'

'I'm sure there's a Ray Cooney production in one of the theatres. Don't worry, I'll fix it,' Antonia promised.

'Then that's settled,' Quentin said with a satisfied smile. 'On Thursday night we'll have a real celebration.'

The rest of the weekend passed peaceably, and for Antonia it provided the rest and quiet she badly needed. She slept late, took Amber, Jacko and Rags for long walks, sat on the terrace talking to her father, gossiped with her mother as she helped her do some weeding, and listened to Roland as he poured out his heart about how disillusioned he felt over Jinny.

Nevertheless, there was a nagging anxiety tugging at the back of her mind all the time, part fear at what Colin Holbrook might do next, and part disquiet at having to keep something from her family for the first time in her life. His last words on the phone kept repeating themselves.

'I intend to have you, Susan. You must understand that. You've started something and it must be finished.'

Petrified, she'd said, 'I want nothing to do with you. Leave me alone.'

'But you wanted to meet me.' His voice was low, husky

and teasing. 'What's changed your mind?'

Antonia longed to scream: *Because you broke into my flat. Because you dared to invade my space. Because you're mad and dangerous. Because you've already killed three women who were stupid enough to get involved with you.* But she didn't. She closed her eyes for a moment and felt soiled. She *had* started all this. She had wanted a man in her life. She'd even advertised for one. If his crime was obsessive lunacy that led to the murder of innocent women, hers was sinking into a depth of desperation she'd never thought possible. Roland had warned her, but the desire for a man in her life, a lover, a husband and someone who would father her children before she got too old, was so great that she'd been prepared to go to any lengths to make it happen. There had been a point when she'd bitterly regretted the time and effort she'd spent on building her career. She could have been having a normal social life throughout her twenties, meeting people in the usual way, but instead she'd strived for financial success.

In the end, she had said to Colin Holbrook, with great dignity: '*Everything* has changed my mind.' And with that she'd hung up and then unplugged the phone so he wouldn't be able to call her again.

Her life was in danger, and she had this terrible feeling that she was partly to blame.

'Do you have to go so early, darling?' Hilary asked sadly, as Antonia brought her suitcase down to the hall after lunch on Sunday.

'I'm not off this minute,' she replied, stalling. 'I just

thought I'd load up the car.' Her mother had picked flowers for her to take back to the flat, and a special bunch for Mrs Miller as a thank-you for looking after Crash.

'Come and sit in the garden for a while,' Hilary coaxed. 'You look so much better than you did; it's the country air.'

Antonia slipped her arm through her mother's. 'And being with all of you, and Mrs Evans's cooking, and sleeping in my old room . . .' Her voice drifted off, laughing, wishing for once that she could stay longer. Her reason for leaving early today was because she wanted to be back in her flat while it was still light. The thought of parking her car, then maybe having to walk the length of the street to get to where she lived, before entering her flat, all in pitch darkness, was unnerving. Colin Holbrook could be lurking, watching her, in some doorway, under the trees of the central square: he might even – God forbid – have got into her flat again. What are the police doing? she thought with sudden rage. Why the hell haven't they picked him up?

At three o'clock they all gathered in the drive to see her off.

'See you on Thursday,' Antonia called, through the open window of her car. Plans for her mother's birthday had been finalized. After the matinée, Quentin and Hilary would go on to the Savoy, to settle into their suite and have a rest, while Antonia was going to nip back to the office before going home to change. At seven-thirty, by which time Tristram, Roland and Leo would have arrived in London, they'd all planned to meet for a drink in the American Bar before dinner.

'I can't wait!' Hilary exclaimed, her face wreathed in

smiles. 'It's going to be the most perfect birthday I've ever had.' She leaned against Quentin, who had his arm around her waist. The last Antonia saw of them, they were all waving as she set off down the drive.

By nine o'clock that night, she was beginning to feel like a prisoner in her own flat. How long was this going to go on? No one could phone her, because her house phone was still unplugged and she hadn't given anyone the new ex-directory number of her mobile. She couldn't pop round to see Barbara or Emma or any of her other friends because it was now dark. For the same reason, she couldn't go and see a film or pop along to the shop next to Knightsbridge barracks to hire a video. Stupidly, she hadn't done any shopping either, knowing she'd be away for the weekend, so there was hardly any food in the house.

'I'm bored,' she announced aloud, looking at Crash, who hadn't let her out of his sight since she'd returned. 'And I'm scared,' she added in a small voice.

He chirruped and sprang on to her lap, dislodging a silk sofa cushion which promptly slithered to the floor. Antonia stroked his ears and looked into his golden eyes and told him how beautiful he was. In response he took little sucking bites at the wrist of her sweater, and dribbled cool saliva on her hand.

Eight

The foyer of the Royalty Theatre was crammed with people, making Antonia wonder, as she squeezed her way through the crowds, how so many of them were able to find time to see a show in the middle of the day. She hadn't been to a matinée performance since she'd been in her teens, because once her career had got under way the thought of going to the theatre in the middle of the day had seemed as decadent as eating chocolates when you were on a diet. As Hilary and Quentin hadn't arrived yet, she waited for them on the stairs leading up to the dress circle, watching the jolly jostling groups pour in from the street. They were mostly women, mostly middle-aged and all determined to enjoy themselves. *Cocktails for Two* was a smash hit for people who wanted to have a good laugh.

A minute later her parents arrived, her father's dark head towering over everyone else's. Wearing a dark suit instead of his customary tweeds, he waved as he and Hilary made their way towards her.

'Happy Birthday, Mum!' Antonia kissed her mother on both cheeks.

'Thank you, sweetheart. We're not late, are we?' Hilary,

elegant in pale grey with a long chiffon scarf, looked much younger than her sixty years.

'You're in perfect time. Shall we get out of this scrum?'

She'd managed to get them three seats in the front row of the dress circle, and she'd already bought their programmes.

'Good idea,' Quentin agreed.

They took their seats, and as Hilary looked around at the red plush and gilt auditorium with its dazzling central chandelier, she patted Antonia's hand.

'This is lovely, darling,' she said. 'It's ages since I've been to the theatre. And I'm so looking forward to the dinner tonight. The boys have promised to be up in town by seven-thirty.'

'Is your room at the Savoy OK?' Antonia asked. She'd arranged with the hotel to put flowers, champagne and a jar of caviar in their suite as a welcome present from her and her brothers.

'Sweetheart, it's more than OK,' Hilary exclaimed with feeling. 'Thank you for the champagne and everything. They've given us a suite overlooking the Thames. This is turning out to be the best birthday I've ever had.'

'So it should be,' Antonia said stoutly. 'You don't have a sixtieth birthday every day.'

'Look what your father gave me.' Hilary extended her hand to show a diamond eternity ring which she was wearing next to her wedding ring. 'Isn't it gorgeous?'

'Mum! Talk about being spoiled!' Antonia joked.

'I think she deserves it, don't you?' Quentin said, taking Hilary's hand.

'Yes, I do,' Antonia replied softly, catching her mother's

eye, as they exchanged loving looks, bonded as they'd been since the moment of her birth. 'As you know, you're getting presents from me and the boys at dinner tonight.'

'More delights to look forward to.' Hilary beamed happily.

People were taking their seats now and there was much flapping of programmes and rustling of sweet papers as the audience began to settle in an atmosphere of anticipation that was almost palpable. The house lights started to dip, an expectant hush fluttered through the audience like the fading ripples of a spent wave, and then it was dark.

'I haven't read my programme yet.' Hilary whispered.

'Neither have I.'

Quentin leaned across and spoke in hushed tones. 'The first scene takes place in a country house on a Friday evening in summer.'

'Oh, good,' Hilary whispered back. 'I can tell this is my sort of play.'

With a silent swiftness that took the audience by surprise the heavy red curtains rose, and there was a typical country drawing room, complete with french windows leading to a very well-executed backdrop of an English garden. It was, as Antonia had hoped, high comedy, set on the eve of a wedding, with everything going wrong that could go wrong, and a wonderful mix of characters rushing in and out of doors, in a steady stream of mounting misunderstanding. Soon, the audience were laughing, rocking in their seats, slapping their knees, wiping their eyes, throwing back their heads, loving every moment as the plot became more and more farcical.

At one point the leading lady, in a pink negligée, came running down the 'staircase' of the set, squealing, 'Harry's arrived! You must hide!' Then she tried to push the leading man into a tiny cupboard under the 'stairs'. He was far too big to fit but nevertheless she slammed the door shut, and in doing so, trapped one of his legs and an arm which then stuck out at odd angles. The audience howled with mirth.

Antonia was laughing along with everyone else at the situation when 'Harry' charged on to the set, entering upstage left, dressed as if for cricket. Antonia gasped, and for a moment she thought she was going to faint. Tiny icicles pricked her skin all over and it felt as if the breath had been squeezed from her body. She looked more closely at the actor who was playing Harry, as he delivered his lines with casual aplomb. There was no mistaking that face, or those dark eyes that held laughter in their depths, or that humorous mouth. It was Colin Holbrook.

Stunned, she sat through the remainder of the first act, clutching her programme in her sweating hands, longing for the lights to go up so she could check the cast list. But *of course* it was him. There was no doubt about it. As if she could ever forget that attractive face she'd so longed to meet at the beginning. As if she hadn't thought about him night and day for weeks, first with a strange sense of longing, more recently with a deadly fear.

Hilary and Quentin continued to laugh as the farce unfolded, oblivious of Antonia's shocked state. She sat mesmerized, unable to take her eyes off Colin Holbrook. And as she watched Act One draw to its hilarious close she realized that everything he'd told her must have been a lie. In fact he'd invented a completely different persona for himself. Even his voice had sounded different, allowing for

216

the fact that he was now playing the role of an upper-class twit.

At last the curtain fell, to an explosion of laughter and applause, and the house lights came on. White-faced, she scanned the cast list in her programme, looking for his name against the character of Harry. Then she frowned, bewildered. There was no Colin Holbrook listed. The role of Harry was played by someone called Mark Dryden. In disbelief she stared at the name. Was it his stage name? Or was it his real name but he'd called himself Colin Holbrook when answering her advertisement? She turned towards the back of the programme to look at the brief biographies of the actors. What she saw made her heart lurch with cold shock. The photograph of Mark Dryden was the same one Colin had sent her of himself. And the same one he'd broken into her flat to steal. It was as familiar to her as her own reflection, and as much of a shock as if she'd come face to face with Colin in person. Her eyes skimmed the short résumé of his acting career.

Mark Dryden trained at RADA, before joining the Stratford Shakespeare Society. He has appeared in numerous productions including A Street Car Named Desire *and* The Cherry Orchard . . . *In the television drama* Time is Now, *he played the role of Simon. Films include* A Step in the Dark . . .

Suddenly, Antonia realized the auditorium was emptying for the interval, and her parents were saying something. She glanced up and saw that they were looking at her with puzzled expressions.

'Are you all right, darling?' Hilary asked in concern.

Antonia blinked, feeling dazed. 'Yeah. I'm OK.'

Quentin spoke. 'Would you like something to drink? Mummy and I thought we'd go to the bar for some coffee.'

'No, nothing for me,' she stammered. Her hands were shaking and her heart was pounding. She had to get to a phone.

'If you'll excuse me, I've just remembered I must call the office.'

'All right. We'll meet you in the bar, shall we?'

'Yes, Daddy.' Antonia nodded, distracted. 'I shan't be long.' She had to find some place where she could phone the police on her mobile without being overheard.

Hurrying down to the foyer she went out into the street. There was an alleyway up the side of the theatre which led to the stage door. It was deserted at this hour. Taking her mobile out of her handbag, she dialled the number of her local police station, committed to memory since the burglary.

'I'd like to speak to Detective Chief Inspector Cooper, please,' she said, praying he was on duty. To her relief he answered as soon as she was put through. Then she told him about Mark Dryden, alias Colin Holbrook.

'You're absolutely sure this is the right man?' he asked. There was doubt in his voice.

'I *know* it is,' Antonia insisted impatiently. 'His photograph in the programme is the same one he sent me.'

'Right. You're still at the Royalty Theatre?'

'Yes.'

'Does anyone know you're making this call?'

'No one.'

'We'll place two plain-clothes men in the wings and

218

try to catch him unawares when he comes off stage at the end. Thanks for the tip-off.'

Antonia felt her stomach give a nervous contraction. At last the end of her ordeal was in sight and yet she felt apprehensive. Supposing Colin Holbrook gave them the slip? There was something else, too, that nagged at the back of her mind. Now she'd seen him in the flesh, she realized she found him as attractive as when she'd first seen his picture. He was the type of man she'd always dreamed of marrying, and for that, she couldn't help feeling sad. It was as if she'd lost something before she'd even found it.

'Go back to your seat and watch the second act as if nothing had happened,' the DCI was telling her. 'You can leave it to us now.'

Antonia made her way up to the dress circle bar. It was packed and the air was stifling, thick with cigarette smoke. Quentin and Hilary had managed to secure a little round table in a corner and they'd even kept a chair for her.

'Is everything all right at the office, darling?' Quentin asked.

'You look very flushed, darling,' Hilary observed.

'Everything's fine,' Antonia replied lightly.

'Are you sure you won't change your mind and have a drink?'

'No, really, thanks.' She'd rolled her programme into a tight wad, and she was tapping the palm of her hand with it in a gesture of impatience. Quentin, aware something was wrong, spoke.

'Do you need to get back to your office, Antonia? Mummy and I will quite understand if you want to slip away.'

Antonia looked startled. She thought she'd been putting on a terrific act of appearing serene, but it obviously hadn't fooled her father.

'Of course I don't want to go back to the office,' she said firmly. At least that much was true.

The second act of *Cocktails for Two* seemed to drag endlessly, and because Antonia was keyed up and under stress, her powers of concentration had deserted her. The audience were enjoying themselves with raucous delight, but she might have been looking at an empty stage for all the effect the comedy was having on her. She kept wondering when 'Harry' was going to make his next entrance and every time a door in the set opened for a character to come on stage, her heart leaped in her ribcage. Supposing something went wrong and he gave them the slip? It was a terrifying thought and she resolved to ask for police protection if they failed to detain him for some reason. Taking deep breaths to try and calm herself, Antonia realized her jaws ached from clenching her teeth, and she was getting a splitting headache.

Then just when she thought she couldn't bear the suspense a moment longer, Colin came on stage, wearing a dinner jacket and smoking a cigarette with languid assurance. Delivering his lines with perfect timing, and stealing the limelight from the other actors, he played the part of Harry with total conviction, being both endearing and maddening at the same time in his role.

Antonia found it almost unbearable to watch him. This was a man she had desperately wanted to date. A man who she now knew to be a serial killer. A man who had picked her for his next victim. She looked at her wristwatch surreptitiously, so her parents wouldn't notice, but it was too dark to see the time. Fidgeting in her seat, she wished with all her heart that the play would come to an end. The suspense of watching Colin Holbrook play his part with such verve, unaware that plain-clothes police were waiting in the wings to detain him after the final curtain call was agonizing, like watching a creature walk unheeding into a fatal trap. Little did the audience realize, she thought, as they roared with laughter, that a real-life drama of terrible consequence was happening in their midst.

At last it came to an end, to thunderous applause.

'Wasn't that fun?' Hilary exclaimed, as the cast took their final curtain call. 'I haven't laughed so much for ages.'

'It was great, wasn't it?' Quentin agreed heartily. 'Thank you for bringing us to this, darling,' he continued, turning to Antonia. 'It was a very good choice on your part.'

It took several minutes to leave the theatre, as they inched their way among the departing crowds.

'Do you think we'll ever get a taxi?' Hilary asked anxiously.

'It's all fixed, Mum. I've got a car to meet us,' Antonia replied.

Quentin looked at her admiringly. 'You think of everything.'

She flashed him a quick smile. 'I believe in cutting down on hassle,' she replied, 'and trying to find a taxi at this time in the West End is impossible.'

At last they reached the foyer, where everyone was spilling out into Shaftesbury Avenue.

Antonia pushed ahead. 'I'll see if I can spot Donald. He was going to get as near to the front entrance as possible.'

Her parents followed. As soon as they stepped on to the pavement, Antonia saw a police car, with its blue light flashing on the roof, parked at the entrance to the alleyway which led to the stage door. There was another one behind it, and two police motorcyclists, double-parked. The air hummed with the buzz and crackle of walkie-talkie radios. A crowd had already gathered, curious to see what was going on.

Involuntarily, Antonia gasped aloud and stepped back, under the shadow of the theatre canopy, trying to merge in with the crowds. She had an overpowering desire to hide so that Colin Holbrook would not see her standing there. He had no power to hurt her now, and yet she felt vulnerable and exposed. If it hadn't been for her parents, she'd have turned and run in the opposite direction.

Suddenly, the car siren screamed into action, piercing the air with a frightening wail, so close it seemed to be in her head. Antonia jumped in alarm, jarred by the noise. Then a group of uniformed police appeared from the alleyway, striding purposefully across the pavement to the first car. In their midst and handcuffed to one of them was Mark Dryden. Wearing jeans, trainers and a tee-shirt, he was looking around as if he didn't know what was going on. He was obviously shocked by the sight of the crowds who pressed forward to have a closer look at him. For a second his gaze passed over Antonia's face, but he didn't show a flicker of recognition. A moment later he had been pushed into the car. Two policemen jumped in beside him and with a roar the car surged forward and streaked away, accompanied by the outriders and the second police car. It was all over in less than a minute, but Antonia felt as if she'd endured an ordeal that had lasted for hours.

'Well . . .!' Hilary exclaimed. 'What was *that* all about?'

'There's Donald,' Antonia said with relief, pointing to the limousine as it drew up to the kerb in front of them. 'Let's get in quickly, Mum. He won't be allowed to stop here.'

They clambered in, all three of them able to sit on the back seat.

'To the Savoy, Miss Murray?' Donald asked, as he let in the clutch and the car slid silently forward.

'Yes, please. And then on to the office, please.'

'Well, that *was* an unexpected bit of excitement,' Quentin observed, slipping his arm through Hilary's. 'Who do you suppose that man was? I wonder why they arrested him?'

'Wasn't he one of the actors, dear?' his wife asked. 'I thought I recognized his face.'

Antonia remained silent, too exhausted to want to engage in conversation. It had been a weird and shocking afternoon, and she felt more deeply shaken than she'd have thought possible.

'Here we are,' she heard her father say at last as they entered the forecourt of the Savoy. 'Do you want to stay for a cup of tea, Antonia? They do a marvellous afternoon tea here.'

'No thanks, Daddy. I want to check on a few things at the office, and then go home to change for tonight.'

'Don't forget you're staying the night with us, darling,' Hilary reminded her.

'I haven't forgotten. I'm not going to miss breakfast in the River Room for anything. I'll be back at seven-thirty,' she promised.

'Don't be late! We're starting the evening with your mother's favourite champagne,' said Quentin as he bent to kiss her goodbye.

'Am I ever late?' she quipped, getting back into the car. As Donald did a three-point turn to get out of the courtyard, she watched them enter the luxurious lobby of the hotel and head for the tearoom; a middle-aged couple who were still in love and still knew how to enjoy themselves.

As Donald drove down the Strand to Trafalgar Square, and then along The Mall to Buckingham Palace, Antonia gazed out of the car windows at the lush greenery of St James's Park and realized, almost with a sense of shock, that she had nothing to fear any more. Colin Holbrook had been arrested. She would no longer be followed wherever she went. There would be no more phone calls. No more threats. No more break-ins. She was safe. *Safe*. She could hardly believe it was all over. The sense of relief she felt was enormous, like the sun coming out after a terrible storm. A burst of happiness lifted her spirits, suddenly making her feel light-hearted. Tonight, for the first time in ages, she was going to be able to relax and enjoy herself, although she knew she'd be called upon by the police to give evidence in due course. But not tonight. When she got to the Savoy she could help celebrate her mother's birthday in the knowledge that her own personal nightmare was over.

'Donald,' she said, leaning forward. 'I shan't need you this evening. Or tomorrow either. I shall be using my own car again.'

'Very well, Miss Murray.'

'Thank you for all your help. I've really appreciated it. I'm afraid you've had to hang about waiting for me more than actually driving me, but I'm really grateful.'

'It's been a pleasure, Ma'am. I'll be pleased to drive you at any time.'

'Thank you, Donald.'

Antonia arrived at the offices of Murray Properties a few minutes later. It was so unusual for her to have taken the afternoon off, that her staff greeted her as if she'd been away on holiday.

'Did you have a good time?' Carina asked, almost eagerly.

'Was the play good?' Sally wondered.

'Did your mother enjoy it?' asked Mark.

'What are you doing back here?' Guy demanded jokingly. 'I thought you'd gone for the day and would be knocking back the champagne by now.'

Antonia fended off their banter laughingly, and decided not to make any mention of the police arresting a member of the cast. After all, if she hadn't come out of the theatre at the exact moment Mark Dryden was being escorted to a police car, she'd never have seen the incident. If his arrest got into the newspapers, which it surely would, she could plead ignorance and say she knew nothing about it.

'Mum laughed until she wept!' she said gaily. 'It is a very funny comedy. I can highly recommend it.' Then she turned to Linda, who was finishing a phone call. 'Any messages?'

'A few,' Linda replied. 'Nothing that can't wait until tomorrow, except for this one, that just came in now.'

'What is it?'

Linda consulted her notepad in which she'd been scribbling. 'I'm afraid it's urgent, and you're going to have to make a decision this afternoon.'

'This afternoon?' Antonia looked at her wristwatch. 'What sort of decision? It's already five-thirty and for once I've got to leave early.'

'It shouldn't take long,' Linda assured her. 'In fact you could check it out on your way home. Shawlands & Cross, the flooring people, phoned a few minutes ago to say they've started to put down the parquet floor in the dining room of the Belgrave Square house—'

'Started?' Antonia cut in. 'I thought they were supposed to have finished it by today?'

Linda shrugged. 'Apparently there's a hitch.'

'Don't tell me . . . they've run out of parquet?'

'No.' she replied. 'In fact they haven't started because they're worried you may find the colour of the wood too dark. They need to know urgently, because the man who usually lays the parquet won't be able to do the job if there's a delay while they order a paler colour. He's booked to do the floor in another house next week.'

'Oh, for God's sake! I chose the colour most carefully. How can it be too dark? Unless they've delivered the wrong shade. If they have to reorder that's going to delay my putting it on the market.'

'I know,' Linda agreed. 'They realize that, that's why they want you to look at it as soon as possible.'

'Damn!' Antonia exclaimed in irritation. 'This could be a major disaster.' She looked at her wristwatch. 'I'll go now, on my way home.'

'The head man from Shawlands & Cross will still be there, so you can give him hell if they've got it wrong,' Linda commented.

'Don't worry, I will.' She looked around the office at everyone. 'Good night. I'll see you all in the morning.'

The walk from Sloane Street to Belgrave Square took her ten minutes, and as she approached the house, which was on the far side of the square, she noticed they'd finished painting the exterior. The stucco gleamed white on the decorative mouldings like icing on a cake. Now that the scaffolding could be taken down, she looked forward to the next stage. She'd commissioned John Plested to do the window boxes, and she knew he'd do a sophisticated design of important plants, in keeping with the majestic dignity of the building, rather than pretty-pretty, cottagey flowers.

As she drew closer she saw that the central crystal chandelier was on in the large first-floor reception room. The front door was slightly ajar, so she pushed it open and stepped into the deserted hall. She beheld the familiar scene: ladders, propped against one wall, buckets, tins of paint and some large kitchen units, draped with dust sheets. There was no sign of the stacks of wooden parquet blocks she'd expected to find.

'Hello?' she called out. Her voice echoed through the house, reverberating in the large empty rooms and up the marble staircase to the floors above.

There was no answer. Puzzled, she turned and walked

into the dining room, which was on the left of the front door. It was an oblong room, with windows at each end. She looked down at the floor.

'What the hell . . .?' she exclaimed involuntary. A virgin expanse of perfect honey-gold parquet gleamed from end to end and from side to side. Her head spun in confusion. Was she in the right room? Was she in the right *house*? Had Linda meant the property in Victoria Road? Or the flats by Marble Arch? But those houses weren't even having parquet flooring installed.

Antonia hurried back into the hall. She must find the head man from Shawlands & Cross.

'Are you there?' she shouted, louder than she'd meant to, recognizing the fear in her voice. There was no answer. The house was silent. The draped dust sheets mocked her like watchful ghosts.

'Hello?' Her voice rose, with a sharp edge to it.

The stillness seethed with menace. She held her breath, looking back into the dining room, knowing something was wrong.

'I don't understand . . .' she said aloud.

'Don't you?'

Startled, Antonia spun round. A man stood in the middle of the hall. His skin had the silvery gleam of fish scales and through his brass-rimmed glasses his eyes glittered as if he had a fever.

'Mr Preedy . . .!' She stared back at him. Her heart nearly stopped with fright.

He gave a little twisted smile. 'I thought you would have realized it was me a long time ago. So much for being an upwardly mobile successful businesswoman.'

She realized she'd fallen into a trap. The problem with the flooring had been a set-up. She made a dash for the front door, but he was nearer to it. With surprising agility for a man of his age, he leaped forward and threw himself against it. With a crash the heavy door slammed shut and he jammed the bolts home.

Antonia struggled to keep calm. She raised her chin defiantly. 'What do you want?'

Mr Preedy swallowed and his Adam's apple jerked above the edge of his white collar. 'What I want,' he said heavily, 'is to rid the world of women like *you*. Women who think they're clever. Women who take men's jobs away from them. Women who walk all over others in their pursuit of promotion.' His face had grown red and he was barely able to control his rage. 'A woman like you cost me my job, my home, my wife and my future; everything I worked for.'

'I created my own job,' she said quietly, gripping her hands in front of her to prevent them shaking. 'I haven't taken anyone's job away from them.'

'That's what they all say. I've been watching you. I know what you're up to. You want to take over, like the others I had to get rid of. You're ambitious. You prevent men like me getting the top jobs.' His eyes stared at her.

Antonia stood still, her face white. The blood roared in her ears and for a moment she thought she was going to faint. He'd planned this. She was going to be his next victim. And he was in league with Colin Holbrook . . . who was really an actor called Mark Dryden. She could see it all now. They must have read the lonely hearts columns and picked out the women who appeared career-orientated. Hadn't her own advertisement stressed . . . *Career Girl . . . With Own Company* . . . ? God, she'd fitted the bill as far as they'd been concerned. Then, because Mark was young and attractive, it had been his photograph they'd sent; and him she'd spoken to on the phone. He may even have written the first letter that had so appealed to her. And *that* was why he'd never turned up for their dates. She leaned against the lintel of the dining-room door and closed her eyes for a moment, feeling crushed. Why had Mark Dryden become an accomplice?

Then she heard Mr Preedy move and her eyes flew open again. He was taking a length of white cord from his pocket. He wound the ends around each of his hands and then tugged them gently apart as if testing the strength of the cord. Then he spoke, as if he knew what she'd been thinking.

'You haven't met Colin Holbrook, have you?'

'No,' she replied, playing for time.

'Colin and Susan!' he mocked. 'That's what you called yourself, didn't you?'

'Yes.'

'And you thought, when you got his photograph . . . now he's a sexy-looking young man, didn't you? One you could go out on dates with? A suitable husband, eh?'

She remained silent.

'So you did fancy him?' Mr Preedy was staring at her and she gritted her teeth, hated to think what lewd thoughts were passing through his mind.

'He looked . . . interesting.' If she could keep him talking, get him into some sort of conversation, maybe she could

offer to find him a good job and he'd let her go? It was a
wild thought and she knew it, but she was prepared to say
anything to get out of the house.

'Only . . . interesting? Dear me, I must do better next
time,' he said self-deprecatingly.

'Have you known him long?'

'Not very. You enjoyed talking to him on the phone, did
you? Disappointed when he failed to turn up for your dates?'

Antonia frowned. Something was wrong. She wasn't sure
what but every instinct told her that Mr Preedy was playing
a game, and it was a sick game, designed to maximize her
terror. He'd probably found out that Colin – or rather Mark
Dryden had been arrested an hour ago. Enlightenment flooded
her brain, filling her with fresh fear. *That* was why he'd
tricked her into coming here tonight; to get his revenge for
what she'd done to Colin.

'Weren't you upset he never turned up to meet you?' Mr
Preedy barked.

She nodded but said nothing.

'But he did, you know. Every time,' he added slowly.

'But I never saw—'

'Ah, but you were looking for the handsome young man
in the photograph, weren't you?'

She stared back at him, her eyes wide.

A smirk of bitter satisfaction contorted the lower half of
his face. 'I thought so. But you were always destined to be
disappointed, because there's no such person as Colin
Holbrook. It was I who wrote to you. Talked to you on the
phone. Made arrangements for us to meet. I *was* there, each
time, to see what you looked like. Followed you the first

time to see where you lived. Followed you again to see where you worked. And decided that you were exactly the type of woman who deserved to be eliminated; but only after I'd had a little sport pretending to be a handsome young man, and watch your face go sad when he failed to turn up.'

'But the photograph . . .!' she protested, without being able to stop herself.

'It's a piece of cake to get hold of photographs of actors. Any agent will let you have one if you say you're a casting director,' he sneered. 'I thought you were cleverer than *that*.'

Her mind reeled. So Mark Dryden had nothing to do with any of this! He was innocent but she'd got him arrested. She'd been so sure he was the man who had tormented her for weeks, and now she'd put the police on to a blameless man who would never even have heard of either her or Mr Preedy.

Linda was the last to leave the office that evening. It was six forty-five and it had been a long day. When properties were nearing completion there were so many details to see to, so many last-minute queries, so many loose ends to tie up, that it left her exhausted. All she wanted to do now was go home, have a hot bath and then get into bed to watch the TV. She'd recently rented a studio flat in Fulham, having decided she did not want to return to Robin in spite of his protestations, and she'd begun to realize why Antonia liked her independence so much. Then she switched on the answerphone, turned off the lights and locked the glass doors to the street. As she hurried to the underground station at

Sloane Square, it started to rain.

Tristram, Roland and Leo had decided to drive up to London in one car, because of the difficulty of parking.

'I wish now we'd come up by train,' Tristram grumbled as they entered the outskirts of the city. It was nearly seven o'clock and because of the rain the traffic was almost at a standstill. 'Bloody traffic jams!' He felt hot and sticky. 'I wish we could stop for a drink.'

'Why don't we?' Leo asked. 'There are plenty of pubs around.'

'There isn't time. We're going to be late as it is.' Tristram retorted. 'God, how I hate London.'

'I'd like to live in London,' Leo remarked, peering out through the steamed-up windows. 'It's where's it's all happening.'

'As far as I can see all that's happening is that you get stuck behind a number fourteen bloody bus.'

Leo was not to be put off. 'Yes, but think of all the theatres and cinemas you can go to, and the galleries and exhibitions. Not to mention restaurants of every nationality you've ever heard of, and a few you haven't.'

'Yeah, but think how much eating out in London costs,' Roland reasoned.

'It's a rip-off,' Tristram informed them. He was getting more irritated by the minute. Hilary and Quentin were sticklers for punctuality and tonight was a special night. He patted his inner pocket to make sure he'd got his mother's birthday present: a voucher for two thousand spring bulbs and the services of a gardener to plant them for her.

'I wonder if Antonia's stuck in traffic, too,' said Roland suddenly.

Leo sounded envious. 'She's probably sitting in the warmth and comfort of the Savoy swigging champagne this very minute, while we're still stuck on Putney Bridge.' He looked out through the windscreen and watched the rain falling like little silver darts in the beam of the headlights. 'I hope they don't start dinner without us,' he added in worried tones.

Daylight was fading. As the fast-gathering shadows in the hall closed in around them, they stared at each other, locked in a fearful combat of wills, which only one of them could win. Antonia stood tensely, waiting to see what Mr Preedy would do next. He was blocking her way, standing with his back against the front door which was her only means of escape. He stared malevolently, while his hands kept testing the strength of the cord. It was silent except for the pouring rain, which needled at the window panes and lashed the pavements outside.

What was preventing him striking? Coming forward to whip that cord around her throat and pull it tightly with those big hands of his? Was it because he was enjoying the power he had over her, she wondered? The moments lengthened, becoming minutes. She wanted to scream. *What's stopping you?* Desperation suddenly gave her a kind of courage. She had nothing to lose. Maybe she should try to defuse the situation?

She cleared her throat nervously. 'Would it help if you found a good job in another big company?' Her voice surprised her with its steadiness.

Something in him seemed to click back into life. His face flushed. 'I *had* a good job. It was taken away from me by a woman like you. It's too late now. I can't start again. I just want to make sure there are no more women like you around. You'll never know what it did to me to be superseded by a chit of a girl.' There was a wild, almost hysterical bitterness in his tone.

In spite of everything, Antonia couldn't help feeling a flicker of compassion. She could understand how it must have been for him. The loss. The humiliation. A dream shattered.

'Do you have a wife? And a family?' she asked softly.

'I *had* a wife,' he replied, and for a moment she thought she detected a slight trembling of his lower lip.

It was almost dark. In the deepening shadows the dust sheets the builders had draped around the hall hung in limp, eerie shapes.

'I'm sorry.'

'Why should you care?' His voice was harsh. Then he stepped nearer as if he'd made up his mind, and Antonia braced herself. He was over six foot tall and large-boned. What chance had she of fighting him off? His fists closed tightly on the cord and he raised both hands as if in readiness.

A rush of adrenalin, born of terror, shot through her. She was not going to become his fourth victim. A sense of self-preservation, almost instinctive, made her raise her foot. Then she kicked out with all her strength. The high heel of her shoe caught him unawares. The sharp blow on the bone, just below the knee, took him by surprise. He yelped with pain and shock and his eyes registered bewilderment for a second. Before he could recover himself she turned and fled across the hall. Three high wooden ladders were propped up on one side. Exerting all her strength, she grabbed the rung of the first one and pulled it away from the wall. As it pitched forward, she grabbed the two others, dodging ahead as they crashed thunderously behind her, scattering, as they hit the floor, the metal buckets and pots of paint left by the decorators.

Running, she reached the flight of stone stairs that led down to the basement. As she scurried down to the darkened kitchen, she heard Mr Preedy chasing after her. His footsteps came pounding across the hall floor. Then there was a crash and a heavy thud and a moment later a loud groan of pain. She could hear the clanking of a bucket as it hit the skirting board. He swore furiously, cursing the fallen ladders and moaning, 'Oh Christ! My knee!'

Antonia didn't pause. She'd helped design the layout of the kitchen quarters and she knew her way around as if it were her own flat. Reaching behind the door at the foot of the stairs, she slid back a panel and disconnected the lighting circuit for the whole of the ground floor and basement.

'You won't get away . . .!' Mr Preedy roared, as she heard him stumbling towards the stairs to come after her. She ran to the far side of the kitchen and opened what looked like cupboard doors. Inside was an old-fashioned dumb waiter she'd had restored and modernized, to carry food and dishes to the dining room above.

At that moment she heard Mr Preedy trying to switch on the lights at the top of the stairs. When nothing happened he let out a stream of curses, realizing what she'd done.

'Bitch!' he yelled, infuriated. Then he began to descend cautiously into the darkness.

With only moments to spare, Antonia hoisted herself into the food lift, displacing one of the adjustable shelves as she did so. Curling up in the confined space, she reached for the switch that controlled the dumb waiter. They were set into the kitchen wall just below the opening. Running her fingers over the buttons, she found what she hoped was the Up switch. She pressed it. Then she grabbed the two small doors and pulled them towards her and closed them just as she heard Mr Preedy enter the kitchen. Hugging her knees to her chin she shut her eyes tightly, hoping she'd pressed the right switch. She could hear him striding around. He was opening and shutting cupboard doors. It was vital that she was out of sight before he got to the food-lift doors.

Suddenly, with a faint whining noise, the lift started to shudder upwards, straining under her weight. She found herself holding her breath as if that might make her lighter. As it inched up, she knew she had to stop the lift getting as far as the dining room.

In the pitch dark Antonia reached for the shelf she'd displaced in order to make room for herself, and hoping her aim was right, thrust it into the wooden framework which was fixed to the supporting brick wall. Instantly the dumb waiter jammed, stuck between floors.

If Mr Preedy pressed either the Up or Down switch now, nothing would happen. Wedged between the kitchen and the dining room, she was safe for the moment – as long as her weight didn't bring the whole structure crashing back down again. And as long as the shelf, made of one-inch-thick wood, was strong enough to keep the lift jammed.

Her hands were wet with sweat and her clothes were sticking to her. Crouching in the tiny dark space, her legs ached and her back hurt as she strained to hear what was happening.

Mr Preedy had heard the electric hum of the dumb waiter and now he was stamping around the kitchen, looking for its source.

'I know you're here!' he said in a quiet voice. It was more scary than when he'd bellowed. Antonia held her breath.

'Ah! That's better,' she heard him say. From the direction of his voice she guessed he'd opened the fridge, and the light inside had provided some illumination.

'I'll soon find you now.' There was triumph in his voice. Then she heard the sound of his footsteps crossing the tiled floor. They were coming in the direction of the dumb waiter.

Sitting in an interview room at the Sloane Avenue police station, the man calling himself Mark Dryden was refusing to say anything until his solicitor arrived. The arresting officer, Detective Sergeant Ambrose, had read the charges against him. They included the murders of Pauline Ashford, Valerie Martin and Roxana Birch, the harassment of Antonia Murray coupled with breaking and entering her flat, and false representation.

Meanwhile, Detective Chief Inspector Cooper, who would be interrogating the suspect, had no doubt that they'd arrested the right man. He looked at the photograph of Mark in the theatre programme Ambrose had procured and it was as

Antonia Murray had described Colin Holbrook: a lean, dark-haired man in his thirties with dark eyes and a humorous mouth. But that was insufficient. They needed Miss Murray to come to the police station herself, to identify the photograph formally as being the same as the one she'd been sent, and to make an official statement. He also wanted her to identify the voice.

'Where is Miss Murray?' the DCI asked.

Ambrose looked at him blankly. 'I don't know, sir. Did you want to see her?'

The pale, foxy features of DCI Cooper showed deep irritation. 'I'm not likely to ask where she is if I don't want to see her, Ambrose. She's our main witness at the moment. Our only lead to a possible serial killer. Or should I say, the only witness that's still alive!'

'I'll get her brought in right away, sir.'

'Meanwhile I'll see if I can get anything out of this Mark Dryden, alias Colin Holbrook.'

But the suspect was absolutely refusing to talk. When asked where he'd been on the nights of the three murders, he protested his innocence and begged to call his solicitor. Then he was asked where he'd been at the time Miss Murray's flat had been broken into. Again he gave the same response.

Tight-lipped at these time-wasting tactics, although he knew Mark Dryden was within his rights to refuse to answer questions until he'd taken advice, the DCI left the interview room and ordered the prisoner to be returned to his cell.

Nine

It was nearly eight o'clock and the American Bar at the Savoy was packed with people, meeting their friends, having a drink after work with their colleagues, or a romantic tête-à-tête with a lover. The head barman was giving a display of his expertise as he rattled a silver cocktail shaker like a maraca. Waiters scurried to and fro balancing silver trays of drinks, and depositing bowls of nuts and olives on the small tables.

In an alcove, Quentin looked at his wristwatch again. 'They're very late,' he remarked.

'I expect it's the rain,' Hilary said. 'It always snarls up the traffic.'

'The boys are all coming together, aren't they?'

She nodded, sipped her champagne and spoke. 'They're probably having a terrible time finding somewhere to park. They'll keep our table in the Grill Room, won't they?'

'I might go and tell them we're running late.'

At that moment, Roland and Leo appeared, looking hot and harassed.

'Mum! Happy Birthday. I'm so sorry! The traffic is absolutely hellish.' Roland bent to kiss Hilary on both cheeks.

'I thought we'd never get here,' Leo exclaimed, kissing

her too. They both embraced their father.

'Where's Tristram?' Hilary asked.

'Don't ask! He's in a foul mood. He's been going round and round in circles for the past half-hour, trying to find somewhere to leave the car. He dropped us off and he'll be here as soon as he can.' Leo sank on to the grey velvet banquette beside his mother. 'God, I could do with a drink.'

Roland sat in the chair facing them. 'So could I. We left home *hours* ago.'

'Let's kill this bottle and I'll order another one,' Quentin said, taking the bottle of Bollinger out of the ice bucket.

Leo eyed the bottle with interest. 'You and Ma have certainly made inroads into *that* one! There's hardly any left.'

Quentin grinned. 'Well, it is Ma's birthday.'

'That's right,' Hilary agreed. 'I hope Tristram gets here soon.'

Roland suddenly looked around sharply. 'Where's Antonia?'

Quentin dribbled the last of the champagne into Roland's glass. 'She hasn't turned up yet. Same reason as you, I expect.' He signalled to the waiter for another bottle.

Leo stretched his long legs, suddenly relaxed at the sight of a drink. 'Oh, well. There's no real hurry, is there? We're staying the night here, so it doesn't matter when we eat.'

'Talking of which, I'm going to send a message to tell the head waiter we'll be dining later,' Quentin said.

Leo took a small parcel out of his coat pocket and handed it to Hilary. 'Happy Birthday, Mum.'

Hilary's face lit up, for a second recapturing the animated beauty of her youth. 'Thank you, darling.' Unwrapping the silvery paper she found an antique amethyst and pearl pendant hung on a fine gold chain.

'It's beautiful, Leo. I love it. Thank you so much.' Her eyes were bright and she smiled at him and reached out to squeeze his hand. 'I shall wear it now.'

Leo looked flushed with pleasure. 'I'm glad you like it. It took me ages to find.'

Roland handed her a flat package. 'Here's mine, Ma.'

'This is like Christmas,' Hilary exclaimed. 'I do wish Antonia was here. And Tristram.' Roland's present was a silver frame holding a photograph of Tristram, Antonia, Leo and himself, taken by Quentin the last time they'd spent a weekend together at Clifton Hall as a surprise for their mother.

'Look, Quentin! A picture of the children,' she said in delight.

He laughed. 'You can't call them "the children" when the youngest is twenty-three.'

'Yes, I can,' she replied sparkily. 'To me they'll always be the children. Ah! Here's Tristram. Darling, we're over here.'

He looked flustered. 'I can't tell you how sorry I am,' he said, hurrying over to kiss her, his soft beard brushing against her cheek. 'I'll never bring a car to London again. Is that champagne? I've been going up and down every bloody street in a half-mile radius, thinking of you all tucking into the bubbly. Where's Antonia?' He looked around questioningly.

'She's not arrived yet.' Quentin filled his eldest son's glass. 'Like you, she's probably trying to park.'

'Thanks, Dad.' Tristram gulped his drink thirstily. 'Why on earth is she bringing her car? Surely she'll take a taxi?'

Quentin shrugged. 'Maybe she will. Anyway, I'm sure she'll be here in a minute.'

'Here's your present, Ma.'

Hilary took the envelope Tristram handed her, and gave a gasp of delight when she opened it. 'Spring bulbs! And someone to plant them! Oh, thank you, darling! You remembered my poor old knees.'

As they all continued to chatter, Quentin kept looking at his wristwatch with growing concern. He hadn't been worried about his sons' delayed arrival; they were nearly always late for everything but it was different with Antonia. Like him, she was always punctual. And tonight of all nights she wouldn't have risked being late. As soon as there was a break in the conversation, he leaned forward to speak to Hilary.

'We did arrange to meet Antonia here, in the bar, didn't we?'

Hilary looked startled. 'Yes. I'm sure we did. Where else would we have all met up?'

Quentin rose. 'I'll go and check with the restaurant to make sure she's not waiting for us there. I'll also call her room. Perhaps she decided to change when she got here.'

Hilary felt uneasy as she watched him stride out of the bar. Antonia was so dependable. It was completely out of character for her to be late.

While the three brothers chattered among themselves, Hilary sat waiting for Quentin's return, sipping her champagne which now tasted slightly bitter. There were a lot of comings and goings at this hour in the American Bar, and every time someone entered, she looked up hopefully.

At last Quentin came back, and she could tell by his

expression that he shared her anxiety.

'There's no sign of her,' he said, frowning.

'Isn't that rather odd? She knows it's an important night for Mum,' Leo observed. 'I'm starving. Can't we go and eat? She can join us when she arrives.'

'She's never late as a rule,' Roland pointed out in a reproving voice. 'I'm worried that something has happened.'

Tristram took his mobile phone out of his pocket. 'I'll ring her flat. Perhaps she's been delayed by a client.'

Meanwhile, thoughts that were too unbearable to seriously contemplate flashed through Hilary's mind. Ever since her children had been small, her vivid imagination had created fearful scenarios of accidents and illness that might befall them. Supposing something dreadful had happened to Antonia tonight?

'She's not at her flat,' Tristram announced, flatly. 'I'll try her new mobile number.' He stabbed at the numbers of his small flat phone with a forefinger that looked enormous by comparison.

'Shall we have some more champers while we're waiting?' Leo asked hopefully.

'No. We'll have wine with dinner,' Quentin snapped with unaccustomed sharpness.

They waited, watching Tristram as he put the phone to his ear. 'Blast!' he swore, holding it away. 'There's terrible static on the line. I can't hear a bloody thing.'

'At least that means she hasn't switched it off,' Quentin observed, looking relieved. 'Why don't you try it again in a few minutes?'

'Yeah. OK. Meanwhile I'll give her office a buzz. Who

knows? She may still be involved in a big deal or something, and can't get away,' Tristram said with forced joviality.

The others nodded, but Hilary knew they were all clutching at straws. Antonia would never do anything, however important it was to her business, to spoil this special night.

Antonia remained crouched, holding her breath and praying Mr Preedy wouldn't be able to dislodge the dumb waiter. She made rapid calculations in her head. The lift was three foot high. Its base was three foot six inches off the kitchen floor; a comfortable height for loading food. The kitchen itself was twelve feet from floor to ceiling. Then there was a further three feet between the kitchen ceiling and the dining room floor above. The shaft was a further six foot six inches to allow for the lift to be in position for the removal of food. She screwed up her face in concentration, wishing she was better at mental arithmetic. By her reckoning, it meant that if she'd managed to jam the lift approximately halfway between the kitchen and the dining room, she'd be beyond arm's length if Mr Preedy tried to reach her from either place. Unless he used a stick or a pole.

A moment later she heard him opening the doors to the dumb waiter. He'd guessed where she was. Sensing him only a few feet below her, she clenched her fists and prayed. She knew that in the darkness he'd be looking into a black hole. And if he reached out, his hand would encounter a brick wall. She heard him grunt and then the cupboard doors slammed shut.

Antonia let out a long breath of relief. Then, just when she thought she was safe – she even harboured the wild hope that he might give up and leave – she heard him hurrying up the stone stairs again.

Suddenly her mobile phone, tucked into the bottom of her shoulder bag, sprang into life with a muffled ring.

'Shit!' she swore under her breath, making a grab for it. The movement made the lift jiggle, but she managed to hang on to the shelf and the lift remained wedged. Then she whipped out the mobile, and, putting it to her ear, switched it on. Instantly, there was loud buzzing on the line, and she pressed it against her ear so Mr Preedy wouldn't hear it. The line continued to crackle in short sharp bursts. Through the disjointed roaring she thought she could just make out a male voice, shouting above the din.

'Help me,' she said desperately, as loud as she dared.

'Help me. I'm at . . .' But the jarring noise got louder and then there was sudden silence. Whoever had phoned had hung up.

Antonia clutched the instrument in momentary despair. Help had seemed so imminent for a moment and now her hopes were dashed. Stuck in this enclosed space between floors, the hope of getting good reception on her mobile was unlikely. She forced herself to face facts. She was entombed in a square wooden coffin in a dark, airless brick vault and if she climbed out of it, she'd be strangled by a psychopath who had already murdered three women. She could dial 999, but her chances of being heard through the static interference were nil. And yet the thought of being marooned here, waiting for Mr Preedy to find a way of getting to her, was unthinkable.

At that moment she heard heavy footsteps in the dining room and then the doors to the dumb waiter above her opened.

A glimmer of fading daylight from the dining-room windows filtered down the lift shaft, picking out the brickwork she faced.

'I know you're down there!' Mr Preedy bellowed suddenly, making her jump. 'Don't think you're going to escape because you're not.'

She knew the lift was beyond his reach. He'd be able to see the top of it from where he stood. There was silence and she imagined him standing in the room above, wondering what to do next. *Please God, make him leave*, she prayed. She knew now that she'd made a tactical error. It would have been better if she'd let the lift go all the way up to the dining room instead of jamming it. Then she might have been able to make her escape through the front door while he floundered in the darkness of the kitchen below. Now she was trapped like a rat between floors and if she went up or let herself drop down, he'd catch her either way.

'Bitch!' he yelled, his voice rising with hysteria. When she heard him go into the hall, she switched on her mobile again, and, thankful for the luminous numbers, dialled 999. A moment later the burst of static almost deafened her. With a sinking heart she switched her phone off. At that moment she heard Mr Preedy coming back down the stone stairs to the kitchen.

'I think we should phone the police,' Hilary said, pushing her coffee cup away. Her face was pale and drawn and she looked exhausted. It was now eleven o'clock at night, and there was no use deluding themselves that Antonia had been delayed.

Quentin nodded. 'Let's go up to our room and make the calls from there.' He rose stiffly. They'd had an excellent dinner, but now he wished they'd got on to the police earlier to see if any accidents had been reported.

'Dad, I'm going to go to her flat,' Tristram said, taking his car keys out of his pocket.

'But you don't have a key.'

'Maybe she's fallen and hurt herself and can't get to the phone.'

'How will it help if you can't get in?' Quentin pointed out.

'I'll rouse her neighbour, Mrs Miller. She has a key to Antonia's flat, doesn't she?'

'I don't know.'

'OK.' Tristram was keen to be off. 'I'll see you later.'

Leo stepped forward. 'I'll come with you.'

As Quentin, Hilary and Roland went up to their rooms on the fourth floor, Roland put forward a suggestion.

'Dad, shall I phone the hospitals while you phone the police?'

'Good idea, old chap. It'll save time.'

Hilary slid her hand into the crook of Quentin's elbow. Her lips were trembling. 'Nothing can *really* have happened to Antonia, can it?'

Quentin looked down at her, his face grave but tender. 'I'm sure we're all getting worked up over nothing,' he said, gently. 'Try not to upset yourself, darling. There's bound to be a perfectly simple explanation. She's probably got herself locked in somewhere and hasn't got the right key to get out.'

Hilary knew he was trying to comfort her and she squeezed

his arm. 'I thought she said she was going to pop in to the office for a few minutes before going home to change.'

'She did, but something may have come up,' Quentin said.

'That's right,' Roland remarked encouragingly. 'I know it's unlike her to go missing, but I wouldn't worry too much, Ma,' he added gently.

Hilary didn't reply. She knew they were trying to reassure her, but she couldn't be comforted. Deep in her bones she felt something awful had happened, and with a mother's instinct knew also that she wouldn't rest until Antonia was back with them.

Their rooms were next to each other.

'I'll come to you as soon as I've made the calls,' Roland assured his parents. 'There are only two hospitals that have got casualty departments in central London anyway, so it won't take long.

Quentin paused, his key in the lock. 'Which police station should I call?' He'd lived for so long in the country that he felt out of touch, as if he were in unknown territory.

'The hotel switchboard will tell you,' Roland advised.

Entering their suite, Hilary saw the flowers and champagne Antonia had ordered, and as she sank on to the cushioned sofa, a small sob escaped from her throat. Immediately Quentin went over and laid his hand tenderly on her shoulder.

'Sweetheart, don't get upset. I'm sure we'll find out where she is in a few minutes.'

She gave him a haunted look. 'That's what I'm afraid of,' she said, her voice quavering. 'I have this terrible feeling that something has happened. When have you ever known

Antonia to be unreliable? When she dropped us off here after the theatre, she distinctly said she was going to the office, then home to change before coming back here.'

'I know.' He stood up and went over to the ornate desk in the window and picked up the phone.

Hilary went to the bathroom, unable to bear sitting and listening while he talked to the police. She bathed her face with a cloth wrung out in cold water and tried to breathe deeply to steady her nerves. There had only ever been one thing in her life she was truly frightened of, and that was something happening to one of her children. Other disasters, even, she reflected guiltily, the death of Quentin, she knew she could cope with. But not her beloved children. Nature did not intend for the old ones to outlive the young ones, but nature was not always in control. Life was not like her garden, where the seasons followed each other in an orderly way, where the spent leaves dropped off to make room for the young shoots, and the petals scattered on the ground to replenish the earth.

When Hilary went back into the drawing room of their suite Quentin was coming off the phone.

'Yes?' she spoke the single word tightly.

'Nothing, darling. There have been no incidents or accidents that they know of. It's much to soon to have her listed as a missing person, especially as she's an adult. I left them our number here so that if there is any news they can contact us, but the chap I spoke to seemed to think we were fussing over nothing.'

'He wouldn't say that if he knew Antonia.'

'I know.'

At that moment there was a knock at their door. It was Roland.

'No news must be good news,' he said cheerfully, when Quentin let him in. 'She's not been admitted to either of the hospitals.'

'What do we do now?' Hilary asked.

'What can we do? Shall I order something from room service while we wait for Tristram and Leo?' Quentin suggested.

'Good idea.'

They sat around drinking tea, each immersed in their own thoughts. Quentin was beginning to think they were all overreacting, while Hilary was equally convinced something dreadful had happened. Roland had his own private thoughts which, out of loyalty to his sister, he felt unable to voice. He'd never forgotten that evening, some months ago, when he'd opened her hall cupboard and out had tumbled all those replies and photographs from men who'd answered her advertisement. He'd been appalled at the time that she would do such a thing but she'd begged him not to tell anyone. He'd respected her wishes but now he wondered if perhaps she'd got involved with one of those men. If that was the case, anything might have happened. He wondered if this was the moment to break that promise to her.

Antonia knew Mr Preedy still loitered in the kitchen because she could hear him shuffling around, searching, she guessed, for the main fuse box, so he could turn on the lights again. The pain in her leg was agonizing from being cramped in such a small space for so long. Yet she daren't try to change her position for fear of dislodging the food lift. The base of her spine felt numb, her neck ached because she had to bend forward to avoid hitting her head on the ceiling of the lift, and she was longing to go to the loo. She'd lost all track of time, and uppermost in her mind was the knowledge that her family would be going crazy with worry.

Only Linda knew she'd been going to the Belgrave Square house on the way home, and she wouldn't be back in the office until morning. It was possible that Roland, who knew her office staff better than anyone else in her family, would think to contact Linda, but he'd try her at home. And she was no longer there, and her ex-husband might not know where she was.

Antonia racked her brains, trying to think what else they might do. Go to her flat? Only Crash – she nearly let out a little cry but smothered it with her hand in time – Crash would be there; and he'd be so hungry! He wouldn't have had anything to eat since this morning. She'd planned to feed him when she went home to change. Mrs Miller wouldn't know where she was, either. It scared her to realize that as far as other people were concerned, she'd vanished. And if Mr Preedy got hold of her – she closed her eyes in momentary terror – by this time tomorrow the news would be that a fourth woman had been murdered near her work place.

She began to tremble; from fear and tiredness and cold. Her feet were icy and so were her hands. The confined space was so claustrophobic it was becoming difficult to breathe. Inching her feet forward she tried to turn sideways, so she could lie curled up on her left side, but her legs were too long and her knees grazed the brickwork facing her. The ripple of laddering tights surged up her thighs. Deciding to get into the food lift had been a disastrous mistake and she bitterly regretted it now.

She could still hear Mr Preedy messing about upstairs again. She was torn between staying where she was, cramped and in agony but beyond his reach, or removing the shelf that wedged the lift, in the hope it might descend to the kitchen again; then she could make a run for it . . . but where would she run to? The back door was locked and bolted and the windows had iron bars across them on the outside. There was nowhere to run to.

It was now nearly midnight and at the police station, not only had Mark Dryden's solicitor not materialized, but neither had they been able to contact Antonia. When Detective Sergeant Ambrose came over to the DCI's desk, he had something else to tell him as well.

Cooper looked up. 'What is it?'

'Apparently a Mr Quentin Murray has phoned in enquiring about his daughter Miss Antonia Murray. He wanted to report her as missing.'

DCI Cooper looked foxier than ever. His small grey eyes were like glass buttons. 'Missing? What do you mean . . . missing? I talked to her myself this afternoon. Where was her father calling from?'

'The Savoy Hotel, sir. She was expected for dinner; they're having a family get-together but she never showed.'

'She was at the theatre this afternoon,' Cooper snapped accusingly. 'She can't have gone far.'

'There's no answer from her home, her office or her

mobile, sir. Her parents seem very worried; said it was unlike her not to turn up.'

'OK, OK.' The DCI was rattled. Heads would roll, and he'd make damn sure it wasn't *his* if this case got screwed up. If the accused man in the holding cell was the serial killer they'd been after for two months, they were going to need Antonia Murray to give evidence as to his methods of latching on to single career women. So far, she seemed to be the only victim of his nasty little grudge who was still alive. Without her they didn't have a case.

'Get me Antonia Murray's father on the phone, Ambrose.'

Hilary's face lit up with relief, as if a terrible burden had been lifted from her shoulders.

'That'll be Antonia!' she exclaimed when the phone in their suite rang.

Quentin's long arm made a snatch for the instrument.

A moment later the atmosphere in the suite had changed as it became obvious that it wasn't Antonia, but the police. Hilary's shoulders drooped and Roland sprang to his feet as if he'd be better able to face bad news from an upright position. They both watched Quentin's face anxiously, rigid with tension.

'I'm sorry, but I don't know what you're talking about,' he said in bewilderment after a moment. 'My daughter never phoned you from the theatre this afternoon. Yes, we did see police cars when we left the Royalty, but it had nothing to do with us. No. Absolutely not. That's impossible. You're barking up the wrong tree,' he added angrily.

'What is it?' Hilary whispered. 'What's wrong?'

'I don't understand . . .' Quentin burst out indignantly. He put his hand over the mouthpiece. 'It's someone at the police station saying he wants to get hold of Antonia urgently. They're holding the man who answered her advertisement in a lonely hearts column on a charge of murder. They need her to make a statement.'

Roland froze, his face white.

'I'll talk to them, Dad,' he said, reaching for the phone.

'What's going on?' Quentin asked suspiciously.

'I don't know exactly, but I've got some idea.'

His father relinquished the handset reluctantly and stood, looking lost and helpless, while Roland talked to the police. When he'd finished he turned to his parents, trying to hide the anguish he felt.

'Roland, what's happened?' Hilary asked. There was a catch in her voice.

He rubbed his forehead distractedly. 'It's very serious . . .'

'For God's sake, *tell* us!' Quentin said sharply.

Roland flopped on to the sofa. 'Some months ago Antonia put an advertisement for . . . well, for a young man, maybe someone she could have a relationship with, in the lonely hearts column of the *Telegraph*.'

There was a stunned silence. Roland struggled on.

'She got a lot of answers. I saw them at her flat. But I made her promise she wouldn't answer any of them.'

'She gave out her address?' Hilary asked, appalled.

'No. They went to a PO box number.' Roland reached for his drink, his hand trembling. 'Apparently she *did* reply to one of them. When her flat was burgled the other day she told the police about the man she'd contacted. She said he'd been stalking her . . .'

'Oh, my God.'

'He's . . . the police think he's the same man who answered similar advertisements, all from career women, all looking for husbands.'

'And . . .?' Quentin looked at Roland. The air between them jangled with the thought of a thousand terrible possibilities.

'He's killed three of the women so far.'

Hilary's hands flew to her face, covering her eyes, trying to blot out the visions that stormed her senses. 'No! Oh, God, *no*!'

'The thing is . . .' Roland began painfully. 'Antonia recognized him from his photograph this afternoon. He's an actor. He was in the show you saw.'

'He's the one they arrested?' Quentin asked.

'Yes.'

Hilary looked deeply hurt. 'Why didn't she tell me? I'm her mother. Why did she keep all this from us?'

The men ignored her for the moment, contemplating the darker implications of what was happening.

'But if this . . . this man has been under arrest since this afternoon,' Quentin said slowly, 'He can't have anything to do with Antonia's disappearance this evening, can he?'

'Bloody hell!' Tristram slowed down as they approached Antonia's flat. 'What are *they* doing here?'

There were two police cars, blue lights revolving dizzily on their roofs. Several policemen stood in the hallway of her building, and on the front steps.

'You don't think they've found . . .?' Leo gasped.

Tristram didn't wait to speculate. He shot out of his car and, charging across the pavement, went up to the senior police officer.

They turned to regard him suspiciously. 'Can we help you, sir?'

'I'm looking for my sister. Antonia Murray. She lives on the first floor. She was supposed to turn up for dinner this evening . . .' His voice trailed away. His reasons sounded feeble.

'We're looking for her too, sir. She's not in her flat. No one's seen her this evening. Her neighbour thinks she went out this morning and hasn't been back since,' the detective sergeant informed him.

'She's got a noisy cat, hasn't she?' a plain-clothes policeman remarked. Their manner was friendlier now. Less guarded.

Tristram nodded, distrait.

'What do you think has happened to her?' Leo asked, wide-eyed.

'That's what we're trying to find out, sir.'

'We thought we'd go and see if she's at her office,' Leo continued.

'Some of our people have already done that,' the police sergeant informed them. 'The place is in darkness. I don't suppose you have a key, do you, sir?'

The brothers shook their heads. 'I don't know what else we can do,' Tristram said, stroking his beard absently.

'She works in property, doesn't she?'

'Yes.'

'Is it possible she's at one of the properties? What sort of thing does she specialize in?'

Tristram spread his hands, shrugging. 'Flats. Houses. Sometimes she converts big buildings into smaller units. It's all residential property.'

'Could she possibly be in one of these residences? Maybe she got locked in by accident?' The police sergeant pulled a small notebook from his back trouser pocket.

'I suppose it's possible,' Tristram sounded doubtful. 'But I've no idea what properties she's handling at the moment.'

'Any way of finding out, sir?'

'Not until the morning. All the details are in her office.'

There was no sleep for any of them that night. When Tristram and Leo got back to the Savoy with the disturbing news that Antonia couldn't be found, and Roland had told them what he knew about her putting an advertisement in the *Telegraph*, they all continued to sit around in a state of shock, oblivious of the time.

'I'd no idea she was so desperate to get married,' Tristram lamented. 'She was always so independent . . . she loved her freedom.'

'Will you stop talking about her in the past tense!' Leo snapped.

'I knew she wanted a husband and children,' Hilary said. 'But I never knew she'd go to these lengths to find one.' She felt both saddened and shocked by what Antonia had done. And devastated now by the consequences.

'What do we do now?' Roland asked. 'Can't we break

into her office and find out the current list of houses she's handling? Then at least we could go round them all, and see if she's got stuck in one of them. We don't *know* anything awful has happened to her, do we?'

'That's true.' Tristram sounded more hopeful. 'I bet she's got herself locked in somewhere and can't get out.'

'But she'd have her mobile with her. Why hasn't she phoned us?' Leo asked.

'Perhaps she couldn't get through,' Roland pointed out. 'Remember we tried to phone her, and there was terrible interference on the line.'

They continued to speculate, constantly reassuring themselves that nothing awful could have happened, that they were making a fuss over nothing, that the solution would be so simple when it came they'd sit back, laughing with relief, and for years to come they'd be saying to one another, 'Do you remember that night . . .?'

'I'm going to lie down for a while,' Hilary said eventually, getting up and going into their adjoining bedroom. 'You all stay here, unless you want to go to bed, but let me know if there's any news.'

Quentin hauled himself to his feet. He was grey with exhaustion, and his long legs felt as if they were filled with lead.

'Are you all right, darling?' he asked anxiously, going and putting his arm around her.

Hilary looked into his face and her lips trembled. 'Just terribly frightened,' she whispered brokenly.

'I know, sweetheart.' He held her close. 'But I'm sure you've no need to be. Antonia has always been able to look after herself, hasn't she? She's strong and clever and streetwise. I'm sure we'll see her tomorrow morning, and if I know Antonia, she'll be spitting with rage at having missed your birthday dinner.'

'I hope you're right,' Hilary murmured, as she lay down on top of the king-size bed. Quentin tucked a large cashmere rug around her.

'Try and have a little sleep, darling,' he said, as he walked softly out of the room.

She didn't reply. Sleep would be impossible, but the quiet of the bedroom, away from her sons all talking at once, would bring her a measure of peace during what had turned out to be the worst night of her life. She didn't dare think about tomorrow. If there was no sign of Antonia in the morning with some simple explanation of what had happened, she didn't know what she would do.

Below the level of her fear was another emotion; a deep sorrow that her daughter had wanted to get married so badly that she'd been prepared to meet complete strangers, in the hope that one of them would feel the same. In her days things had been so different. There had always been lots of young men around, and the girls, with nothing but marriage on their minds, had been able to pick and choose, as she herself had done; the nicest, the handsomest, the kindest and the most eligible bachelor on the scene. And they'd lived happily ever after. Girls, like Antonia, were too busy with their careers to have *time* to meet lots of suitable young men these days. Her daughter, she knew, was only one of a large group of women who were heading for a lonely old age, without children, unless they soon found someone to share their lives with.

But this wasn't the way to do it, Hilary thought, her eyes filling with tears. Putting an advertisement in a newspaper was asking for trouble.

The violent crash came suddenly, without warning, petrifying Antonia. She could hear Mr Preedy, leaning into the open shaft of the food lift above her. He was trying to smash the top of the dumb waiter with a pole of some kind.

The heavy blows to the woodwork were inches from her head. Involuntarily, she gave a scream of terror.

'I'll get you out of there,' he roared. The lift rocked, threatening to become dislodged. She gripped the shelf she'd used as a wedge. The surrounding darkness was a solid mass, stifling her, closing in on her, making her choke. Like an animal stuck deep in its warren she was being pursued, and it was a race to the kill. Whether she went up or down she'd surely meet her end.

More hammer blows rained down just above her head, and only a slab of two-inch-thick wood protected her from having a cracked skull. Panic seized her, making her weak with despair. Whatever Mr Preedy was using to try to get to her was heavy. Each frenzied smash made the lift judder.

'Don't think you can hide in there for ever,' he yelled, excited in pursuit of his prey. His voice was close, a few feet above. 'If it takes all night I'll get to you.'

In a wild paroxysm of terror, Antonia managed to shift her position, and, swivelling on her bottom, with her knees almost touching her shoulders, she pressed her feet against the brick side of the shaft. The shelf was still wedged tightly. If she braced her back against the side of the lift and her bare feet against the wall, it might help keep the dumb waiter in position.

There was a sudden pause, and silence. The sweat was running down her neck and body and she could smell her own fear in it. A wave of nausea nearly made her gag. It was the sheer helplessness of her position that made her want to sob with frustration. If only she had a weapon; something to protect herself with. She knew she wouldn't be afraid to use it, either. Her loathing for Mr Preedy made her feel murderous. Three women had already died because of him. Sudden resolution, born of terror, made her swear she wouldn't be the fourth.

The silence continued, unnerving in its intensity. She imagined his creeping around, planning another attack, looking for something else with which to dislodge her. She strained to listen. There was nothing. In her dark, cramped box, she might have been entombed deep underground, unaware of what was going on above. The nightmare of her situation brought feelings of desperation, and she was having to look deeply into herself to find the courage she needed if she wasn't going to crack up. She had to search for the strength to keep going or she'd be lost. All sense of time had deserted her. She was on her own and she knew no one was coming to rescue her, because no one knew where she was. Her mobile phone was useless, and anyway her shoulder bag had slipped behind her back and she daren't let go of the shelf to reach it.

Lack of air, heat and exhaustion made her close her eyes. She wondered how much longer she could last without seizing up with the pain in her back and her legs. Her head felt heavy, and only fear prevented her from becoming unconscious. This was a new threat she hadn't thought of before. Suppose she suffocated?

Her eyes drooped again and she was unable to keep them open. Her concentration was sliding away from her like fine sand trickling through her fingers . . . a sense of unreality drifted over her and she began to believe she was having a nightmare . . .

Then it happened. With shocking suddenness, her senses jolted back into consciousness and she gave a scream. She was being lifted . . . felt herself rising. Then realized it was the lift going up, slowly, jerkily, inch by inch. The shelf toppled from her grip. The soles of her feet scraped against the brick shaft . . .

'No . . .!' Her shriek rang out, reverberating in the confined space. 'No . . .!' Was Mr Preedy waiting for her in the dining room? Twisting that white cord in his hands, that mad expression in his eyes? She reached for the shaft as if to stop the lift ascending any more, but she grazed her knuckles. They stung with pain. She felt crushed and beaten. He'd won.

'. . . Come down, you bitch!'

She jumped from shock. His voice was directly underneath her . . . there was a dull thumping sound on the bottom of the lift. She realized he was back in the kitchen, that he was leaning into the shaft looking upwards, probing the dumb waiter in an effort to bring it down again.

Now she prayed for it to continue moving up. If she could get to the dining room before him . . . smash her way out of the house through a window . . . anything to get away . . .

Without warning the lift trembled, halted, then smashed back downwards, slamming against the base of the shaft with such violence Antonia felt like a rag doll being thrown about.

Her cry of alarm mingled with another cry. It was like the howl of a dog in agony. Her blood seemed to turn to ice surging sluggishly through her body. Then she peered cautiously out of the lift. The fridge door was still open. The small electric bulb inside was like a dazzling beam, until her eyes became accustomed to the light. Then she realized the dumb waiter had not reached the bottom of the shaft. It was nearly a foot above the base. Enough room for her to squeeze out through the opening, providing she ducked her head.

Gingerly sliding her feet out first, she suddenly drew back with a gasp of horror. She was sliding out over Mr Preedy's body. His top half had been trapped under the lift when it had smashed down. His bottom half hung limp, his feet dangling, barely touching the floor. In reaching up in an effort to dislodge her, he'd been taken by surprise when the lift had descended so suddenly.

'Oh, Christ . . .' Antonia whispered, trembling. She had to get out. She had to get away from here. With one swift movement, she pointed her feet at the floor, slithered forward, feeling the base of Mr Preedy's back against her own as she slid over him. Then she collapsed on the kitchen floor, her legs giving way beneath her. She couldn't stand. She could barely move. Hours of being curled up had left her legs numb, useless, the joints in agony.

A second later, the dumb waiter, relieved of her weight,

rose a few inches, and in so doing released Mr Preedy from underneath it. With a sickening thud, his body fell backwards, tumbling heavily on to the floor beside her. His head hit the tiles with a loud crack, splattering her with blood. She glanced fearfully at him. He lay still, his glasses shattered, his eyes shut, his face a bleeding pulp.

Staggering to her feet, Antonia straightened up slowly and painfully, grasping one of the lift doors for support. Somehow, exerting her last remnants of resolve, she managed to step over his body to reach into the lift for her handbag. Sobbing with weakness and shock, she opened it and took out her mobile. Then she stepped back and nearly tripped over his sprawled legs. Her one thought was to phone the police. Unsteadily, Antonia shuffled towards the stairs but her legs wouldn't support her. She stumbled and fell forward, landing on her hands and knees. Dragging herself forward on all fours, she glanced back at Mr Preedy. His eyes were open and he was watching her.

Ten

'My dear boy, what's this all about?' Tod Sylvester trotted into the interview room, his anxious face gathered like shiny pink silk into a rosette of a small mouth. Small and rotund, with blue eyes which, magnified by his glasses, seemed much too big for his face, he oozed concern and bewilderment.

'Where the hell have you been?' Mark Dryden cried. 'I rang your office *hours* ago. Sheila said she'd get hold of you right away; have you found a solicitor for me?' Tod Sylvester had been Mark's agent for the past nine years, and they had something of a love-hate relationship.

Flustered, Tod sat down facing him. 'I'm sorry, Mark—'

'Have you any idea what I've been through? They're accusing me of murdering three women and attempting to murder another, and they won't believe me when I say I don't know what they're talking about! And what about the evening performance? Did my understudy go on? Why have you taken *seven* hours to get here, for God's sake?' He was scarlet with frustration. 'Where's the solicitor?'

Tod swallowed and clasped his pudgy hands together.

'He'll be here in a minute. Everything's under control, Mark. Jake Hudson's on his way, too.' Jake was the company manager of *Cocktails for Two*. 'It seems to me,' Tod continued, 'that what you need more than anything is a character reference. This is obviously a case of mistaken identity.'

'You can say that again,' Mark said desperately.

'Don't worry, dear boy.' Tod's eyes seemed to pop behind the strong lenses. 'Brian Eccles, my solicitor, is on his way. He'll tell you what to say. We'll soon have you out of here.'

'Just tell them what you told me,' Brian Eccles advised Mark, half an hour later. 'There's nothing as good as the truth.' He was a young, go-ahead solicitor with an eager manner and driving ambition. When Tod Sylvester had woken him up sometime after midnight and asked him to come over to the Westminster police station to advise a young actor who seemed to be in a spot of trouble, Brian's heart had sunk. He was not into showbiz people, and presumed he was going to have to deal with some sort of gay drama. On second thoughts, however, he decided it might be a good opportunity to get some publicity for himself. Actors in trouble were always great fodder for the media.

Mark felt traumatized by his arrest, and now he knew he had to face being grilled by Detective Chief Inspector Cooper. The interview room was bare, except for a table with a cassette recorder on it, and three chairs. While Tod Sylvester, with Brian Eccles and Jake Hudson sat outside waiting, Cooper took his place opposite Mark, his face white and skeletal under the single overhead light. A uniformed policeman stood by the closed door. Cooper spoke first.

'Interview with Mark Dryden alias Colin Holbrook,' he began, 'on July twenty-first in the presence of DCI Cooper and Constable Coleman. Time: one thirty-six a.m.' He paused for a moment, looked searchingly into Mark's eyes and began.

'Your name?'

'Mark Dryden.'

'Age?'

'Thirty-four.'

'Address?'

'328, Battersea Bridge Road.'

'Occupation?'

'Actor.'

'Do you ever go under the name of Colin Holbrook?'

'No.'

'Or James Maxwell?'

Mark shook his head. 'No.

'Have you at any time bought or rented a flat or room at 26 Cloudesley Road, Islington?'

'Never. I've been in Battersea for the past eight years.'

'Do you know a woman called Pauline Ashford?'

'No.'

'Or Valerie Martin?'

Mark frowned, puzzled. 'No, I told you, I've never heard of any of these names.'

'Roxana Birch?'

'No.'

Cooper continued, never slacking the pace. 'Where were you on the night of the seventh of February?'

'On stage at the Royalty Theatre.'

'What about the night of the eleventh of April? Can you

remember what you were doing then?'

'Yes. I was on stage. I've been in *Cocktails for Two* for the past seven months.'

'What were you doing on the night of the eighteenth April?'

Mark tried to be patient. 'I was on stage.'

'And after that? What do you do after the curtain comes down?'

'I usually go to a restaurant with friends.'

'I shall want to know who these friends are but meanwhile, where were you on the night of the twelfth June?'

'The same.'

'What does that mean?'

'I was also on stage that night.'

'But only until, what, ten-thirty?'

'Yes, and I always go out afterwards.'

'*Every* night?' Cooper spoke as if such extravagance was a wicked, unheard-of luxury.

'I only have a light snack before a show,' Mark pointed out. 'Then I eat properly afterwards.'

DCI Cooper changed tack. 'Are you in the habit of mailing lots of photographs of yourself to just anyone who asks?'

On and on the interrogation went, drilling into Mark's tired mind until he felt like crying. Cooper's questions sounded as if he thought Mark came from another planet; did this crafty-looking rodent-faced man know *anything* about the theatre, Mark wondered?

'I'll have to get all this verified,' Cooper said at last, in a tone that suggested it was very unlikely he'd be able to do so. He switched off the recorder, having announced that the 'interview ended at two-twenty-three a.m'. Then he rose to leave.

'My agent, Tod Sylvester and the company manager, Jake Hudson will be able to confirm everything I've told you,' Mark said, raising his chin and looking Cooper straight in the eye.

'Well, we'll see about that,' the DCI replied dismissively.

Terror gave Antonia the strength she needed. Without a backward glance she made for the stairs on her hands and knees, her breath coming in sobbing gasps. Her legs felt as if they were made of rubber, but she grasped the black iron handrail and managed to pull herself up the flight of stone stairs, step by painful step. Her progress seemed torturously slow. Every muscle from her waist down felt as if it were being torn by hot pincers. Only the thought of Mr Preedy catching up with her kept her going. There were only five . . . four more steps to go. She was nearly at the top.

Then she heard movements behind her. She didn't dare look back, down into the murky depths of the kitchen.

'Oh God . . .' she said under her breath. 'Oh, please God . . .'

Desperation helped her conquer the last three steps. The sweat was pouring down her back from the effort, and her legs felt on fire, but she was now in the darkness of the hall. The sprawling ladders and overturned paint pots that she'd scattered in her wake formed a barrier between her and the front door.

Somehow she had to get over them in order to escape. Inching forward, she accidentally kicked a galvanized pail.

It rolled away with a clanking sound and hit the skirting board. The only illumination came from a street lamp shining through the dining-room windows, spilling through the open doorway into the hall. The front door was less than thirty feet away. Antonia knew she must be careful not to trip on one of the rungs of a ladder or slip on the spilled paint. Her heart hammered against her ribcage, and there was a roaring, like the sea, in her ears. Frightened she might faint, she took deep breaths, and tried to quell the dizziness that threatened to make her black out. She stepped over the first ladder, as gingerly as if it had been a landmine. Pausing for a second, trying to gather herself together, she heard the sound of feet shuffling up the stairs from the kitchen. He was coming after her. In spite of his injuries, *he was coming after her.* For a moment total terror nearly made her collapse. When would this nightmare end? The footsteps came nearer. Now she knew she'd never make it to the front door in time.

Antonia acted quickly and without hesitation. Picking up a five-gallon tin of gloss paint from the floor, she staggered under its weight as she made her way back to the top of the stairs. She peered down to the shadowy depths below. Mr Preedy, grotesque-looking and bloodied, was swaying as he clung to the banister. Then he lurched forward, coming nearer. A length of white cord was still wrapped around one of his hands. Seeing her, he pulled himself up another step. There was not a moment to lose. Raising the heavy tin in both hands, she flung it at him with all her strength. As she turned to rush back towards the front door she heard a piercing screech. Then the tumbling and thudding of a body falling back helplessly down the stairs.

Grabbing her phone from where she'd dropped it, she fled across the darkened hall. The bolts of the street door slid back as smoothly as silk. Wrenching the door open, the fresh cold night air took her breath away and made her feel dizzy.

'Please help me . . .' she sobbed, stumbling down the wide steps to the pavement, as she punched out 999. 'For God's sake someone, please come and help me . . .'

Eleven

Antonia shuddered and her teeth started to chatter, as an icy wind blasted across the wide expanse of Belgrave Square. It was still dark but only just. The first pearly-grey light of a summer's day was beginning to change the tops of the trees from black to a pale glimmer of green. In the distance she could hear the piercing scream of police sirens coming nearer. She clutched her arms tighter across her front, holding the warmth of her stomach to herself, bowing her head forward, closing her eyes and silently thanking God that rescue was on its way. When she'd escaped she'd staggered along the pavement to a house four doors away, and it was in the shelter of its pillared portico that she crouched now, hidden from Mr Preedy in case he should come after her.

Help is on its way, she thought. But she was so numbed by shock that a sense of unreality made her feel detached; had she endured nearly twelve hours of being threatened? Hours when she'd believed her life to be in danger? And had she really managed to escape? It seemed at this moment as if the terrible ordeal she'd been through had happened to someone else. She could hardly believe that she was still alive and that her nerves hadn't completely cracked. But there was Mr Preedy; was he dead? What in God's name would happen if she'd actually killed him?

Antonia bit her lip, determined not to give way now. The police were on their way and they would have to deal with Mr Preedy. She would be able to let go, at last, and relinquish all responsibility for him and for herself. The thought should have brought relief, but instead she felt nothing. Except cold, and immensely weary.

A car came hurtling round the wide road that circled the two-acre gardens in the middle of Belgrave Square. Its headlights were blazing. They were looking at her. Her nerves, as if reactivated by an electric shock, were set jangling once more, and she started shaking. This wasn't a police car. There was no reassuring flashing blue light on the roof or white paintwork. This was an ordinary and rather grubby Ford Escort, and it was squealing to a halt, the brakes slammed on, and the man in the front passenger seat was already half out of the door on his side.

As it halted yards away from her, he jumped out and raced across the pavement to where she crouched. In the murky light she saw that he was wearing a tracksuit and trainers.

'Are you all right?' He spoke urgently.

Antonia looked up at him, shocked. The second man came leaping up the steps.

'We're plain-clothes police officers,' he said hurriedly, seeing her expression. 'Have you been hurt?' His dark eyes were full of concern as he gazed down at her.

'I'm . . . I'm fine,' she replied, finding her voice.

At that moment the street became a chaotic mêlée of police cars and vans, their sirens petering out to a whimper as the vehicles stopped, forming a blockade across the road. Uniformed officers swarmed out like black beetles. Motorcyclists roared up, their helmets gleaming, their radios crackling in the cold morning air. There were shouted orders from the police officers and two constables were unwinding large rolls of blue and white tape, which they were stretching between railings and lamp-posts as they cordoned off the area.

Dazed, Antonia watched the activity of the uniformed and the plain-clothes police from where she sat. Then, recognizing DCI Cooper with his distinctive pinched face, she emerged slowly from her hiding place and walked towards them.

He didn't notice her for a moment, and then he blinked as if startled to see her, his eyes sharp in the growing light.

'I thought it was *this* house . . .?' he said sharply, pointing to the building where Mr Preedy lay.

'It is,' she replied in a small voice. 'He's . . . Mr Preedy's in the basement. I don't know whether . . .'

'Is he armed?' Cooper demanded roughly.

'I think he's . . . *dead*.'

Like a banshee mourning the dead and dying, the wail of an ambulance added to the noise and bustle of activity that had now spread along the west side of the square.

Cooper's expression didn't flicker. 'Let's go in then.' An ambulance came swerving round the square and stopped a few feet away. 'I'll get the paramedics to take care of you,' he said, turning to Antonia.

'I'm really OK,' Antonia said, but she didn't feel it.

The ground was cold beneath her bare feet and she suddenly felt sick with tiredness. Swaying, she reached out to hold on to the bonnet of one of the police cars to stop herself falling.

At a signal from the DCI, two burly paramedics, who had jumped out of the back of the ambulance, hurried to her side, each taking one of her arms. 'Why don't you come and sit down for a few minutes, Miss?' They half lifted her into the vehicle. 'We'll just check you over.'

Unresisting, she submitted herself to their cheerful ministrations as they settled her on the bench inside the vehicle, took her blood pressure and gave her a glass of water.

'This will have ruined my mother's birthday dinner,' she said regretfully. 'I must phone them to say I'm all right.'

'You can go in a few minutes,' the older one reassured her. 'Your blood pressure's normal, but you should rest.'

The water revived her and she began to feel the strength returning to her limbs. She removed her torn tights and one of them dabbed her grazed knees and knuckles with disinfectant.

'I'm OK now, really,' she said, rising. 'I've left my mobile on the doorstep and I want to phone my family.'

As she stepped out of the ambulance she glanced at the house where the police were still milling around. At that moment they were bringing Mr Preedy out on a stretcher. He was covered with a blanket and she couldn't see his face.

'Is he dead?' she asked, stricken.

No one answered her. The paramedics from the second ambulance were grouped around the stretcher-bearers and after a moment, they all got into the vehicle and the doors were slammed shut. Then it streaked away into the blue dawn, its siren rending the still morning air.

DCI Cooper strode up to her. 'We'll have to send someone into the house later on today to gather evidence,' he announced in a calm voice, as if no more than a domestic burglary had taken place. 'Do you know how this man got in, in the first place?'

'He probably fooled the builders, as he did my assistant, by saying he was from the flooring company we were using.'

'Have you got a key to the premises, Miss Murray? We'll need to secure it for the time being.'

'Yes. I'll get it for you.' She started padding towards the house. He suddenly noticed her feet were bare.

'You've got no shoes,' he exclaimed.

'My shoes are in the house. So is my handbag with the keys. I still have to get my phone so I can tell my family I'm all right. I was supposed to—'

'They've been informed that you're safe.' When Antonia looked surprised, he added, 'Your father reported you as missing at midnight.'

'Oh, poor Daddy!' She was appalled, but not surprised. She'd spent a lot of the night worrying about *them* being worried.

'One of my men will get your things for you.' The DCI's tone was kindly, satisfied. It would go down on record that he'd been the one to arrest the dangerous serial killer of lonely career women; it would no doubt lead to a commendation.

Antonia spoke firmly. 'No. I'll go.'

He started to protest. 'But I don't think—'

'This is something I have to do. Houses are my business and if I don't go in there now . . .' She looked over to the open front door through which she'd run screaming only a short while ago. 'Well . . . I'll be scared of going into empty houses for the rest of my life.'

The DCI wasn't convinced. 'There's no electricity,' he protested. 'My men had a hell of a job finding their way about.'

'I know. I disconnected it.' She hurried up the front steps, past a group of policemen who were looking at her with puzzled expressions.

They'd cleared a pathway through the debris in the hall, pushing the ladders and paint pots to either side, to enable them to bring Mr Preedy out. One of them shone a bright torch to help her pick her way. Then, borrowing the torch, she strode silently along the hall and started to make her way to the kitchen. It was a bad moment. In her mind's eye she could still see Mr Preedy, with his face smashed, coming up the stairs to get her.

Antonia braced herself, knowing she'd be lost if she let her imagination get a hold. The worst was over. She had to tell herself that all she had to do now was come to terms with the memories.

In the kitchen the fridge door was still wide open, its light revealing the blood on the terracotta tiles where he'd lain when he'd fallen out of the dumb waiter. The doors to the lift were still gaping wide, the dark confined space where she'd hidden for nearly eleven hours hollow and empty.

Antonia had to reach deep into herself, in order not to go running back up the stairs screaming. Terror gripped her again as she fought to gain control. This nightmare *had* to be exorcised or she knew she'd get a phobia about basements . . . especially in empty houses. With a quick decisive movement, she reached for the sliding panel behind the kitchen door, opened it, and threw the switch. Instantly the place was flooded with light. Suddenly the kitchen looked strangely ordinary and normal, with its smoked-oak units and stainless-steel fittings. Even the dumb waiter looked like a practical piece of catering equipment and nothing more. Nevertheless, she grabbed her handbag and her shoes from the floor and turned and hurried back up the stairs, not stopping until she was in the street again.

Hilary was still awake, lying on top of the bed in her best dinner dress, when the phone on the beside table gave a shrill ring. Startled, her heart suddenly pounding, she reached for it, but Quentin, in the next room, had already picked it up. A moment later she heard him exclaim, 'Antonia!'

Hilary clambered off the bed and hurried into the sitting room, hardly daring to believe that her daughter was really on the line. She looked at Quentin and he nodded, his eyes shining.

'I'll pass you over to Mummy,' she heard him say, handing her the receiver.

'Darling?' Hilary found she was shaking so much she had to sit down. 'Are you all right, darling? You've no idea how worried we've been.' At the sound of Antonia's voice she started weeping. 'Oh! My baby . . .'

Quentin dropped limply on to the sofa. He seemed to have aged ten years in the last few hours. Tristram, sitting beside him, put his hand on his shoulder in an almost paternal gesture.

'Are you bearing up all right, Dad?'

Quentin nodded. 'She's on her way to the police station to make a statement. She'll come here as soon as she can.'

'Is she really OK?' Roland was blaming himself, to a certain extent, for what had happened. He should have kept closer to Antonia to make sure she didn't get involved with a stranger, but then he'd underestimated her need for someone. With the wonderful lifestyle she'd created for herself she was the envy of most of her young friends; no one, not even he, had realized how deep was her longing to have someone to share it with.

'Antonia sounded fine, but exhausted, of course,' Quentin replied. 'She kept saying she was sorry for not turning up tonight. She said she'd tell us all about it when she sees us.'

Hilary came off the phone at that moment, half laughing and half crying. 'Oh, isn't that wonderful?' She wiped her cheeks with her fingertips. 'She's safe. She's all right. Apparently she's been stuck in one of her houses all night, with this man who wanted to kill her. Oh! My God, I thought we'd never see her again.' Her voice wobbled dangerously.

Tristram rose to his feet and went and perched on the arm of her chair, and gave her a hug. The child had become the parent to both his mother and father.

'Shall I order some coffee?' Leo asked, anxious to be helpful.

'That's a good idea, old boy,' Quentin replied. 'We're not going to get any sleep now, so we may as well stay thoroughly awake.'

Roland, hunched morosely in a deep armchair, spoke. 'I feel strung out. My head's splitting. I cannot *believe* what's happened. Did she really sound all right, Ma?'

Composed again, Hilary's smile was still wan. 'Yes, she did. But you know Antonia; she always puts a plucky face on everything.'

Antonia sat in the back of DCI Cooper's car as they sped through the empty streets to the police station, where she was going to make her statement. As they drove away from Belgrave Square the dawn chorus of blackbird and thrush, from the high perches of the trees in the middle garden, was in full spate. In Grosvenor Place they passed an early lone red bus with only three passengers on board. Londoners were beginning to awaken to a new day, and Antonia wondered when she was going to get a chance to go to bed and get some sleep.

'We're just finishing the paperwork and then you'll be able to go,' Detective Sergeant Ambrose informed Mark Dryden, who was still sitting waiting in the interview room at the police station.

Mark half rose. 'I can leave . . .?' His eyes lit up with relief. 'Thank God for that.'

'Yes, sir. We've verified your statement, with the help of Mr Sylvester and Mr Hudson. You're in the clear, sir.'

'Is my agent still here?'

'Yes, Mr Sylvester's waiting outside, sir. He thought you might like a lift home.'

Mark found Tod sitting with Jake Hudson and Brian Eccles on a bench in the general waiting area. As soon as they saw him, Tod gave a loud exclamation of delight.

'Ah! Dear boy, there you are! They tell me you can go

home as soon as they've got through the red tape! Come and sit down. Listen, do you know the whole story? Have they told you what was behind your arrest?' Like a gossiping old woman, his mouth pursed tighter than ever, his blue eyes popping behind his glasses, he launched into what he had to say without giving either Jake Hudson or the solicitor a chance to speak.

'You know you were saying how you wanted to write a film script, but you couldn't find a good story? Well, dear boy, *this is it*! It's got *everything*: rich, successful young woman . . . great settings in big mansions . . . a serial killer who has already committed three murders . . . mistaken identity . . . she's held hostage in a lift . . .!'

'Steady on, Tod. Start from the beginning. Which young woman are you talking about?'

'The one that set the police on to *you*, dear boy. Do concentrate. Listen, I believe she's on her way *here*, to make a statement. You can see her for yourself. Apparently . . .' and Tod was off again, jabbering rapidly as he repeated the gist of what he'd found out, as he'd sat watching and listening with the avid curiosity of an old cat. Detective Sergeant Ambrose had let slip a few details, too, and ever the opportunist, Tod Sylvester saw the whole incident as an opportunity to promote his client, and at the same time, provide him with a plot for his proposed film script.

When Tod finally came to the end, pausing to look at Mark questioningly and obviously waiting to be congratulated on his brilliant suggestion, Mark crinkled his brow and looked far from enthusiastic.

'Well? Don't you think it's *great*?' Tod insisted. 'You

could play yourself, dear boy. We'd have to cast this girl, whatever her name is . . . Annabel or Antonia or something . . . with a big box-office name. I wonder who we should go for? Emma Thompson is not glamorous enough; what about Claudia Schiffer?'

'Hang on a minute,' Mark protested. 'We can't hijack someone's terrible experience and turn it into a script, just like that!'

Tod's face was blank with astonishment. 'Why not?'

'Because you can't. It's not on, Tod. The last thing this young woman is going to want is to have her story made into a film. Think about it! It would be a terrible intrusion into her private life. There's no way I could do such a thing.' Mark spoke quite heatedly.

'Well, I think it's very silly of you to turn down an opportunity like this, without even *thinking* about it,' Tod snapped huffily. 'You wouldn't even have to do any research.'

'I think you should give it serious consideration,' Brian Eccles remarked, resting his elbows on his shiny briefcase, which was on his knee. Mark noticed that, in the light of the day, his suit was shiny, too.

'Think of the publicity!' Brian continued, eagerly. 'The Americans would love it because it'd be based on fact, and that goes down so well these days.'

Jake Hudson, who kept the company of *Cocktails for Two* on an even keel, said nothing but he gave Mark a sympathetic wink to signify that he agreed with him.

At that moment Detective Sergeant Ambrose came forward with Mark's discharge papers and he was free to go.

'Do you want a lift home?' Tod asked.

'That's OK, I'll pick up a cab,' Mark replied. 'Thanks for coming to my rescue, Tod. I really appreciate it.'

'Then I'll be off.' Both he and Jake creaked to their feet, two men who liked to pretend they were much younger than they were, caught out now by a long night of real drama.

'If you need any further help give me a call,' Brian Eccles said, flashing his business card under Mark's nose. 'I'm always ready to help.'

Yes, and to charge me through the nose, Mark inwardly reflected, not liking the solicitor at all.

They departed, anxious to be off, while Mark said goodbye to Detective Sergeant Ambrose. Then, as he turned to leave the station, a group of police officers arrived with a young woman in their midst. She was tall and very slender and Mark had an impression of pale, delicate features with large dark eyes, a shoulder-length sweep of dark hair and long shapely legs. Without being told, he knew instinctively that she was the girl in the story Tod had just told him. But Tod hadn't known about her beauty, or her mixture of vulnerability and strength, which gave her an air of dignity, even in her crumpled suit.

Then she saw him, and for a second she froze as their eyes locked.

'Oh, you must let him go!' Antonia turned to Cooper in agitation. 'He's innocent! I got it terribly wrong. You're not charging him, are you? Mr Preedy confessed that Colin Holbrook didn't exist . . . that he only used Mark Dryden's photograph!' She was red in the face and gesticulating with her hands.

'We're not detaining Mr Dryden,' Cooper replied, calmly. 'He's no longer a suspect.'

Antonia exhaled with relief. 'Oh, thank God!' Then she turned to Mark and he had the feeling, as he looked into her eyes, that he'd known her for a long time. 'I'm really sorry,' she said contritely. 'I was so *sure* . . . Oh! it must have been a nightmare for you. I feel dreadful now.'

He smiled gently, wanting to reassure her. 'You weren't to know. I gather you've been through a much worse experience.'

A shadow passed across her face and he noticed her grazed knuckles as she placed the flat of her hand on her upper chest, as if to still her heart.

'Yes,' she said simply, dropping her gaze to the floor.

'Will you come this way, please, Miss Murray,' DCI Cooper interjected, as he led the way along a corridor. For a moment she recovered herself, and followed the detective into a room. A moment later the door closed behind her and she was gone.

Mark turned away and was about to leave, find himself a taxi and get back to his Battersea flat, when a sudden compulsion to stay overtook him. Fate had inextricably linked him to Antonia Murray under bizarre circumstances, and he felt a sense of responsibility towards her. After all, it was *his* photograph that had set her on such a disastrous route, although he'd had no part in sending it to her. And she'd thought she was meeting *him* when she arranged her dates with Colin Holbrook!

He returned to the bench and sat down again, knowing he couldn't simply walk away and leave her here, to be interrogated by the foxy-faced Cooper, as she made her statement. She'd looked on the point of collapse, although she'd held her head high, but her face showed the stress she'd been suffering during her long night of terror, and Mark's heart went out to her.

Detective Sergeant Ambrose strolled past on his way off duty. 'You're free to go, you know, sir,' he pointed out, looking puzzled at seeing Mark still sitting there.

'I thought I'd wait for Antonia Murray. Say I'm sorry for what happened,' Mark replied.

Ambrose gave a quirky smile. 'Say *you're* sorry? It was thanks to Miss Murray that you were arrested. You've no reason to apologize to her, sir.'

'It looks like we were both victims,' Mark replied. 'What's happened to the man who's responsible for all this?'

'As far as I know he hasn't regained consciousness. They've taken him to Chelsea and Westminster Hospital.' Ambrose shuffled from one foot to the other, anxious to leave. 'Let's hope he doesn't die, or Miss Murray could be up on a charge of manslaughter. Goodbye, sir. I'll be off now.'

Mark watched him go, his last words digging a hole deep in his brain. Manslaughter. That would be the worst injustice in the world.

Antonia's statement, taken down in minute detail, was completed, ready for her to sign. It had taken over two hours of questioning, but finally DCI Cooper, looking more gaunt and ashen than ever, laid the computer printout in front of her, admonishing her first to read it through carefully. From years of practice at reading surveyors' reports and builders' estimates, she read it swiftly and then, borrowing Cooper's pen, signed her name with a flourish.

'Can I go now? I want to see my family. They've been waiting for me since seven-thirty last night,' she said, plaintively.

'Yes, of course. We all have homes to go to, don't we?' For the first time, he gave a weary smile. 'Thank you for your cooperation, Miss Murray. I'll keep in close touch. A lot will depend on when, or *if*, Alec Preedy regains consciousness. As I expect you know, it could be very serious for you if he were to die.' He paused and the silence between them grew heavy.

For a second Antonia covered her face with her hands. Then she looked up at him, composed and in control. 'I'll face that eventuality when – and if – it comes.'

As he escorted her to the main entrance, she saw with astonishment that Mark was still sitting on the hard wooden bench.

'Are you still here?' she exclaimed. 'I thought they'd said you could leave hours ago?'

He rose, smiling. 'They did, but I was waiting for you.'

'Oh!' Her expression melted from curious, to warmly appreciative. 'That's so nice of you, I'd no idea . . .' She was lost for further words, submerged in the eyes she already knew so well, and the humorous mouth she'd found so attractive in the photograph. For a long moment they stared at each other, forgetting their surroundings, forgetting DCI Cooper, who was fidgeting to leave, unaware of everything except each other.

'Can I give you a lift?' he asked, breaking the spell.

'Thank you,' she replied automatically. A sense of unreality enveloped her, and as she followed him on to the street and watched as he hailed a passing taxi, a voice in her head kept saying, *This can't be happening. This is the man I chose to meet . . . The man I've dreamed about . . .*

As she stepped into the taxi her face was flushed, and she could barely bring herself to look at him.

'Where to?'

'Oh, the Savoy, please.'

'Right.' A flicker of surprise showed in his eyes, as he climbed in beside her.

'My parents are staying there, with my brothers,' she explained hurriedly. 'It was my mother's birthday dinner last night, and I was supposed to join them . . .' Her voice drifted away as she sat staring out of the window, as the taxi bowled along the Mall, past the morning greenness of St James's Park. She was still feeling too strung out to be relaxed. The impact of meeting Mark face to face had shaken her deeply and now she had this new worry: what if Mr Preedy died? She was only half paying attention to what Mark was saying, but suddenly his words had meaning, took form, required an answer.

'Yes, I'll give you my phone number,' she heard herself say.

'Perhaps we could meet after the show tonight?' He paused and then added touchingly, 'I'd like to tell you, properly, how really distressed I am about all this.'

She glanced at him, enthralled that he was just the sort of person she thought he'd be.

'And I have to say how sorry I am that I set the police on

you. It must have been an awful shock. You must have wondered what on earth was going on.'

'I can understand how it happened, though. It was my photograph you were sent. It's no wonder you thought I was responsible for what happened.'

'I thought we were having long phone conversations, too.' She shook her head. 'I really thought I knew you; now I know why you didn't recognize me when you left the theatre under police escort.'

He raised his dark, dart-shaped eyebrows and looked at her curiously. 'You were there?'

'Yes. I was with my parents and you glanced in my direction. It surprised me at the time that you didn't recognize me.'

'So can we meet tonight?' Mark asked softly.

Suddenly the tension in the small confines of the taxi made Antonia's heart thump uncomfortably. Mark was looking at her with those glinting dark eyes she already knew so well, and the corners of his mouth were turning up attractively.

'Yes,' she said simply, because there was no other possible answer.

'Why don't you come backstage after the show? The curtain comes down at ten-fifteen. We can have a drink and then go on to a restaurant.'

'That sounds great,' Antonia agreed, smiling limply. 'That is, if I'm still standing by then!'

'You should get some rest today. Can you go home to bed after you've seen your parents?'

'Probably,' she said vaguely.

The taxi entered the Savoy's courtyard and swerved to a

stop by the revolving glass doors, on either side of which stood neat bay trees, stiff as sentries.

Mark got out of the taxi and then escorted Antonia to the entrance. 'I'll see you tonight, then.'

'Yes.' For once Antonia didn't care that she looked a mess in her crumpled suit, with grazed knees and hands, unbrushed hair and wrecked make-up.

The uniformed doorman was looking at her strangely.

'It's all right,' she informed him blithely, as she turned away from Mark, 'I'm expected for dinner, and I'm only fourteen hours late!'

It was late-morning by the time Antonia finished telling her family the whole story. After she'd phoned a horrified Linda to tell her what had happened, and to say she wouldn't be in today, she filled in the missing gaps of what her family already knew.

'And it's far from over,' she concluded. 'If this man Mr Preedy dies, I'm in very serious trouble.'

'But you were defending yourself,' Quentin protested.

'I could still be on a charge of manslaughter.' Suddenly she covered her face with her hands, and she was shaking all over. 'If only I hadn't thrown the pot of paint at him! I think I'd have still got out of that house without doing that, but I was so *scared*.'

Hilary went and put her arms around her. 'Those are mitigating circumstances after all he'd subjected you to,' she said firmly. 'Daddy will get on to his old friend, Edward Crosby. He's a brilliant QC. He'll look after you, if needs be.'

'I really doubt if the police will bring charges, Antonia,' Tristram said. 'What were you supposed to do? Hang around and let this maniac kill you?'

She raised her head to look at him, her eyes full of pain. 'I was warned, at the police station this morning, that I could be in trouble.'

'Then I'll get on to Edward today,' Quentin assured her.

Antonia went to the bathroom to wash her face and borrow her mother's hairbrush, and when she returned to the sitting room, they were talking quietly among themselves about what had happened.

'I *knew* she was taking a risk . . .' she heard Roland say, then he broke off when he saw her.

'You're right,' Antonia told him. 'I was taking a risk and I'm sorry I didn't tell you I was going ahead anyway, but I knew you wouldn't approve and I didn't want to worry you.'

Quentin looked at her and spoke compassionately. 'It's not a case of approving or disapproving, darling girl. I'm so sorry you felt the need to find someone in that way. We'd no idea you felt so lonely.'

'It's more than loneliness,' Antonia replied, lying back on one of the sofas while Roland sat by her bare feet. 'It's a sense of failure, a gradual feeling that descends that there must be something wrong with me.'

Hilary, shocked by this, started to protest, but Antonia shook her head.

'You don't understand, Ma. I know there's nothing *actually* wrong with me; it's just that I'm at risk of missing the boat. In your day girls didn't work as hard as we do now and the work they did was a way of passing the time until they got married. Women have careers now, not just jobs. Apart from that romance I had a few years ago, which was going *nowhere*, I've never had the time to get to know anyone well enough to develop a proper relationship. I'm not complaining because I wanted to concentrate on getting Murray Properties up and running, and that's what I've done, but somehow I'd assumed I'd get married by the time I was thirty. Then suddenly I'm thirty-one, thirty-two, and all the men I meet are either married, gay, or absolute dweebs. You've no idea how out of it I felt at Susan Sinclair's wedding. Everyone seemed to be married and to have children, and there was I, on my own as usual.'

'You shouldn't worry about what other people think,' Tristram remarked. At thirty-four he rather prided himself on still being single in spite of there always being droves of girls after him.

Antonia sat up straight. 'I don't. But the time has come when I long for someone special in my life. I also want children before I get too old.'

The yearning in her voice made Hilary feel wrenched with pity. What Antonia had said was true. Her generation had been able to devote most of their time to presenting themselves, looking pretty, at scores of parties attended by eligible young men who were also wanting to marry. It was the top priority for girls, their whole *raison d'être*. No one, but absolutely no one, in her day, would have resorted to going on a blind date through a highly organized marriage bureau, far less to putting an advertisement in a national newspaper. But then none of her friends had wanted a serious career either.

Leo leaned forward, fascinated. 'So what's this Mark Dryden like?' he asked, curiously.

Antonia, to her annoyance, found herself flushing. 'He's very nice,' she said curtly.

'Are you seeing him again?'

Antonia hesitated, not wanting her youngest brother probing into something so new and tender.

Leo continued bluntly, 'After all, he's the one you chose from all the applicants. You must have found him attractive?'

'That's enough, Leo,' Quentin said firmly. 'Antonia needs to rest. You should go home, darling girl, and—'

Antonia gave a little scream and clapped her hand over her mouth.

'What's the matter?' Hilary asked, alarmed.

Antonia jumped to her feet, scrabbling for her shoes. 'I've forgotten about Crash! He won't have been fed since I left the flat yesterday morning. I must go, Ma. I must get back and feed him.'

Roland clambered off the sofa. 'I'm coming with you.'

'There's no need.'

'I want to,' he insisted. 'I'm not having you go home alone, after all you've been through.'

'And I suppose we should be getting back to the country,' Hilary remarked sadly.

Antonia's eyes were bright with unshed tears as she hugged her parents, and then Tristram and Leo.

'I've really screwed up Mummy's birthday celebrations, haven't I?' she said, trying to cover up her emotional state by being jokey. 'We'll have to do the whole thing again, on me next time, and I promise not to stay out all night.'

They laughed with her, determined to keep the mood light for her sake, because it was obvious the least thing would crack wide her determination to remain controlled.

'I'll be down at the weekend,' she promised.

'That *will* be lovely, darling,' Quentin said warmly. 'And try not to worry about this man, Preedy. He's sure to be all right, and if he's not, no one will blame you for what happened. You did what you had to do.'

Antonia nodded, unable to speak.

'Of course you'll be OK,' Tristram said stoutly.

'Now hurry along and feed that little furry animal of yours,' Hilary urged gently.

As the taxi sped along the Strand, heading for the Mall, Antonia suddenly saw, on a street vendor's kiosk, a pile of *Evening Standard*s. Mark's picture was on the cover, under the banner headline WEST END STAR ARRESTED.

She gripped Roland's arm. 'God! Look at that! Now I suppose the whole story will come out!'

Roland craned his neck to get a better look. 'I guess Mark Dryden's publicity machine has gone into overdrive. People will be queuing round the block to see *Cocktails for Two* after this.'

When they arrived at her flat, Antonia hurried ahead while her brother paid the cab. When she opened the front door, Crash came trotting towards her, miaowing loudly.

'Oh, my baby!' She dropped to her knees, picked him up and held him close. 'I'm so glad to see you again.' He purred loudly in appreciation and started kneading her shoulder with pinprick claws. 'You must be starving.' Getting up, she carried him along the corridor to the kitchen.

The door was open and she stood stock-still, looking around in astonishment. 'What the . . .?'

The fridge door was open, and the kitchen floor was strewn with chicken bones, the empty wrapping from a pound of Harrods' sausages and most of the contents of the two bottom shelves, which included a spilled jug of cream.

With a cheerful chirrup, Crash struggled out of her arms, and jumping down to the floor, continued to scavenge with a blissful expression on his face.

'Well, you needn't have worried about *him* starving to death,' Roland remarked from the doorway, where he stood surveying the mess. 'While you've been in jeopardy he's obviously been having the picnic of a lifetime.' He tweaked the cat's ear affectionately. 'You know how to look after yourself, don't you, old mate?'

'Now he knows how to open the fridge I'll have to get a lock for it,' Antonia laughed indulgently, as she got out a dustpan and brush.

'Here, let me. You go and have a bath and a rest.' Roland spoke with unusual firmness. She could hardly hide her relief.

'Are you *sure*, Ro? The floor's going to need washing . . .'

The ringing of the phone made her break off in mid-sentence. She looked at it nervously.

'I'll get it for you,' said Roland. A few moments later he handed it to her. 'It's Mark Dryden,' he mouthed discreetly.

'Antonia?' Mark sounded fraught. 'God! I'm sorry! I could *kill* my agent for giving the story to the newspapers. Have you seen it?'

'I haven't read it but I caught a glimpse of the front page on my way home,' she said coolly.

'I would never have let this happen if that scumbag had told me what he was going to do. I can't tell you how badly I feel.'

Listening to him, Antonia realized he was genuinely shocked and upset. 'I wish it hadn't happened either, especially in this sensational way,' she admitted. 'I suppose I was naive to think there'd be no mention at all, but I didn't expect this.'

'Neither did I. There was no need for this. I don't know what to do, now. If I deny the story it will only make things worse. I've had the satisfaction of giving Tod the boot, but that's no consolation to you, and doesn't make up for having your name plastered all over the papers,' he added in distress.

'At least they haven't got my photograph,' she said drily.

There was a pause, then he spoke. 'There *is* a picture of you actually. Looking wonderful, in a big cream hat with roses . . .'

Antonia remembered she'd been photographed in that hat at Susan Sinclair's wedding. 'Oh, well . . .!' she began to laugh softly. 'That's it then. There's nothing we can do except ride out the storm. What is it they say? Today's news is tomorrow's fish and chip wrapping? Hopefully people will have forgotten by this time next week.'

'I hope you're right. Listen, the paparazzi are going to be hanging around the stage door tonight, so instead of coming to the theatre, why don't we meet in a quiet restaurant? How about Santini's, in Ebury Street?'

'Yes, OK. I suppose it won't take much for them to find out where I live.'

'I'm really sorry, Antonia.'

'It's not your fault.' When she'd bid him goodbye, she went back to the kitchen. Roland had swept up the mess and was now tackling the floor with a mop and bucket, while Crash had left in a huff.

The phone rang again while she was in the bath. A few minutes later Roland announced through the bathroom door that Barbara was coming round for a drink, when she'd finished work.

'She's seen the newspapers and she's horrified at what you've been through. She rang up to ask how you were and if there was anything she could do.'

'That's nice of her,' Antonia agreed. 'Was she surprised to find you here?'

'Sort of.' He sounded, she thought with amusement, very pleased with himself.

'Is it all right,' he continued to shout through the door, 'if I stay the night on your sofa? I thought I might take Barbara out for a bite of food, after we've had drinks.'

'Be my guest!' Antonia replied gaily, glad he couldn't see her grinning face.

Twelve

Antonia knew she ought to rest, but she was still on an adrenalin high, with scenes from the previous night replaying over and over in her head. Sleep would be impossible if she did lie down, and so she decided to go over to the office to see what was happening.

'You're mad,' Roland informed her. 'You'll collapse at this rate. You're running away from what happened when you should be relaxing and taking stock.'

'Since when have you become a psychiatrist?' she demanded. 'I'm only going to stay at the office for an hour or so.'

'Then do you mind if I lie on your bed for a kip?' he asked, with a slightly embarrassed air. 'I'm bushed by being up all night, wondering what had happened to you.'

'You obviously feel worse than I do,' she said with an irony that was lost on him.

Antonia's arrival at the office was greeted with stunned looks and cries of amazement. She also noticed copies of the *Evening Standard* lying around.

'What are you doing here?' Linda exclaimed. 'My God, are you all right, Antonia?'

They all grouped around her, looking at her with concern.

'We didn't expect to see you for days,' said Sally. 'I can't believe what happened.'

Linda looked crushed. 'It was my fault you went round to Belgrave Square.'

'You weren't to know,' Antonia assured her. 'If I'd told you what was going on none of this might have happened. I thought it was a man called Colin Holbrook who was stalking me.'

'We'd have rumbled Mr Preedy this morning, as a matter of fact,' Guy remarked, picking up a letter from his desk. 'The cheque he gave as a deposit on Wilton Place has just been returned. It bounced higher than a ball at Wimbledon.'

'So his time *was* running out,' Antonia said thoughtfully. 'That's why he probably decided to strike last night.' Then she turned to Linda. 'Could you ring the Chelsea and Westminster Hospital and ask how he is? I'm desperately afraid he's going to die, and you realize I'll be on a charge of manslaughter if he does?'

Linda shot her a look of sympathy and without saying a word, dialled the hospital number. The silence in the office was suddenly oppressive as everyone stopped work to listen. Computers rested, the fax machine was still, the photocopier immobilized and the other phones silent. Antonia went and sat at her desk because she was afraid her legs were going to give way and she felt sick. How was she going to cope with this new terror? she asked herself. It seemed the nightmare was never going to end, and she felt wretched at the threat of this new injustice.

When Linda put the phone down, they all turned to look

at her. She spoke without expression.

'There's no change in his condition. He's still unconscious.'

Icy prickles swept through Antonia and she clenched her fists, fighting the rising panic, but said nothing.

'Shall I get you some coffee?' Linda asked, solicitously. 'You must be done in.'

'Yes, please.'

'You should go home to bed.'

Antonia shrugged. 'Everyone keeps telling me that, but I can't relax. I want to get through the rest of today, and tonight I'll catch up on sleep even if I have to take a knockout pill!'

Barbara arrived at the flat just after six, carrying an enormous bunch of pink and white roses and lilies, which she thrust at Antonia.

'How *are* you, love?' she said anxiously. 'I can't *bear* to think how unlucky you've been. You know Susan Sinclair met Andrew Armitage through computer dating? And that worked out blissfully?'

'Susan . . .?' Antonia's jaw dropped. 'You're not serious?'

Barbara's neat little face was composed in earnest lines. 'I promise you. Susan's admitting to it openly, now they're married. It's nothing to be ashamed of these days.'

Antonia could sense Roland's restlessness by the way he jingled the small change in his trouser pocket and shuffled from foot to foot. Suddenly he spoke.

'I hope you're not doing anything like that, Barbara?'

She looked surprised, delicate blonde eyebrows raised.

'Not so far,' she replied lightly, 'although I've got nothing against it. Antonia's just had rotten luck. It is a bit of a lucky dip, isn't it?'

When the two of them left to go out to dinner an hour later, Antonia noticed with amusement that he was holding Barbara's hand in a very possessive way.

Santini's was a pool of exotic darkness with shafts of light trained on tables covered with white cloths, crystal glass, the glint of silver and exquisite arrangements of flowers. The place was redolent with the fragrance of wealth; of rich food and fresh herbs, newly laundered damask and hothouse lilies, fruity wine and cool air-conditioning. She looked around. There was no sign of Mark Dryden. For a moment she had the uncomfortable pumping feeling in her chest that history was repeating itself. Then Mark came bounding out of the darkness, through the restaurant doors from the street, rushing up to her. He looked hot and dishevelled.

'I'm sorry I'm late,' he sounded as if he'd been running. 'I had a hell of a job getting out of the theatre because the press were six deep outside the stage door, and it was almost impossible to avoid them.' He grinned apologetically, touching her lightly on the arm. 'I felt like Joan Collins! In the end they had to sneak me out the front way, as soon as the theatre had emptied, but then I had to walk, or rather run, for miles to find a cab.'

Antonia smiled. The moment of tension she'd felt that morning in the taxi came back, but now it was tinged by an edge of excitement and again she had the strange feeling that she already knew him well. It was almost like meeting the other half of herself. Shocked by the strength of her emotions she moved in a daze as he escorted her to their table, asked her what she'd like to drink, and then set about ordering from the menu. And as she looked into his expressive face with their dark, intelligent eyes she knew, without a shadow of a doubt, that this was the man she wanted to spend the rest of her life with. He caught her looking at him and smiled, too.

The journey had begun along the path to declaration and fulfilment, and she was happy to take it at an easy pace.

The next morning she was told that Alec Preedy had regained consciousness and was in a stable condition. The relief was so great that when she'd finished talking to the ward sister, she allowed herself to do something she hadn't done for years. She gave herself the day off. The tiredness had begun to hit her, in the early hours, like a dose of flu, and as Roland had returned to the country, having dropped in to wish her a sheepish goodbye, and 'Yes, Barbara and I had a very nice time last night', Antonia decided to stay in bed. Maria, her cleaning lady whom she hardly ever saw, brought her coffee and toast while she read the newspapers, propped up by a mound of pillows. They were, of course, still full of the case of Mr Preedy and herself, and how Mark had been wrongfully arrested. Her private life had been spread out in graphic terms for all to see, but she thought, what the hell? Being discreet and secretive had nearly cost her her life. Sleepily, she skimmed them through, switched off the phone and then fell asleep again, with Crash curled up against the small of her back.

The first thing Antonia knew about it was three weeks later

when Linda handed her the *Daily Mail* as she arrived at the office.

'Have you seen this, Antonia?'

In a heart-stopping moment Antonia grabbed the newspaper. The thick dark headline seemed to spring off the page and overwhelm her. PREEDY DEAD.

'Oh, no!' she gave a sharp intake of breath. Then she caught the word *suicide*. 'I don't believe it.'

She'd heard that he'd been discharged from hospital and sent to a psychiatric unit while he awaited trial. With a sinking feeling in her stomach and her mind caught in a tangle of horror, she tried to make sense of the newsprint as it danced and flickered before her eyes.

'. . . "After confessing to the murders of Pauline Ashford, Valerie Martin and Roxana Birch, and the attempted murder of Antonia Murray,"' she read aloud, perched on the edge of her desk, '". . . Alec Preedy, fifty-seven, of Hornchurch, hung himself from the central light fitting in his cell . . ."' her words became hurried, as if by blurring over them they might have less meaning. There was a pause, and then she dropped the newspaper on to her desk.

'Oh, my God, how dreadful!'

'At least you won't even have to give evidence in court now,' Linda pointed out pragmatically. 'This should be the end of it as far as you're concerned.'

'I thought they took precautions to make sure nothing like this could happen,' Antonia said, not listening.

'But isn't it better this way? What had he to live for? He'd lost absolutely everything and he was going to be put away for life, in any case.'

Antonia said nothing. Linda was right, of course, but right now she couldn't bring herself to agree. Alec Preedy's mind had been turned by the shock and grief and anger of not getting the promotion he'd so long expected. His overreaction had been insane, of course, and perhaps, in the first place, he shouldn't have attached such importance to his job, but who was she to criticize anyone for doing just that? He'd brought tragedy to his victims and their families and she'd been lucky to escape, but he'd also brought about his own destruction and for that he'd be forever damned.

'There's a call for you,' Linda said, breaking into her thoughts. 'It's Mark.'

'I know,' Antonia replied, not knowing at all, yet knowing absolutely, because during the past three weeks she and Mark had become linked by an invisible thread, aware of each other's movements and thoughts, attuned to each other's moods.

'Hello,' Antonia said without preamble, her voice low. 'You've seen the newspapers.' It was a statement, not a question.

'Yup.' Mark didn't even sound surprised that she'd guessed what he was ringing up about. 'Ghastly business. And very careless of the authorities to let it happen.'

'I know. I suppose he couldn't face going on.'

'Poor bugger. He was obviously demented. At least he did one good thing in his life.'

Antonia smiled, inclining her heard towards the earpiece, knowing exactly what he meant. 'In bringing us together? Yes, he got that right.'

'Thank God it's over, darling. Now we can move forward;

get on with the rest of our lives.'

'I know.'

'I'll see you tonight after the show. At the usual time.' Mark's tone was intimate, his voice husky. They'd been having late suppers together every evening since that first dinner at Santini's. Sometimes she went backstage after the curtain came down and they went on to a Chinese or Italian restaurant in Soho, and other times she cooked for him at the flat.

'I'll see you tonight,' Antonia replied softly.

Mark stayed that night, for the first time. Antonia had been right when she'd sensed at the beginning of their relationship that they were embarking on a slow and gentle journey of exploration. They had spent the past few weeks telling each other about themselves and their families and as they exchanged their views on life and love, marriage, fidelity and careers, Antonia became filled with wonder at how much they had in common. Every nuance and change of mood from light to dark that passed between them seemed to bring them closer and she loved the way they made each other laugh, sharing the same sense of humour. Bit by bit, like putting a giant jigsaw puzzle together, they realized that all the pieces fitted. Exactly and perfectly. For Antonia, the miracle she'd hoped for had happened, as she discovered they'd become committed to each other, totally and for ever. The waiting had sharpened their mutual desire, too, and as Antonia lay beside Mark she felt driven by a great encompassing wave of love that, once released, swept her uncontrollably forward. His arms were strong and his kisses tender. Although she'd been sure he'd be a skilful lover, the gentle passion and mastery with which he took her still came as a shock. Hungry for her, still he held his passion unselfishly in check until he had made her come, and she heard herself sobbing, 'I love you ... love you ... love you,' while the tears streamed down her cheeks, and he gave himself to her with a potency that made her shudder.

Later, much later, as they lay talking quietly, they felt Crash stepping daintily but surely up the bed, making little noises of contentment.

Antonia started laughing. 'I never thought he'd accept anyone else in my life, but he's certainly taken to you.'

Mark stroked the cat's head and Crash started to purr.

'Nothing like a few Dublin Bay prawns to get on the right side of this little fellow,' he confessed with a grin.

What a difference a year makes! Antonia thought, as she stood by Mark's side in the crowded marquee, as they were about to cut their wedding cake. Twelve months ago she'd attended Susan Sinclair's marriage to Andrew Armitage and now here she was, in a confection of white wild silk, with a lace veil held in place by Granny's pearl and diamond tiara, hardly able to believe this was really happening to her. So many people who had been at that wedding were here, today, too; some more settled in their marriages, others disillusioned and contemplating separation, some newly pregnant, others showing off the babies they'd been expecting last year. Susan herself was pregnant, and so, to her intense surprise, was Jane.

'I don't know how it happened; I've been on the pill, but then I did forget to take it for a couple of days . . .' she informed them brightly and happily.

Hilary, looking relaxed and elegant in beige, and delighted at having the opportunity of arranging a traditional wedding at last, was busy gathering the family together for the speeches. Antonia's godfather had been invited to say a few words, and Quentin insisted that he honour his only daughter, too, on such an auspicious occasion. Tristram had been selected, as the eldest brother, to read out the telegrams, while the best man, Mark's brother Charles, was going to propose a toast to the bridesmaids, a collection of small children who were the offspring of Antonia's friends. Except for the chief bridesmaid.

'Darling, I'm much too old!' Barbara had exclaimed when Antonia had first invited her. But when Roland pointed out that it would be her last opportunity because in three months' time she'd be the bride when *they* got married, she relented in paroxysms of shocked but delighted giggles. 'What a way to propose!' she shrieked, by way of saying yes.

The blue and white marquee, fragrant with the smell of trodden grass and the white roses which garlanded the tent poles, was packed as all the guests crammed into it, eager to drink Antonia and Mark's health.

The ringing tones of the Honourable Mrs Henry Cope could be heard as she held court in one corner. '. . . About time too! Antonia took so long to find a husband I thought she'd be left on the shelf . . .!'

'Granny, shall I get you some more champagne?' Leo hurriedly offered.

'You'd better make sure everyone has a full glass for the toasts,' Quentin advised. Denise drifted past, her smouldering cigarette held aloft, her latest girlfriend following behind. 'Oh, God! *None* of Mark's friends are gay!' Quentin overheard her say. 'I thought *all* actors were gay!' Emma, being chatted up by an elderly gentleman, was asked the same question Antonia had been asked the previous year. 'And which one is *your* husband, my dear?' Emma's grief at being dumped was still acute and so she turned away, not answering.

'Congratulations. You look wonderful,' Antonia heard someone say, and she spun round to see Linda grinning at her. She was not alone.

'Robin!' Antonia exclaimed. He was smiling sheepishly and he had his arm round Linda's waist. He didn't show the faintest flicker of embarrassment at seeing her again, and Antonia was thankful.

'We're together again,' Linda explained. Her face was flushed and her eyes were blazing with joy. 'It's only happened last night, but we wanted to come today to wish you both every happiness.'

Antonia spoke with sincerity as she kissed her warmly on both cheeks. 'Linda, I'm more delighted than I can say.' She'd recently appointed Linda a director of Murray Properties and she'd be running the company while she and Mark honeymooned in St Lucia.

'Ladies and gentlemen . . .' It was time to cut the three-tiered cake, iced with white sugar roses; to have the speeches and drink the toasts; and for Mark to say what would be the most clichéd line of his career, but which was guaranteed to produce a laugh: 'My wife and I . . .' And for Antonia to hope that the film Mark had scripted, at her insistence, based on how they'd met would serve as much as an inspiration as well as a warning, that another cliché was true: be careful how you go about it but remember, there really *is* someone for everyone, if you can just find them.

If you enjoyed this book here is a selection of other bestselling titles from Headline

THE REAL THING	Catherine Alliott	£5.99 ☐
DOUBLE TROUBLE	Val Corbett, Joyce Hopkirk & Eve Pollard	£5.99 ☐
THREE WISHES	Barbara Delinsky	£5.99 ☐
THE SWEET CARESS	Roberta Latow	£5.99 ☐
CLOUD MOUNTAIN	Aimee Liu	£5.99 ☐
THE RUNAWAY	Martina Cole	£5.99 ☐
A DRY SPELL	Susie Moloney	£5.99 ☐
TAKING CONTROL	Una-Mary Parker	£5.99 ☐
A FEW LATE ROSES	Anne Doughty	£5.99 ☐
THE PROMISE	Mary Ryan	£5.99 ☐
MIXED DOUBLES	Jill Mansell	£5.99 ☐
WHEN TOMORROW DAWNS	Lyn Andrews	£5.99 ☐

Headline books are available at your local bookshop or newsagent. Alternatively, books can be ordered direct from the publisher. Just tick the titles you want and fill in the form below. Prices and availability subject to change without notice.

Buy four books from the selection above and get free postage and packaging and delivery within 48 hours. Just send a cheque or postal order made payable to Bookpoint Ltd to the value of the total cover price of the four books. Alternatively, if you wish to buy fewer than four books the following postage and packaging applies:

UK and BFPO £4.30 for one book; £6.30 for two books; £8.30 for three books.

Overseas and Eire: £4.80 for one book; £7.10 for 2 or 3 books (surface mail).

Please enclose a cheque or postal order made payable to *Bookpoint Limited*, and send to: Headline Publishing Ltd, 39 Milton Park, Abingdon, OXON OX14 4TD, UK.
Email Address: orders@bookpoint.co.uk

If you would prefer to pay by credit card, our call team would be delighted to take your order by telephone. Our direct line is 01235 400 414 (lines open 9.00 am–6.00 pm Monday to Saturday 24 hour message answering service). Alternatively you can send a fax on 01235 400 454.

Name ....

Address ....

....

....

If you would prefer to pay by credit card, please complete:
Please debit my Visa/Access/Diner's Card/American Express (delete as applicable) card number:

Signature .... Expiry Date ....